A Beautiful White Cat Walks with Me

Youssef Fadel

Translated by
Alexander E. Elinson

hoopoe
AN IMPRINT OF AUC PRESS

Quotation on page viii: Cited in Bertrand Fessard de Foucault, "La question du Sahara espagnol (I)." *Revue Française d'Etudes Politiques Africaines*, 10th year, no. 119 (November 1975): 78.

First published in 2016 by
Hoopoe
113 Sharia Kasr el Aini, Cairo, Egypt
420 Fifth Avenue, New York, 10018
www.hoopoefiction.com

Hoopoe is an imprint of the American University in Cairo Press
www.aucpress.com

Exclusive distribution outside Egypt and North America by I.B.Tauris & Co Ltd., 6 Salem Road, London, W4 2BU

Dar el Kutub No. 25738/15
ISBN 978 977 416 776 8

Dar el Kutub Cataloging-in-Publication Data

Fadel, Youssef
        A Beautiful White Cat Walks with Me / Youssef Fadel.—Cairo: The
American University in Cairo Press, 2016.
        p.   cm.
        ISBN 978 977 416 776 8
        1. Arabic Fiction –Translation into English
        2. Arabic Fiction
        I. Title
        892.73

1 2 3 4 5   20 19 18 17 16

Designed by Adam el-Sehemy
Printed in the United States of America

They say: 'Our Lord! Hasten for us our sentence
even before the Day of Reckoning!'
(Qur'an 38:16)

Foreword

ON NOVEMBER 6, 1975, a mass government-orchestrated demonstration saw 350,000 Moroccans cross Morocco's southern border into what was then the Spanish-occupied Sahara. The goal was to pressure Spain to withdraw from the territory it had occupied and administered since 1884. The Green March (so named for the color of Islam symbolizing the Islamic rhetoric with which Morocco's King Hassan II imbued the action) was preceded by a movement of armed Moroccan troops into the territory the week before on October 31, 1975. Facing pressure from the Sahrawi nationalist Polisario Front, as well as from the United Nations and the Moroccan government, Spain finally withdrew on November 14, 1975. Morocco and Mauritania moved in to take control, but under continued pressure from the Polisario, Mauritania withdrew in August 1979. As the sole remaining power in the territory, Morocco became the target of an armed struggle for Sahrawi independence that continued until the UN-brokered a ceasefire in 1991 with the promise of a referendum for or against independence. Neither side has been able to agree on the terms of the referendum, most notably the definition of eligible voters, and the referendum has yet to occur, with Morocco's official stance now a proposal for autonomous Sahrawi governance under Moroccan rule.

The status of the Western Sahara (or Southern Provinces as it is referred to in official Moroccan parlance) remains highly contested, as Morocco has viewed the territory as part of Greater

Morocco since before it gained independence from the French in 1956. Immediately following independence, Istiqlal (Independence) Party leader Allal al-Fassi proclaimed on June 19, 1956: "If Morocco is independent, it is not completely unified. Moroccans will continue the struggle until Tangier, the Sahara from Tindouf to Colomb-Bechar, Touat, Kenadza, Mauritania are liberated and unified. Our independence will only be complete with the Sahara!" This notion was embraced both by King Muhammad V and his son Hassan II, who ascended to the throne in 1961, and in fact, the Sahara issue served him well as a patriotic rallying cry to solidify support for his rule.

Following coup attempts on July 10, 1971 and August 16, 1972, Hassan II purged his military of several high-ranking officers. He faced a general crisis of confidence, and took a series of measures to try to reestablish his authority and popularity among Moroccans. He instituted a land reform program aiming to 'Moroccanize' farms and small businesses still held by non-Moroccans, and in 1973 he sent Moroccan troops to Egypt and Syria to join the fight with Israel in an attempt to shore up his anti-Zionist credentials. Arguably his boldest and most effective move, however, was to ramp up rhetoric in the summer of 1974 in support of Spanish withdrawal from the Western Sahara and its (re-)incorporation into Greater Morocco. These efforts built upon already enthusiastic popular support for the territory's liberation from Spain and (re-)integration into Morocco. Hassan II eventually gained approval for his claim from most Arab countries, as well as from the United States and France.

This enthusiasm, however, was met with opposition from the indigenous Sahrawis. The Polisario Front, established in 1973 as a nationalist resistance movement that aimed to expel the Spanish from the region, refocused its attentions and activities on Morocco and Mauritania until its pullout in 1979. By April 1976, as the conflict escalated, much of the Western Sahara's local population had left the region, with tens of thousands settled in Polisario-administered camps in Tindouf, Algeria. Inside the Moroccan-controlled territories, Morocco faced increasing guerilla attacks that it countered with troop build-ups and the building of security walls that aimed to stem the outflow of refugees and prevent attacks against Moroccan forces. Although the Moroccan military held a material advantage over the Sahrawi resistance, Moroccan troops—largely peasants from the north and urban conscripts—were at a distinct disadvantage, unaccustomed as they were to the extreme weather conditions and geography of the desert. These conscripts and their commanders were also unable to adapt to the guerilla warfare used by the resistance. Sahrawi fighters were familiar with the terrain and territory, were able to move about largely undetected, and were thus able to keep the Moroccan troops on the defensive, with little to do but wait for the next attack.

This war resulted in a dramatic increase in the size of the Moroccan military, from 56,000 troops in 1974 to 141,000 in 1982. The increase in military expenditures, combined with growing economic troubles that were exacerbated by population growth outpacing agricultural output, crop failures, and drought in the early 1980s, all led to a serious national crisis. The heady days of patriotic fervor that had immediately followed the Green March in 1975 had given way to a precarious economic and social situation that severely tested Moroccans' faith in their country, their political leaders, and their king.

King Hassan II (r. 1961–99) ruled Morocco with an iron fist, responding to challenges to his rule from military leaders and leftist/Marxist activists with mass arbitrary imprisonment, mock trials, torture, and forced disappearances. The Years of Lead in the 1970s and 1980s were a time considerable brutality and fear in Morocco, and it was only in the 1990s that Morocco's human rights record began to improve. Despite considerable progress in terms of human rights and press freedoms, limits remain. Journalists and activists still routinely face fines and jail time for transgressing article 41 of the Moroccan Press Code that prohibits anyone from questioning the sanctity of "the Islamic religion, the monarchy, or Morocco's territorial unity." Vague as this prohibition is, writers are constantly testing its limits. In the Western Sahara itself, there continue to be reports that torture and forced confessions are still practiced by Moroccan authorities against Sahrawi advocates for independence and human rights.

Hassan, one of two narrators in *A Beautiful White Cat Walks with Me* is a comedy performer with leftist tendencies who finds himself drafted into Moroccan military service and sent off to the desert to fight a war that he and his fellow conscripts do not understand, against an enemy that is elusive and really no different from themselves. His father, Balloute, is a jester in the royal court whose proximity to the king offers a rare glimpse into the monarch's inner circle, his habits, his sense of humor, his flaws, and the rewards and dangers of living so close to power. Their narratives intertwine not only as those of a son and his father, but as complementary views of the kingdom from both inside and outside the palace walls.

This novel depicts Morocco in the 1980s during the war in the Sahara, and is about how the war, and rule of Hassan II, permeated every aspect of Moroccan life. *A Beautiful White Cat Walks with Me* combines comedy and tragedy to examine the role of violence, power, and authoritarian control. One might recognize real historical figures, such as Hassan II, General Ahmed Dlimi (d. 1983) who was the king's right-hand man and commander of forces in the Sahara, the king's real court jester Mohammed Binebine (d. 2008), and others. What is remarkable about this novel is that Youssef Fadel has created a fictional world that evokes these personalities and this time, but is not bound by them. With characters comic and tragic in their humanity and in their attempts to find respect and love in a place where power is concentrated in the hands of the very few, the novel depicts life as so unpredictable, cruel, and ridiculous, it is difficult to know when to laugh, and when to cry.

Alexander E. Elinson

1

Day One

I HAD DREAMED OF THE desert, almost like the one surrounding me now. A desert slapped by blazing whips of sunlight. A fort, a burning tavern, a purple road like a thin strip along the horizon. I saw all of this in the dream, months before actually finding myself here. I hadn't set foot in any desert before that dream. I had never passed by any fort or gone into any tavern. All of this I saw in the dream. It was just like this, in almost the same baffling order. The burning tavern first, then the fort made of clay, then the road, the same purple shade tending toward blue, and the same sun whose heat continued to burn in one's memory long after it was gone. There were soldiers playing cards, unaware of the fire consuming the tavern and of the pillars of smoke rising from holes in the foundation and walls, making it difficult to see. And there I was, calmly searching under tables and between legs for something I was unable to find, not even knowing what I was looking for. Neither the fire's smoke nor the noise of the card players distracted me. I saw all of this in the dream, just like I said. How could I possibly have imagined that a few months later I would find myself sitting in the same tavern I had seen in the dream, a few dozen meters from the fort made of clay, that I had also seen in the dream, watching over the road stretched out like a thin line drawn on the horizon?

I'm now sitting in the same tavern, but without the fire, and without the smoke. I'm watching the same road, but it's not deserted. There are trucks passing by from time to time. For their part, the soldiers are standing at the counter drinking indifferently rather than playing cards, and I'm not searching for anything, neither under tables nor between legs. Rather, I'm thinking of Zineb.

In the dream I hadn't seen the waterwheel whose water had dried up long ago, nor had I heard the sound of the turning axle moving uselessly, perhaps only because of the small breeze still softly and mercifully blowing. Purple stone everywhere. An expanse of purple stone starts immediately behind the tavern. Purple stone, a purple sky, and an evening not too different in color. The air is heavy. We can barely breathe. A faint breeze blows through the small, narrow window. Stone, a sky, an evening. And this tavern resembling a wooden hut cast out into the empty waste, with a narrow window looking out toward the fort, the six date palms, and the stone road—purple, distant, and aligned with the horizon that separates the purple stone from the purple sky. I don't see the waterwheel because it's on the other side.

Not too far away, a soldier plays his stringed instrument. His name is Haris Sahrawi, and he is the guard. He sits at the fort's door covered with a cloak that has acquired a gray tinge—the color of the desert evening descending upon him. It is his turn to serve sentry duty. Whenever evening falls upon him during guard duty, he thinks about his wife and children back on the islands off the coast, and intense longing overwhelms him. Every once in a while an argument rises up inside the fort between the soldiers playing cards at Sergeant Bouzide's place, followed by the sound of a passing truck in the distance. It's carrying water to a base farther down the road. The truck doesn't turn toward our fort. We get our share of water from the well.

That's it. The fort, the tavern next to it, an argument, the purple hue spreading out in every direction, and the four of us at the counter.

Coincidence and military service have gathered us together here. A conscript named Brahim is blowing cigarette smoke at a small turtle crawling along the bar. He waits for it to walk a little bit before returning it to where it had started, then he blows smoke on it again, laughing. Mohamed Ali doesn't laugh because he doesn't like joking around. He's from Zagoura, in his fifth month here. And there's Naafi. Naafi is a conscript from Marrakech, like me. We arrived on the same day two months ago. His bed is next to mine. He's a student who has finished his first year. He knows the area because during summer vacations he worked as a tourist guide. He loves the desert and he adores Fifi, the tavern's owner. Whenever he's not on guard duty or cleaning the courtyard, he's leaning on the counter suggesting changes he'll make to the bar after he and Fifi get married. She tells him she's going to go back to Tangier and come up with some sort of plan once she gathers enough money here, if the war continues for another few years, but Naafi doesn't pay any attention to what she says. He goes into the kitchen and comes out with his mouth full, jaws working indifferently, as if he was in his own house. Or he wanders around the tables of the dining room, smoking and moving with deliberate steps. It's not the walk of a soldier or of a civilian. Rather, it's the walk of Alain Delon, just as he saw him in one of his films.

Then there's Brigadier Omar, whom no one likes simply because he's a malicious person. He likes to do wicked things for no real reason. Two steps away from me he sways, almost falling over, but is saved by the bar that continues to prop him up as he curses a devil only he can see. And Fifi stands there like a man, cigarette not leaving her lips that are stained blue by cheap wine, disdainfully watching what Brahim is doing with the turtle, yet unable to kick him out because he spends what little money he has there. No one knows her real name. They call her Fifi. She's beautiful, no older than thirty. Her face has light freckles. Her hair is blond and her smile provides a bit of cheer to this place. She came from Tangier two years ago, and is not allowed to sell the soldiers drinks, cheap or not. Therefore, she serves them "under the table," as they say. Captain Hammouda tolerates her because of her smile and the light freckles on her face. So, there's Fifi, Brigadier Omar, the conscript Brahim, the soldier Mohamed Ali, and Naafi. And then there's me, wondering how I found myself in a place I saw in a dream six or seven months ago.

The picture of Alain Delon never leaves Naafi's pocket. He has a color picture of him and a mirror he uses to comb his hair back when he wakes up, the same way Alain Delon does. When he sleeps, he places his pants under the quilt so that the crease remains visible and straight, just like Alain Delon's pants. And when he sits at the counter to smoke, he waits for Fifi to turn toward him so he can raise his right eyebrow, just as he saw Alain Delon do in one of his first films. Fifi is only interested in him as someone who says funny things. Of greater importance to her is what she nervously follows Brahim doing with the poor turtle. When Brahim is sure she is watching him with those nervous eyes, he places his hand on its back like a civilized person who loves turtles. She approaches him, fills his glass while drawing on her cigarette, and seizes the opportunity to return the turtle to a little plate of palm leaves, placing it on the inside corner of the counter. Brigadier Omar, who is still not sure whether he's going to fall or not, finally falls. He shoots a glance at everyone, wondering which of us made him fall. Then he grabs his glass, holding on to it as if it will help him get up, and there he remains, wondering whether he'll be able to get up or not. Finally, he gets up.

I'm not thinking about life at the base, or the desert I saw in the dream. Rather, I'm thinking about military service. "Eighteen months. Just eighteen months, after which you can return to civilian life and continue performing your sketches in cabarets and private salons as you were doing before. But military service is obligatory!" That's what the commanding

4

officer made clear when we were in the capital. Everything was going just fine for me at the time, just about. I had left Zineb sick and bedridden, and work wasn't going as I would have liked, but I had high hopes for the future. In the last few months I had been able to put on a few private performances in front of a group of engineers and doctors. In those shows I made fun of the prime minister, who had suggested his government prepare an educational curriculum enumerating the virtues of fasting, which he would then distribute to schools and institutes with the goal of having people forgo the habit of eating, because of the exorbitant cost of wheat to the national treasury. I also had jokes about hard currency and other stories that resonate among the elite. I had been performing this sketch for a while now because the audience I performed for knew it, had memorized it, and came to expect it. Many of my sketches contain the same elements. They always resonated with large numbers of people, and the press wrote about their boldness, considering them politically committed works, just as some considered me a leftist. I'd be a leftist if they insisted, but on my own terms.

As I said, everything was going just fine. It couldn't have been that these sketches, meant to make people laugh, were the reason behind the call to duty. I don't have enemies who would want to send me to the front. Surely my father couldn't be behind it. I was twelve or thirteen years old when he left his wife's bed; when he disappeared from the house for good. I'm twenty-seven now. That year, the year of his disappearance, my mother maintained that he still set up his performance circle in the Djemaa El-Fna square. But after a year, he disappeared from there too. Where did he go? God only knows. Then we heard that he had become a jester in the king's palace. We left him in his palace and no longer thought of him. We forgot him just as he forgot us. I didn't think of him when my sister Fadila had an epileptic seizure in the middle of the alley and fell convulsing into the dirt, the neighbors carrying her unconscious back to our house. I didn't think about his absence from our table. I didn't think about him when my mother joined the traditional arts collective in order to provide for us. And I didn't think of him when I received that sudden call, at a time when everything was basically going all right, despite Zineb's illness. I had been completely engrossed in preparing a new show about Tariq bin Ziyad, the Berber who, despite not knowing Arabic, wrote his famous speech. In the end, I blamed it on the dream. As long as I dreamed of this place, and as long as this place existed, I would have to see it one way or another. But how would I have seen it without being forced to? Is there a more direct way to get there than through compulsory military service? Compulsory and obligatory, no way around it, just as the officer had said.

2

YES, I'M A JESTER. IT fills me with pride to hear people guffawing, torrents of laughter crashing down everywhere, clusters
of joy hanging all around me, happiness swimming in the air,
and the wings of intoxication fluttering. A hurricane that fills
veins, eyes, and mouths. It squeezes one man's midsection,
his cheeks reddening and the blood almost bursting from his
pores. He looks as if he's about to explode. It is truly something strange to watch a group of people laugh. Their bodies
seem oblivious to anyone watching. When they laugh, people
turn into something else entirely. How interesting it is to make
people feel happy and unrestrained when they're together—
usually with simple words that wouldn't make someone laugh
were you to say them to him on his own. But when they're
together, their masks fall, to the point that you don't recognize them anymore. This one produces a sound resembling
a horse's whinny. That one reminds you of a donkey's bray.
Then there's the laugh that resembles a dog's howl or a saw
working its way through a piece of wood. A strange carnival
of sounds, from the clucking of a chicken to the cackle of a
hyena, and every form of laughter strives to outdo the others.

The jester has no family. His family is his occupation.
This is what I've come to understand after years of work.
The nature of his work has him on call at the palace round
the clock, as sometimes late at night sleep eludes His Majesty,
or he wants to extend a soiree into the wee hours. Yes, I'm

a jester, and my mission is to make the king laugh. Despite my sixty years, I'm still needed, thank God. Work still has me by the neck. They say that my face is gloomy and that's what causes people to laugh. They say that whoever looks at me thinks I'm crying, so they laugh. But I don't listen to a word they say about me. Why don't I cry when I see my face reflected in the mirror? Why doesn't my face make me laugh whenever I look at it? People say all sorts of nonsense that would never occur to me. Let them talk. I'm only interested in one thing: pleasing His Majesty.

I consider myself lucky, and I'm not just saying this. Is it possible for anyone else to gain such proximity to him? Someone like me, with essentially no trade or craft. No high pedigree or family tree with deep roots. Someone like me, who has memorized only a few lines of poetry and a couple of verses from the Qur'an. I was nothing more than a street performer in Djemaa El-Fna before becoming, all at once, a jester for the king. I eat with him and drink with him, accompany him on his trips and hunting expeditions, entertain him when he wakes up and before he goes to sleep. How many people have been granted the likes of this honor? Not too many, in any case. There are some professional actors and singers, but they only appear during holidays and official functions. They present what they have in terms of new jokes or they sing their enthusiastic songs, then they leave. There are some politicians who might come close, but how quickly they become boring. There's Said Jilali who brings the water for ablutions to His Majesty. This man used to sell donkeys before luck smiled upon him, all because his aunt was employed as a cook in the palace for a little while, and during that time she worked on his behalf to get him this job. His greatest wish when he was hired at the palace was to kiss His Majesty's hand. As time passed, the wish faded away, and in the end it was replaced with the wish to celebrate *me* and kiss *my* hand.

Then there's Zerwal the hunchback, although I don't take him into account. I don't consider him lucky like me because God already provided him with the necessary weapons for permanent and eternal success. His hump and his deformity are the two things that guarantee his livelihood, and this livelihood will never be cut off as long as his hump remains on his back. His head, which resembles a pear, is extra capital that will accompany him to the grave. God created him in this deformed way as if He were handing him a precious gift—a treasure he would benefit from for his entire life, eat from without worry, like a landowner or someone who holds an exclusive license for cutting stone or deep-sea fishing. I don't have any of these special things—neither a license, nor a hump, nor any deformity at all. I'm well formed and can't complain of any deficiency. My professional success relies more on my rhetorical ability, if I say so myself, than on any external appearance. Moreover, Zerwal's constant presence in the palace is more a curiosity than anything else. The king is obsessed with science and scientists, and he is interested in this clown as a specimen with which he and his scientists, on Friday afternoons, can study the natural and unnatural changes that occur in the human body. Zerwal the hunchback is my closest enemy; my only competitor, to be exact. For his part, he considers me an enemy and a competitor too. I know that he spends his time setting traps for me, and even though his ruses haven't succeeded yet, it doesn't mean he has stopped plotting. Even if he gives the impression that he's tending toward rapprochement, that doesn't mean that his intentions are to be believed, that he is not secretly planning something for me, and that he won't succeed tomorrow or the day after if I let my guard down and allow my vigilance to flag.

The sultan's jester *is* the sultan. I know things about him he doesn't know about himself, and he knows things about me that never occurred to me. I say what I'm thinking to him without worry. This is natural as long as we complement one another. I can say what I wish without fear. Once he told me that his soldiers slave their whole lives away and don't earn a tenth of what I do per minute, to which I immediately responded, "My task isn't easy. There's nothing harder than making a smile bloom on the lips of a tyrant such as yourself." He let out a loud chuckle and walked out. I said this because I knew exactly what his reaction would be because, as I said, I understand him as he understands me.

But what's important is that I must never stop being entertaining and funny, and must always remain open to mockery. I must never forget this. The day His Majesty stops making fun of me and laughing at me and at every word that comes out of my mouth, the day the flame that provides my silliness with the necessary strength dies out, that's when I'll consider myself done. That day has not come yet, thank God, even though I'm constantly thinking about it. I think about what happened to Dr. Rahhali, who was on the verge of being thrown into one of His Majesty's prisons for something or another. They call him doctor, but he didn't work in a clinic. Maybe it's because of the long period of time he spent so close to the king. No one even knows what his job inside the palace was. He was always seen with His Majesty, but can anyone actually remember what exactly he did? Now he's sitting at home waiting for his fate to be decided, perhaps praying day and night that the king has forgotten him, while he waits for a punishment to be meted out for something that no one has any knowledge of. That's what I imagine. I'm not interested in him; not interested in whether he's standing up straight or bent over in prayer. However, I do picture him sitting on his sheepskin rug begging God to lift this misfortune from him. I try hard not to think of him, but he imposes himself on me every time I lie down in bed. Dr. Rahhali, whom everyone revered and respected and whose friendship they bought, look what's happened to him! I do everything I can to stay under His Majesty's protection, sharpening my wit day and night, firing up my intellect with my whip-smart memory until I find something sufficiently entertaining. When I can't, I go to the house of my old friend Si Hussein the barber. He has enough jokes and stories to keep me fed for days. I don't see any other fate for myself. Sometimes I can't sleep, thinking about the day when . . . I just hope that day never comes. Allegiance to the palace is like walking on shifting sands, and I need to love my shifting sands, to swim in them with the current, as they say. This is how it goes and I need to go along with it, and to thank God for it. Even with all the caution it requires daily, for years on end, diving into these sands is not safe.

All in all, these aren't complaints. When I see the esteem for me in the eyes of my friend Si Hussein the barber's customers, or the jealousy in the looks of people I bump into on the street, I see that I am closer to His Majesty than anyone else in the world; closer than his ministers, his high-ranking officers, his chamberlain, and his private guard. Si Hussein the barber is an old friend from my days of hanging around the Djemaa El-Fna when I was just a street performer. In his store or his house in the Sammarin district I would gather my provision of stories and strange tales for the days that my well ran dry. Si Hussein is a bachelor, like the cobbler he shares a living space with. The cobbler, like Si Hussein, is in his fifties and loves smoking kif, playing the oud, and spending time in the company of young men. When the two of them smoke hashish, Si Hussein grabs his instrument and together they sing the poems of Ben Brahim. Sometimes they sing exceedingly erotic melhoun poems, along with *The Boasting Match between Young Men and Slave Girls*, the book by al-Jahiz that both of them have committed to memory. I have memorized many poems from these two, and from them I learned an essential aspect of my work: to recite love poetry and accompany it with the oud, because many of those I visit in their palaces love this.

The jester's task is not always enjoyable. Besides entertaining his master and his guests and making them laugh by recounting strange tales, he should have committed the Qur'an and hadith to memory, and possess a tremendous number of stories, jokes, and poems. In the moments when he is least expecting it, he has to be able to invent entertaining ruses and games on the spot. Sometimes he has to display great talent and spontaneity by inventing something entertaining, totally unprepared, that is appropriate for a particular moment or that corresponds to some sort of emergency or the arrival of one person or another. I'm like that actor whose worries are hidden when he casts off all his daily cares in order to free himself up for the task of alleviating those of the audience. That's not to mention those times during the day when boredom bears down and they pelt me with fruit peels, or sometimes with empty, or even full, glasses. Once they asked me to throw myself naked into the palace pool at midnight, and as soon as I jumped into the pool they took off with my clothes. I have to accept this with an open mind because all of it is part of my profession. I'm not going to balk at such trifling matters. Nothing in this is what would be called strange. Rather, it's part of my job. Incidents such as these are as much a part of palace life as the walls and the garden and the water cistern. They're always to be found with the king, all around him; with all kings, in fact.

Instead of complaining, I need to hold fast to this opportunity. Every day when the sun rises I say to myself that this is my opportunity and I need to hold on to it. Let them hit me, let them pour water on me or piss on me. This is part of my job and I need to accept it as a gift because tomorrow, and the day after that, and on all the mornings that God creates, I'll sit on the balcony of the Renaissance Café watching Marrakech from above and all around me the customers will turn and point to where I'm sitting. "Who's the man wearing the djellaba and the red tarboosh?" "The one sitting there? Don't you know? Why that's Balloute, the king's private jester!"

In the past few years, with seniority, and because I have become His Majesty's favorite jester, there are no longer that many people bold enough to cross the line with me as they did before when they took off with my clothes or pelted me with fruit peels, even if they are still tempted to do so. They do that with Zerwal now. They hit him on his hump or pull his shirt off in order to use the hump as a dry ablution stone. Despite all of this, I always say that a profession such as this is tempting for important men such as ministers and generals. I've seen some of them clucking like a chicken laying an egg just to get the king to smile. And there are those who will act like a monkey, pretending to pick through the hair on their bellies in a government meeting during which important matters such as the state budget are being discussed. All of this behavior seems strange to me when it comes from important people such as ministers and general secretaries. Making the king laugh has never been a part of their jobs and this makes me hate them even more. I always have to hide my true feelings and accept the mockery and abuse of others good-naturedly. This is all part of my job. I am a jester, true, but behind the mask of the silly jester there lies a deep indignation. My hatred for humanity knows no limit.

Laughter gives life and brings death. He who does not want to die from laughter wants to be made healthy by it. That's because laughter, if it doesn't kill, cures, just as it did with the king whose kingdom was saved by a single fart. This king was bedridden because of an illness that responded to no treatment. None of the doctors of the kingdom were able to prescribe medication that would bring about his recovery. After a few weeks, the illness got worse and he was on the verge of death. All across the land the weepers wept and the mourners mourned. Then it happened one day that his jester was sitting on the edge of his bed crying. The sight of the jester caused the king to let out a resounding laugh, and with it a huge fart that allowed his entire body to breathe easy. Things didn't happen exactly as described; a few details have escaped me and maybe I'll remember them later. The important thing is that the very next day, the king felt better, as if he had never been at the edge of his grave.

While you might find a person who has never cried in his life, you won't find a person who has never laughed. Animals don't laugh. Laughter is for humans. If someone doesn't laugh out of happiness, he'll laugh out of worry. He'll laugh about sitting and about standing, about silence and speaking. Laughter is in the heart and in the mind. However, even if a person is extremely prone to laughter, he cannot make himself laugh all by himself. He can tickle himself as much as he wants, but he still won't laugh. He might think hard about where laughter comes from and squeeze his heart and tickle himself under his arms and on other parts of the body, but he'll never laugh. He needs someone to stimulate that strange gland—the laughter gland—and as long as things remain thus, we, the jesters, will have a prominent place in people's lives and hearts.

3

Day One (Conclusion)

THREE TRUCKS PASSED BY, THEN two more, all of them carrying water. Where were they heading? Somewhere in the sprawling desert there were soldiers waiting for water. We weren't waiting for water. We were waiting to visit our families. The fort is close to the well that brings us water. Thirty kilometers of sand and stone separate us from it. We were in the tavern celebrating the furlough we'd received. The conscript Brahim, the one who was playing with the turtle—his vacation would be spent on the road. He's from Oujda. Two days to get there and two days to come back, maybe more, depending on the road's mood; if it isn't cut off, or a tire doesn't blow, or the bus isn't late, he'll have just enough time to see his parents and ask them to look for a wife for him for whenever he returns. He thought about all of this while he played with the turtle. He returned it to where it belonged whenever it strayed too far, to remind it, and himself, of their ridiculous journey. The conscript Mohamed Ali wasn't laughing. He's from Zagoura and doesn't like kidding around. He was thinking about his French wife he left behind there. He's got a store where he sells his drawings and this Frenchwoman had passed by the store and liked the paintings. Then she sat down to drink tea with him and stayed in Zagoura. Her name is Françoise and she is the apple of his eye. He was thinking about the days he'll spend with her.

And Naafi? He was leaning on the counter studying Fifi and counting in his head the number of tourists he'd bring here when the war ended and he married Fifi. So, there was the conscript Brahim, who was playing with the turtle; the conscript Mohamed Ali, who found no reason to laugh and whose heart burned for Françoise; Naafi, who was feeling his way to Fifi's heart; and there was me, thinking about Zineb. Zineb, who I left sick and lying in bed without the smile that was usually on her lips. There wasn't even a phone here I could use to call her to make sure she was okay, to hear her voice and be satisfied that she was in good health. I'd written two letters since arriving. I hadn't received a response and I didn't expect one because she doesn't like writing letters. I requested a special leave in order to see her. The next day I would leave the barracks. That's why we were in the tavern, drinking toasts to the upcoming vacation I'd been anticipating for a while now, and whose time had finally come.

Brigadier Omar rose, holding on to his glass as if it would help him get up. He turned in our direction, firing a look as if he were trying to figure out which one of us had caused him to fall.

Aiming the words at me, he said, "Do you know what's waiting for you, Hassan?"

"I don't know what's waiting for me, and I don't care to know, Brigadier Omar, because I'm traveling tomorrow."

"So you don't know? Better for you."

There was something resembling a smirk on his face, or a muffled laugh that knows there's a hole in front of you, but that doesn't want to point it out before you fall in. Then he told me: My leave had been revoked, and that we would set off, the four of us, at midnight, so as to reach the well in the morning to get water.

"But do you know what sort of weapon the enemy uses?"

No one responded to his question because Brahim was still busy with the turtle, or at least that's the impression he was giving. Mohamed Ali put his head down like someone whose head had started to hurt all of a sudden and Naafi was counting his tourists. The brigadier leaned on the counter again and lifted his empty glass to his mouth, then slammed it down violently on the wooden counter. Fifi came over and put another bottle in front of him. He filled his glass until the foam spilled over the edge. He lifted it to his mouth and this time the beer spilled all over his uniform.

"They use Kalashnikovs," he said. "New, Russian-made Kalashnikovs. Have you guys ever seen one?"

I hadn't seen one, but I didn't tell that to the brigadier. I had seen the rifle that Naafi used to hunt the gazelles that he'd give to Fifi as a gift. As for the enemy? The enemy's weapon? No. But I didn't say anything. I was waiting for him to finish, as were the others. Or maybe I wasn't waiting for anything anymore after the devastating news I had just heard. As for Brigadier Omar, his unjustified victory made him laugh. It wasn't us who caused him to fall to the ground. That's what I was about to say, but he continued, intoxicated by what he was saying, even more so now that what he was saying was getting through to us.

"And do you know where they are? The enemy? At the well. Guarding the well itself. Tomorrow they'll wait for you so you can see them up close, or maybe they'll wait for you to *not* see him, just like before."

He laughed. He drank from his glass, pushed it toward Fifi, and left before falling over for a third time.

I wasn't thinking about the well or about the thirty kilometers that separated us from it that we would cross at night. I wasn't thinking about the enemy and whether or not they would appear. The time for this had not yet come. My mind was preoccupied with Zineb. We hadn't parted under the best of circumstances. I told myself that this was because of her illness. I had thought that she was pregnant for a second time and, rather than being happy like any other woman would be, the news unraveled her nerves. It wasn't the first time she had gotten pregnant. The first miscarriage had made her permanently apprehensive. But no, she was just tired, I told myself.

What worried me more, though, was that she would be on her own, in bed. I asked her to go to her sister Leila's in Bab Aghmat. Her sister is a housewife. She doesn't go out at all. She'd be able to take care of her more than anyone else would, but Zineb refused, with the excuse that the never-ending noise of her three children would drive her crazy. Or she could go stay with my mother and sister Fadila in Sidi Benslimane. No, she didn't want to put anyone out.

In the end, she said that the doctor would visit her whenever he could. The doctor and his wife are friends whom Zineb had met back in the days of the cinema club, before she met me. Then I met them, through her. They're true friends, as she says, despite the relationship we have with them, which has not always been great. There were some violent rumblings at one point and, another time, a complete breakdown. However, the waters of friendship flowed between us once again, and when she asked them to visit her from time to time, they said they'd come to keep her company every day after work. Zineb opposed this suggestion too. She saw it as too great a commitment on their part, but they insisted on staying late into the night with Zineb since they had no children waiting at home for them, allowing them to spend most of their time after work going from one friend's house to another's. They said that the only time they relaxed was when they were with Zineb, and that Zineb was the only person they knew who deserved this sacrifice of their time.

"Isn't that so, Zineb my dear?"

Collective laughter. Then the doctor said, turning to her, "The soldier will be gone, but the artist will remain here."

I met Zineb four years ago. She was twenty-two and we were getting ready to participate in a television talent show, Zineb as a singer and me as a comedian. I wouldn't have met Zineb were it not for the chance I was given to be in that show, and this is one of the mysteries that continues to perplex me, just like the desert I saw in the dream. I keep saying to myself that if I hadn't been a part of that very program, I never would have met her. If I had stopped and hesitated in front of the television studio door and turned back down the stairs, if I had told the program director not to nominate me (just to see what would happen, as they said), and if she had not looked at me with that encouraging look while I was preparing to stand in front of the camera for the first time in front of a new audience filling the studio, then I would now be sitting in that remote tavern on the edge of the desert and not thinking about any girl, or thinking about another girl. She might be beautiful, but she wouldn't be Zineb. She might even work in a nightclub like the one Zineb works in, but she wouldn't be the woman I love, who I'm thinking of now as I sit at Fifi's counter watching Brahim stare at the turtle walking away from him.

Whoever was watching television that night saw a young man of twenty-three performing his sketches on a brightly lit stage. That viewer might or might not have been laughing, but he wouldn't have known what I had been concerned with just moments before. I was standing behind the curtain, filled with self-doubt, studying the room I was about to plunge into, reviewing the sketch I was going to present, and not even thinking about whether it would please the committee. My main concern was that it would please Zineb because I had fallen in love with her the moment I saw her. My heart had never beaten the way it beat at that moment. Nothing like that had ever happened to me before. Prior to that moment, I had never felt attached to a girl. This inner turmoil and shock was happening to me for the first time, in a room filled to the rafters with an audience of young men and women, as well as middle-aged men and women, some wearing djellabas and others not. I turned to my left and saw her. She wasn't thinking about what she was going to perform for the audience like I was. She was neither surprised nor scared. She was calm, just focused on the task at hand. She was a singer at the Shahrazade Cabaret and she was intent on appearing on the program in order to become a professional singer. I'm not sure how sound her thinking was. As for me, I didn't gain fame or fortune from this television appearance, but what I did gain was Zineb, and that's the important thing. I gained everything that night, to the point where, a few months later, I realized the most beautiful thing that could happen to me was that I marry Zineb.

The night of the show I was really rattled and couldn't say whether her singing had moved me or not. I wouldn't know that until a few days later at the Shahrazade. Of all the things that happened that night at the studio, I only remember one thing: her encouraging, optimistic smile and the colored lights reflecting off her face like little lanterns. She dragged a stool over to me and sat on it, and I sat as well. When I gazed at her face, my whole being was filled with tranquility, as if a hidden bond had been formed at that very instant. I left the television studio singing. Life seemed full of promise and, without knowing why, I lifted my eyes to the sky. It was blue and clear, magnificent. It seemed to me that those passing in the street knew my secret, and they were happy, satisfied in knowing it.

I remember the first time I kissed her, months later. When her moist lips touched mine and quenched the thirst of those arid years, a fever came over my entire body. A heat spread over the skin of my face. I felt a light trembling. It was pitiful, ridiculous. Luckily we were in a dimly lit place. I remember her in the days that followed—normal days for the most part—sitting in front of me, leaning her head on her hand, putting her little finger between her lips and staying like that, studying me for a long time, while I was drowning in a sweet happiness that didn't give me the time to wonder: "What is Zineb thinking about right now?" We were sharing the same shyness, the same awkwardness, the same desire. Or perhaps in these special moments, we didn't have a defined idea about "us"; we were without concerns, and perhaps even without any desire except for that which had to do with our being together in the same place, sharing those moments. After these four years, despite the storms we have weathered together, there's no doubt that her tender body remembers the scent of blossoms that floated around us the day we kissed for the first time.

4

AZIZA, MY THIRD WIFE, IS a young woman who isn't more than
twenty-four years of age. She's been good to me, so far. I know
her mother controls her and that she goads her to try and fleece
me every chance she gets. Until now, Aziza has remained reasonable. She hasn't yet been bold enough to actually do this,
but how long will she resist? I can't picture things going on like
this forever. Sooner or later, she'll show her teeth. Anything
else would be strange and unusual, and I wouldn't expect it.
I'm sixty years old and Aziza is twenty-four. When I first met
her mother, she didn't ask me the usual questions: How did
you meet my daughter? Where? What are your intentions?
No. She went right into talking about herself, her humble
family, my status at the palace, and her husband the butcher
who left home and abandoned them—her along with two sons
and four daughters—with no support. All of this before he
remarried and rented a house not far away, his life continuing
normally as if he had never met any of them. What was she
expecting from me? To become a husband to her daughter
and to provide for her and her kids? She didn't ask about Aziza
and our future together. Instead, she kept on talking to me
about her pitiful life, as well as that of her husband the butcher
who had forgotten all about them. "He opens his shop every
morning, you know, and he closes it every evening, like someone without a care in the world, and he doesn't provide them
with a single morsel of meat, despite how hungry they are."

When she heard what her mother said, Aziza provided commentary. Laughing, she said to me, "Now that you have entered our lives, you won't get out unscathed." What could she have possibly meant by this nonsense?

I always wonder what her mother has in store for me. I wouldn't go so far as to say that Aziza loves me, despite all the appreciation she has shown me up until now. I'm not so foolish as to be convinced that she accepted marriage to a man approaching sixty because of my good looks and charm, or because of my status and position, or even because of the respect she saw in peoples' behavior toward me. Oh no. It is because she's poor and she saw that marrying me was an opportunity for her little fingers to grab onto some prestige and for her to know what fortune feels like. I see this especially in the eyes of her mother who has come to view my inevitable death as some sort of deliverance. I picture her praying morning and night that what she wants might finally come to pass.

For the past couple of days, I have thought of telling her that I have children with another woman, just to skew her calculations and keep her forever in my control. It is the first time I've thought of them in a long time. However, I'm afraid of making Aziza angry. Her mother thinks I'm sitting on top of the treasures of Solomon, that I'm stingy, and that I would be of more use to them dead. I'm not sure where she gets these ideas and I always wonder why she behaves this way toward me. We've never delved into the matter directly, but we think about it. Each one of us sees it in the eyes of the other. I meet my obligations toward her daughter, and provide her with some largesse as well by buying her a sheep every year for the Eid feast. Despite that, she never lets an opportunity pass to spread gossip all over the neighborhood and beyond about my unfair treatment toward her and her family. Women are strange beings, and the reason for her hatred toward me will remain forever unknown, just as this marriage will remain one of Aziza's secrets, or one of their secrets. Aziza hesitated for a long time before agreeing to marry me, but in the end she agreed, and that's all that matters.

This wicked mother of hers once told me Aziza had a relationship with a young man she was going to marry. I think she invents these stories whenever she decides to visit us, just to darken what's left of the day. She said that Aziza might still love that young man, or that she may have just left him temporarily because he didn't quite understand her, yet there remained something inside her that longed for him. She said that her daughter was desperate.

"Why is she desperate? What is she missing?" I asked.

"That's exactly what I don't understand," she said, and added that she was doing everything in her power for me to take that young man's place in Aziza's heart. She'd make Aziza love me more than she had loved that young man whose name she didn't want to say out loud, out of respect and appreciation for me. This woman is no idiot. She didn't forget to add in the end that she'd keep to her promise as long as I paid her the necessary attention. That was how she began taking advantage of me. From then on, she did with me as she pleased. She would take my wallet whenever she wanted and buy things she didn't need, with me paying for them willingly, throwing money out the window, as they say. And me, what could I do other than wait for God to deal kindly with her and with us?

Good days nonetheless. I like it when Aziza sits facing me, when she moves in front me shaking her buttocks, proudly showing off her lithe body. When she irons my clothes, I love her because she's Aziza, because she's twenty-four years old, because I become ravenous whenever I see her and whenever I think of her, because I can't picture life without her; without women in general, for that matter. I have crossed enough barren deserts to make me weigh every word I say carefully. I'm not speaking of love. I'll leave matters of love to adolescents and sentimentalists. What is the meaning of this love that I hear about everywhere? This thing that we can neither touch nor see? If you open up a human being's heart and dissect it, you won't find a single atom of the love people talk about everywhere and in every book; you'll just find blood and sinews and veins. You won't find a word written about it there or in the mind or liver or in any of its cells. Can you love a woman who doesn't sleep in your bed, whose neck you can't caress, whose breasts you can't kiss? Can you love a woman whose fruits you cannot savor anytime you want? The love I know, and with which I love Aziza, is her lying on the bed waiting for me to come to her, or sitting next to me waiting for me to take her hand and lead her to the bedroom. Women are bodies created for us, the tribe of men, to rub against as we like, to eat and to drink and to till as we like. Man has always been this way, no matter where, and whoever says otherwise is sick or deranged.

Thursday is a long day, the longest day of the week. From the morning, my mind is preoccupied with thoughts of her body. It gets into my blood and my whole being thumps to the rhythm that anticipates the evening when I'll sleep with Aziza. I picture Aziza all day as she sits preparing to go to the hammam accompanied by her mother, as she walks around the house, as she lies down in the steam room. Aziza moves in my imagination like a happy dream from Thursday morning until evening. She warbles in my head endlessly like a goldfinch. I don't do any work. I want to think of nothing but her. I listen to Abdel-Wahhab sing his old songs, which fill me with longing, and I wait for eight o'clock to arrive, at which time I will sleep with Aziza. Nothing in the world compares to these moments, when she's in the hammam, in the steam room getting ready. She has brought her mother with her to rub down her body and prepare it for tonight while she spits venomous and deadly thoughts into Aziza's head. She has brought enough perfume and venom with her to fill an entire night. But the night is still there waiting at the other end of the day. I can't stand her mother, can't bear even looking at her, but she rubs her daughter's body, despite her venom, despite the black clouds she places between us. Everything is good, bearable, as long as this evil creature remains far away in her son's house on the other side of the city.

In order to make the day pass quickly I go to the café and play cards with Si Abbas and the café's owner. Because I'm completely preoccupied, I lose. My thoughts are scattered, which makes me joyful and lightheaded, so I laugh. My two friends note that I am particularly happy today. Of course. It's Thursday, and already four o'clock in the afternoon. I turn my head to look at the clock on the café wall, blackened by cigarettes and kif smoke. I see that it's only three o'clock, not yet four. In good spirits, I continue to lose, waiting for evening to arrive.

What more could a man of sixty want? What more could he hope for other than that his final days be calm, that pleasant moments such as these last for as long as possible, and that his life ends normally—as any man would hope for—without back or joint pain, or at least with no *major* problems. I try to give them the impression that my fortune does not actually comprise a fortune, as Aziza and her mother think, so as to grasp a moment of calm. Despite that, I'm not saying that I expect things to end badly. Not at all. After all of the Thursdays that have passed, all I hope for is to spend what remains of my life as I am now, in Aziza's arms, no more, no less.

When I go, I won't leave them a thing to remember me by save for the few jokes that made the king laugh and that the government repeated during a discussion of the state budget. I won't leave them a fortune that Aziza's mother could boast of, telling the neighbors that she had hastened sending me to hell in order to enjoy the money before it was too late. I would prefer feeding it to rats. Sometimes I sit looking at them and say to myself, "If only you knew that you won't inherit a thing, that neither you nor your wicked mother will get anything." In any case, whatever they have in mind, they envision a fortune I do not possess. I have this high status, some money in the bank, this house that I'll sell soon, a villa still under construction that they don't know about, and these gifts I have received from the palace, or from this or that important person: wall clocks, valuable rugs, and trays made of silver or fine porcelain. If it were enough for her mother to simply steal some of these gifts, I wouldn't have any problem. However, what her mother wants is to get her hands on everything that I own. The jingling of dirhams in her hands makes her delirious. I have never seen a woman who so loses her bearings and her ability to focus on anything by the mere sound of coins clinking together. The sound of money makes her happy in a way that defies the imagination. When she hears stories of the wealthy and the talents they possess for spending, it throws her off balance and her thoughts are derailed. Her deficient thought processes simply cannot absorb the fact that people spend their money as if they had found it in an alley. As for Aziza, until now she hasn't displayed the same endless yearning or overtly hateful propensity for thievery as her mother.

Today I began to execute my plan.

Man's condition seems truly strange to me. Sometimes life smiles upon him and fate shines on his face as if he were in the springtime of his life. Other times his skies are obscured by thick black clouds to the point where you'd say that bad luck has taken hold of him and won't let go. When that happens, his only hope is a faraway exile or a flash of lightning.

On one of those hot summer days in Marrakech, Zerwal the hunchback and I were sitting in the Café les Négociants, and I heard him ask me, just like that, without any preamble, whether I had a son named Hassan. I was surprised by the question.

"Uh, yes. Hassan. I haven't seen him for ages, for so long that I'd forgotten all about him. What about him?"

He seemed uninterested in my response. He added another question to his first one, as if he were constructing another floor from which to throw me.

"And does he still perform sketches insulting the government of His Majesty the king?"

It was as if he had lit a fire inside my head. I felt it burn the roots of my hair. This hunchback didn't waste any time. He'd dug away at my life story in order to find the stake that he would drive into my heart. And with a stake of this size, you are sure to feel the pain when it's pounded into your bones.

"I have no idea how Hassan is doing, or what has become of his family. I don't know where they are or what they're doing. I don't even know if they're still alive, or whether they still live in the same place. I had forgotten them. Only now do you remind me of them, Zerwal my friend."

I think about Hassan from time to time, but when I do, I don't see him as grown up. I always picture him as a child, yet here he appears in another form, as a young man writing slanderous things about people he doesn't know. Why would Hassan insult the government? I left him when he was young, forgot about him and his tribe, and here he was, sent back to me in the form of a threat that the hunchback sitting by my side in the Café les Négociants fired at me with a nonchalance that hides his true intentions. His seeming indifference makes his threat that much more potent. What concerned me most of all was: where did he meet Hassan? Did they meet in a public place or did he visit him at home? Were there others who knew the story of the son who insulted the government? I wouldn't ask Zerwal, sitting next to me and waiting for me to do so. I wouldn't ask him because I didn't want to give him the impression that I was afraid of him. Then he would grab my neck even tighter than he had it already. I didn't want to give him the opportunity. What needed to be done next was for me to observe him more closely.

I invited him to my house, welcoming him warmly, and presented him with a wall clock that pleased him. This wasn't the house I shared with my wife, Aziza. No. For some time now I have borrowed a garçonnière, where I find refuge every once in a while. I hadn't opened it up for any man before, but now I hand the key to the hunchback with peace of mind. Completely contrary to what I had pictured, I discovered that he was an insatiable philanderer, but as long as women rejected him and were stricken by true fear at the mere sight of his form, he found in my friendship a means of catching his prey and in my house the nest where he could attend to his vices without any hindrance. From the moment I brought him into my house, he didn't mention the story of Hassan or his sketches to me, which worried me to no end, my fear increasing rather than dissipating.

I don't like him, especially now that I have let him into my house so he can entertain his prostitutes there. I have always considered him an enemy, my number-one enemy. I started to invite him to my house so that I could see what his intentions were. Before then, I didn't know how far he had gone with his plan. How could I know? But here in my house I had a rare opportunity to take a picture of him naked in the arms of one of his prostitutes, and to leak it to the press. I mulled the idea over more than once, but then dropped it. The picture might have the opposite effect of what I expected. The picture could cause waves of laughter to swell among the very circles I sent the picture to, resulting in his speedy promotion rather than demotion. Besides, he no longer mentioned the story of Hassan and his plays in which he insulted the government.

Nevertheless, it was like I was swimming in a closed, airtight tank, every movement a useless effort that sapped my strength. I thought seriously about how to cause his downfall before he caused mine. I spent my nights dreaming but one dream: that I was burying Zerwal in a hole under my bed. I would remove his clothes, obscure the features of his face, and strip him of anything that would allow him to be identified. I would throw him into the hole and cover him with a mixture of iron and cement, and then I would go to sleep on top of him. I had the same dream so many times that I would spend my days wondering whether I had actually committed the crime. Sometimes I was so confused between the dream and reality that I would jump from my bed and crawl underneath looking for traces of the hole.

That day, I began to implement my plan to bring him down. I didn't take naked pictures of him. I didn't splatter the porch of his house with blood, nor did I place amulets in hidden corners to bring evil on him. No. I didn't succumb to any of this. Rather, I introduced him to a whore whom he immediately liked, a young girl I found in one of the bars in the Gueliz neighborhood. She was no more than sixteen, beautiful and kind, but she had syphilis, and the best thing about this particular disease is that its symptoms don't appear until it's too late for treatment. And so I waited.

In the royal palace, I observe Zerwal's body. Is there any change in the color of his skin? Have any blisters or abscesses appeared? Nothing has shown up yet and that's for the best. The longer the symptoms take to show, the deeper the disease will have burrowed its way in. I hope that it has made its way into his blood and into all his cells. At the same time, I observe His Majesty's behavior. I analyze the way he looks at me. Has there been any change? So far, I haven't been able to spot anything specific.

Our king is a great king, but he's a tyrant, and I know what fate his enemies and their families have met, and that this is his right. He has sentenced all who have opposed him to death, expulsion, and banishment, in order to perpetuate the awesome power of the Makhzen, as it was in the days of the great sultans. But I'm not opposed to him, and I'll wash my hands of my son in front of His Majesty and in front of witnesses in the event that the boy's damned activities come to his attention. The weather is calm now, with no storm on the horizon. The hunchback has not taken up full arms against me in battle. I'm the one who knows the king best. I can be sure that his anger is fierce, and that his tyranny in these sorts of situations is even stronger. When he sends someone to one of his prisons, he will never appear again. May God save you and us both. This severity is what has convinced his enemies and those who oppose him that there's no use attempting a coup against him. Our war in the Sahara is an opportunity for everyone to gather under his shadow. His severity is what allows him to control everything. But there are those who know nothing and think that such actions are no longer appropriate. I think the opposite is true. The regime is really ruling now. It's a wonderful idea, this war.

All sorts of people flock to the palace—high-ranking officers, professional politicians, ministers, honored guests—and they all resemble one another to a great degree. In fact, it is difficult to distinguish one from the other. I don't understand why His Majesty considers them necessary when they don't do anything useful. They are nothing more than a bunch of creeps who spend their time trying to ingratiate themselves with the king. Oh, how I hate them. Stupid people who never stop frowning and furrowing their brows. And when they do laugh or imitate a chicken laying an egg or a monkey picking at its hair, it's all to put their master in a good mood. Some of them ruin royal dinners with their gloominess. They don't find pleasure in anything. At the sight of their serious miens anything pleasurable prefers to turn its back rather than look at their depressing faces. It's as if they're terminally constipated. It would be best if they just retreated to the desert to take pleasure in their frowns and depressive states until the end of time. I always wonder where this terminal gloom comes from, this blight that banishes all of life's pleasures, for what meaning does life have without a desire for those pleasures in the first place?

But it is not sadness that haunts their faces and makes their lives miserable. Rather, it is because they are always scared of losing their positions. That's the reason. Their handkerchiefs never leave their hands because they're constantly sweating. Their eyes dart in every direction, scared as they enter the palace and still scared as they leave it, not breathing until they are sufficiently far from it. Even then, they keep looking over their shoulders wondering whether they have gone far enough. This is how they pass their lives, as if walking in a minefield. In the palace they nod their heads like trained monkeys. They leave every decision to the king so as not to make a slip and be flogged or cast out like their predecessors. Thus they are tortured. Whenever I think about it, I'm struck with the same fear. When I think about Zerwal I break out in a cold sweat and anxiety eats away at my nerves. I think about him all the time. I think about him when he's with me in the palace, but he worries me even more when I leave him behind in the house rolling around in the arms of prostitutes.

Other than providing solace to His Majesty, my one pleasure in this world is Aziza, my life's single joy. I use all sorts of fruits and vegetables that enhance sexual appetite in order to remain in control of things at home, and there's no shame in this. It's not as if I'm like Zerwal, who's up to his ears in depravity. I can only love one woman at a time. When I went off with Drissiya, when I decided to live with her, I left my first wife and children. I fell in love with her the moment I saw her and I sacrificed everything for her—my house, my wife, my children. That was all many years ago.

One morning I just left the house and never went back. All I possessed was a palm-leaf basket that I'd sit on in the square under the burning Marrakech sun, and a small teapot that I would fill with water, and when I poured it out into cups, sometimes it came out yellow, and other times green—childish toys that no one would envy. I would finish my days just as I had started them, with empty pockets. But all around me there were other performers who were successful at what they did, and next to all of these people there stood this woman, Drissiya, another one who knew what she was doing. She had a megaphone that carried her voice to every corner of the square. She set up her spot next to mine. A woman with a lovable plumpness, selling amulets and remedies that she said she had gotten from the Hijaz. She had placed a hat like that of a cowboy's upon her head. She had black sunglasses and a Mercedes, and she loved to laugh. Her teeth were white and they shone. She loved to laugh in order to show her beautiful white teeth. She said that she had been watching me for some time, and I said the same thing to her. Then she said that she loved me, and I said the same, so we got married and it lasted a full year.

With her, I roamed the country from one end to the other in the Mercedes she drove, always wearing her black sunglasses. We would sell her herbal remedies in different markets, and then we'd move on. Then one day, her husband showed up. I hadn't known that she was married, she hadn't said a word about it, but there he was standing right in front of us. There was nothing to do about it as he didn't want to get his wife back. All he wanted was to live with us and eat and drink at our expense. His name was Jimmy. His hair was always slicked back. He looked like a pimp, and maybe that was indeed his line of work. At first he would only appear at the end of the day, to receive his cut, as if it were he who was continuously barking into the megaphone. This didn't bother me as long as Drissiya saw no problem with it. But it came to pass that Drissiya would never leave his side because he started to eat and sleep and spend all day and night with her. And how would they spend their time? Laughing. They spent their time playing and laughing and screwing like cats while I was left shouting into the megaphone.

That was many years ago. I didn't think about marriage again after my experience with Drissiya, and my adventures remained limited—in this regard I don't resemble Zerwal at all—until the day Aziza showed up spreading her lovely scent all around me. Zerwal resembles a goat. His smell is disgusting, and he loves it just like a goat would. He has sex and doesn't wash, so the smell of it clings to him. Aziza's smell is always pleasant.

I met Aziza through a friend of mine two years ago. I didn't pick her up in one of the cabarets. No, I met her with the intention to marry and I told her when we first met that I was only thinking about what was right and honorable. I waited a while for her response, and then I knocked on the door of her house in Bab Aghmat and told her for the thousandth time that I was awaiting her response. I said it to her with an air of concealed threat, not entirely free of a begging tone. As she always did, she pursed her lips. Her mother was unable to convince her. She said, "This girl wants to kill me," and I left the house angrily, dragging myself through the street without paying attention to anyone passing by or greeting me. This wasn't normal for me. I was completely preoccupied with Aziza. She was living in a modest house on a poor street where rats and cats played in front of her door. She was a girl of limited means who only owned two dresses and an old pair of shoes, yet still she refused. I didn't see the waiter as he placed my cup of coffee and water on the table. Perhaps he said hello, to me but I didn't respond. I was preoccupied. Her house had the smell of cheap coffee, of everyday rosewater, of childhood. I hadn't yet reached the age of sixty, like I have now, and my desire was to bury what remained of my years in her succulent youth. The desire itched like a damned illness. My mind and body were empty, or rather, completely filled with her. They were not prepared to do anything that day, and had the king been in his palace, I'm not sure what my stupidity would have driven me to do. My mind was more troubled than ever. Never had I suffered as I did while waiting for Aziza's response. I had never endured a moment like that one, neither with Drissiya, nor with Fatima, my first wife. Maybe it was because of my age.

Aziza never visited my house—she didn't even know my address—and I became obsessed with thinking about when she would knock on my door. I would wake up at dawn and wait like someone who had lost his mind. I would wake up at dawn and sit waiting for a young girl who didn't even know my address to knock on my door. Is there anything crazier than that? I remained clinging to this madness for a while, not wanting to go anywhere, not thinking about anything. My mind was in that filthy house where Aziza lived. My whole being was there. I was hoping she would say that she wanted me as a husband, to put my mind at ease, though I was approaching sixty, though the story would cause people to laugh. If I could have, I would have run to her and thrown myself into her arms and kissed her hands, even though I was the one who was expecting *her* to kiss *my* hands as her savior who would deliver her from poverty. I was like an infatuated teenager. Then, in moments of anger—the anger that lovers feel—I would think about her and picture myself storming her house to force myself on her. I would see myself throwing cash on her naked body and, glaring at her harshly, I'd assure her that I would hate her forever. With the eye that lovers have, I would see her ask me to protect her as a slave girl and kiss my feet, which would only increase my hatred for her.

5

Day Two

WE WALKED AT NIGHT, ONE behind the other, carrying water and provisions, along with a rifle and some bullets, heading toward the well. Me, Brahim, Mohamed Ali, and Naafi. My leave had been canceled at the last moment. We left the other soldiers playing cards at Sergeant Bouzide's as they do when night falls, and we left Brigadier Omar swimming in a fog of drunkenness. The heat rose from the rocks. It descended from the sky. Not a wisp of wind around us, as if we were walking through hot steam. Our bodies took in the heat and then gave it off many times over. We were crossing a road of which we could only see the part that was lit. The moonlight gave the impression that there were things there that actually weren't. Shadows shifted at every turn and the sand dunes moved as if they were the ones walking instead of us. What we thought was a well turned out to be a pile of rocks. We saw a sea and rivers. Sometimes we saw cities that didn't exist. As for the well, we hadn't gotten to it yet. Three hours of walking and there was no well on the horizon. In fact, was there even a horizon or a road? When we began the journey we were singing, but by the time we reached the midway point, we were silent. We left silence behind us, only to meet more, never-ending silence. It was in front of us like a wall, thicker than the one we'd left behind.

Mohamed Ali said, "If we keep walking straight with our backs to the sun, we'll reach Las Palmas. We may not find the well, but Las Palmas is this way, straight ahead," and he pointed in front of him.

I asked him, "What sun? It's the middle of the night," to which he replied that he was speaking in general terms.

"And if there's no sun?" I asked.

Brahim laughed while Naafi looked at his picture of Alain Delon and raised his right eyebrow. Mohamed Ali, who never joked, said he had a friend in Las Palmas and he was the one who told him that. Las Palmas is in the west, always due west. Brahim continued to laugh.

I said, "I've never seen Las Palmas, but I know that it's not located west of anything."

My words made Brahim laugh even harder. With his hand pointing in the same direction, Mohamed Ali said excitedly, "Whichever way you face, Las Palmas is west of you."

Mohamed Ali was beginning to get irritated. He said that his friend knew Las Palmas like the back of his hand; that he'd gone to Las Palmas thirteen times and had built many houses there. He'd built whole cities, in fact, because he was in construction, and his cities attest to the fact that he was there, there in Las Palmas, and he pointed in the same direction. He said that a construction worker doesn't lie because he plants proof everywhere he goes, and his friend's proof is all the cities he has built in Las Palmas.

Brahim continued to laugh, completely indifferent to Mohamed Ali's irritation. I asked, "And the sea? What does your friend do to cross the sea?"

Amazed, he said that his friend never mentioned any sea either before or after Las Palmas, that it's enough to just keep walking with your back to the sun. This time we both laughed, Brahim and I. As for Naafi, he seemed to be somewhere else entirely. Wherever he turned he saw Fifi, so he'd raise his right eyebrow and smile.

We fell silent, and then heard something move nearby. It could have been a snake. Brahim jumped back, as did

Mohamed Ali and I. Naafi grabbed his rifle. The three of us stood behind him. I said, "Snakes are harmless. They're friendly animals." This time, Brahim didn't laugh. He was looking around in terror. He had realized for the first time that he was walking in the desert, and that the desert was a place where more than prophets lived; there are also snakes, scorpions, lizards, bats, and wolves. Naafi was pointing his rifle in every direction while Brahim jumped behind him, shifting his feet and picking them up one at a time as if the snake's poison were already coursing through his veins, even before he'd been bitten.

We didn't know how to use our weapons. We had never carried a weapon in our lives. We were here as conscripts, each seeking the protection of the others because no one had mastered the use of any weapon whatsoever. This is how compulsory military service works: you go to war without having mastered the use of a weapon. You'll always find someone whose hobby is hunting gazelles or rabbits or wild boar, and you'll spend the next eighteen months behind him.

Mohamed Ali didn't utter a word when Brahim exploded into laughter once again. He didn't say a thing about Las Palmas or about his friend who had gone there on foot thirteen times, and I couldn't tell if he was still angry. I tried to bring Brahim back to his senses by asking, "Brahim, what's with you?" but I was unsuccessful. He remained silent for a few seconds before breaking into laughter again. He alternated between giggling softly and guffawing so loudly that you'd swear the man had lost his mind. I asked him to be quiet since we were crossing an area we didn't know at all. The dawn light began to show, making it necessary for us to be extra cautious. Rather than showing caution, however, he burst out laughing. When we could take it no longer he apologized, saying that the turtle was tickling his belly. Brahim wasn't laughing because of Mohamed Ali's stories, or because of the stories of his friend who had erected cities in Las Palmas. Brahim was hiding Fifi's turtle under his shirt and it had been tickling him the whole time. I saw him grab his belly and try to stop himself from laughing, but he couldn't. Naafi ran toward him and lifted the shirt, and even when he pulled the shirt up from the bottom and extracted the turtle from it, Brahim continued to laugh for some time. Then he said apologetically that the turtle helped him keep his mental balance, that it kept him from feeling alone. He seemed to be asking Naafi to return the turtle to him and the two of them started to walk behind us, Naafi first and Brahim following a step behind. They got farther away from us. I saw their shadows only when I turned around and the night carried their whispers to us as if they were coming to some sort of a secret agreement. Then we forgot about them entirely, for silence enveloped them as if Fifi's turtle had taken the place of their need to speak.

In a little while the sun will come up. This is the time when Zineb leaves the cabaret, the Shahrazade Cabaret. I had never set so much as a foot in there before meeting Zineb. Because of the chaos of the crowds, I could never get in. It's springtime. The girls laugh, bunching up in front of the entrance, and the guys play with beer bottles, balancing them on their heads, only to grab them just as they're about to fall. They also laugh loudly, but the bouncers don't do anything. They just stand in front of the door, not saying anything to them. I'm not laughing, even though I am going to see Zineb. I'm more serious than necessary when I'm not at work. Even the sketches I perform are marked by this manner of seriousness. I'm fully aware of it and I make a concerted effort to put serious thought behind every laugh. For this reason, I always say that I don't give people the gift of laughter just for its own sake. The police have summoned me to the station numerous times because of my "subversive stories," as they call them. Some of the workers who control the dressing rooms in the city's concert halls have even banned me. It's not as if I'm a jester!

I was finally able to enter. The crowd dwindled and it didn't seem like the same place where moments before bottles had been flying over the door. Onstage in the dance hall a young man was telling jokes to the small audience drinking there. I sat, calmly watching him. All around me there were customers standing or sitting at tables crowded with bottles and surrounded by girls, most of them no older than sixteen. Their youth made them frivolous, exaggerating everything they did—smoking, drinking, laughing, being indifferent—and the young man onstage continued to tell dirty jokes, but the patrons were laughing. I think they were laughing because of the atmosphere and the girls and the drinking. It wasn't the vulgar talk coming out of the young man's mouth that made them laugh. There are people who are ready to laugh at any moment. They laugh at everything and nothing. They even laugh when they hear someone wishing them good morning. As for me, I don't laugh, either at my own stories or at the stories of others. I felt like an orphan sitting in front of an empty table with a harsh light shining down on me, watching a person tell bad jokes to customers who were laughing for reasons no one knew. Luckily, my head was filled with thoughts of Zineb.

Warm applause rose up when the singer appeared, her brocaded dress shining under the lights. She sang well. The applause wasn't exaggerated. Light as a breeze, airborne like a butterfly, her voice rang through the room like pure crystal. Moments before, the customers had shown no joy on their faces, but now everyone in the cabaret caught their breath as they watched the elegant body move lithely across the stage and listened to the quivering voice, sounding as if it came from a spring of eternal sweetness. And perhaps it is at that moment, as you are taken by this dizziness, that your only desire is to get up on stage and run your hands all over the young woman, to climb down her throat and search her with your eyes, your hands, and your fingernails to find the answer to this baffling and confusing, even nerve-wracking, question:

"Where does this voice come from, and how does it flow from this throat so fluidly, so purely, with such enchantment?" No, the applause was genuine when Zineb appeared onstage.

The applause continued for some time after she finished singing. With the same grace and lightness she had onstage, she moved between the tables and sat at mine. So this is the Zineb who had been standing next to me a few days ago on television, troubled and worried about her future. Her neck was slim and her breasts were small and erect. With a delicate movement she untied the string that was holding her hair up and shook her head a few times, letting her hair fall down over her shoulders, flowing like fields of grain under an evening breeze. She was beautiful, no doubt about it. Not the type of beauty that is brilliant and fades fast. No, there's another kind of beauty that is difficult to describe because it brings calm to the heart rather than confusion, a soothing warmth rather than a burning heat. Zineb's beauty is of this latter type. Her smile, her movements, everything about her gives off a feeling of calm and makes you feel optimistic and happy. I ordered her something to drink but she said that she only drank water. I grabbed a glass of water from another table and gave it to her. She took it from me and thanked me. She drank it and wiped her lips slowly with the back of her hand. She's truly a simple girl. She penetrates your heart from who knows where. When you sit with her you feel as if you've known her for years.

During our second meeting she grabbed my hand, caressed it, then turned it over to read my future, which could be nothing but bright coming from Zineb's lips. And it was just as I expected. I spent months walking on air, not knowing whether I was dreaming while awake, or awake while dreaming. I don't recall many of the details, but I do recall that at seven o'clock in the evening I would park my motorbike, waiting in front of her house to take her to the cabaret. A strange hour, seven in the evening. I would spend the day thinking about it. Seven in the evening, when will seven o'clock come? I would stop in front of her house at ten in the morning to wonder what she was doing at that moment. I would picture her still sleeping. I would picture her washing her face, soapsuds between her fingers and on her forehead. Then I would picture her making her black coffee, and her blue ceramic coffee cup. I would picture her house, and her room. I hadn't yet entered her room. No doubt it's clean and white, with a white bed and a small blue carpet in the middle, and a closet made of juniper wood with two candles brought from Essaouira on it. Then I would pass by at three and stop again, thinking that she might be looking down at me from her balcony, and why not? These things happen every day. While walking across the room, some sort of an alarm would go off in her head telling her that a young man named Hassan was passing by under her balcony at that moment, so she would turn toward the balcony wanting to cast a glance at the street. My heart beat and I saw a shadow pass behind the shade and I told myself that it was Zineb passing close to the balcony, close to my heart.

After three I didn't return to her house. It seemed like seven o'clock was very close, but it was stubborn, seeming to move further away the closer it got. I made the rounds of the streets without any set goal, or more precisely, with only one goal, which was to pass the time, but it didn't pass. The clock's hands had stopped. All the clocks' hands had stopped. They were all pointing to three and sometimes to before three. As for seven, it was far away. I'd never get there. And what was Zineb doing during this time? She was getting ready. She was moving calmly toward seven. Didn't she know that I'd passed under her balcony four or five times? Didn't she know that I'd been waiting for her next to her house for two hours? Four months passed in this way. After seven o'clock, when I took her to the cabaret, I'd sit waiting for her in the café next door. I didn't do anything. I didn't think about my work. I didn't do my regular exercises. I smoked and I waited for Zineb. My entire life boiled down to this waiting for Zineb. I waited with

43

a fluttering heart to take her to the cabaret and I waited with the same anguish to take her home. This schedule filled me with joy. My proximity to her was enough to satisfy me. It permeated my room when I returned alone at the end of the night. It filled my night and what remained of my day. My anguish was proof that I was feeling, living, thinking, and loving. Zineb thought I was neglecting my work, and grew sad. She said that I was neglecting my sketches, and that I was neglecting the regular exercises I used to do at home. This made me happy too, that she was worried about me.

We got married after four months, without a ceremony, without a wedding, without a party, and after we wrote up the contract in the notary's shop, she told me she loved me, and this was enough, more than enough.

Zineb changed once the pregnancy began to show, which is natural. The changes that her body was undergoing were sure to affect her mind. This is what I thought, but I was wrong. The socialist doctor and his wife gave her the idea of getting rid of the fetus. That's what happened. She didn't consult me at all and her dear friends continued to conspire and maneuver behind my back until they convinced her of the uselessness of children.

We walked softly toward the dawn, toward the well whose silhouette had begun to appear.

6

Day Two

GENERALLY, HIS MAJESTY GOES TO his palace in Marrakech when he wants to make an important announcement, and I'm usually right there next to him the whole time he's there. This year, he'll come earlier than usual to stay in the city, before the spring. He's not in the habit of coming before the spring, but this time he's awaiting one of his important guests. Everyone *says* that he's waiting for an important guest, but is he really that important? It is the press that's writing that he's important, and the press lies, this is well known. And it is also the press that's writing that they will discuss the issue of the Sahara, but why? When has His Majesty ever discussed his affairs with anyone? Can His Majesty not solve a minor issue like the Sahara on his own, just as he has done before with everything else he has faced?

Before, I said that those who come to the palace resemble one another quite a bit. Even more than that, they all try to be like His Majesty. They dress like him, they buy the same shoes, they put on the same tie, and they buy the same expensive watches he wears on his wrist. They erect magnificent villas in an attempt to compete with his palaces, and they hold the same refined cigarettes between their fingers that His Majesty smokes. If they could they would own eunuch slaves like those in the palace, but, alas, the law prohibits them to do that, lucky for us. What would it be like if hundreds of effeminate eunuchs with piercing voices were prancing around the city's streets? That would be all we needed!

One day, His Majesty asked one of his ministers about the cost of his new residence. It was an extravagant palace this minister had built. Because he wasn't expecting such a surprising question, and so the king wouldn't accuse him of wasting money, he quoted a low price. Then the king asked the minister if he could visit his palace as soon as possible. The minister returned to his palace trembling and immediately ordered that the walls and ceiling be covered up then painted over with plaster and gypsum in order to hide all signs of ostentation. Before arriving at the minister's house, the king's spies told him about the new wall coverings concealing the rare Italian marble underneath. The king made a careful inspection of the palace's many wings and at the end of the tour, he announced that the building was in need of numerous repairs, but that in its current condition he would purchase it for half its value, an amount not even equal to the price of the land it was built on. He is a smart man who knows every detail, large and small, about the men who make up his entourage. I'm sure that, in his heart, he hates them. Naturally, I'm not so stupid as to think that between our master and me there's any sort of resemblance, but I do believe that with certain things, I think the way His Majesty thinks. Neither of us likes the moochers who flock to the palace and who consider themselves indispensable just because they are skilled in the art of playing tricks on one another.

It is truly an important guest who has come. He is the president of a republic, but with his huge entourage and the pageantry surrounding his visit, he is like a king. He has come accompanied by his wife and children, as if they are on vacation even though the visit is part of important negotiations, according to what I heard on the radio. Red carpets are laid down over the entire route from the airport to the palace and the crowds on either side of the road are waving signs and pictures of His Majesty and his guest. Men carry their children on their shoulders and point to the procession so that they will see and remember this momentous day. They jostle one another without paying attention to the metal barriers. They threaten the procession as they hastily rush forward, ignoring the batons of the gendarmes and the police. Military music, youyous, and anthems blare everywhere. Hands are waving and old women are crying because they can't see anything; all they can hear are shouts in honor of His Majesty and his guest. Throats are hoarse from so much yelling. This has never happened with any other guest. Never before have we lived a day like this one. A historic day, the likes of which we'll wait years to experience again.

When the important guest arrived, all of the kingdom's singers and musicians were in the palace's reception hall waiting with their black suits, various instruments, and sullen faces. Some of them were licking their dry lips, while others were chewing on their moustaches or going over their songs in their heads so as not to forget them. Everyone was at the ready. An unforgettable day! I consider the singers a necessity for making His Majesty's intentions known and for vaunting his glories to the people. I understand well why they go with him from palace to palace. Without them, how will the people know the extent of the efforts that His Majesty exerts to improve our image in the eyes of the important guest, and in the eyes of other guests as well? I saw His Majesty in the expansive, well-lit hall speaking with his guest, who was smiling and nodding in agreement with every sentence. He was tall and had to lean over in order to hear what His Majesty was saying. And how could he have behaved any differently, with a king who knows about everything, big and small? He is truly a great man. He loves to talk about the most sensitive matters and to know other peoples' opinions on them, even though he doesn't take them into consideration and hates any opinion that is not his own. Yet he deigns to listen to them.

General Bouricha was sitting on the other side of the table. This officer had submitted his retirement papers years ago, but was still hanging around inside the palace walls waiting to be given some sort of role. He too was nodding his head. His Majesty was not looking at him. He paid no attention to him. For a while now he hasn't trusted his officers. I'm not saying that he was scared of them. He just doesn't like them, and imagines them plotting behind his back. As for Bouricha, the king doesn't like him because of his peasant roots, or maybe it's because of his overly serious demeanor, and probably also because his face is always hidden behind black sunglasses. So for all these reasons he leaves him to nod his head like a horse without paying him the slightest attention. I can't stand him either.

I had never seen him as angry as he was that night. The evening concert began as I was expecting. Musicians and singers filed onto the podium. When it came time for his favorite singer to perform, the guy looked confused, unable to hold his oud properly or find the right rhythm with his voice, and this all happened in front of a guest whom everyone considered important, as evidenced by the unusual pageantry with which he was received. But look at this singer whom His Majesty has long held in high regard, presenting him with mantles and shoes. Look at what he does now! Here he is in front of his guest, trembling and swallowing his sentences like some amateur performer. His Majesty couldn't contain himself. He rose from where he was sitting and grabbed the oud from the singer's hands. He placed it on the chair next to him and demanded that he return the shoes to him. I had never seen him in such a state.

After that, he removed himself along with his guest to another room where they spoke for hours in private. He must have been discussing the issue of the Sahara with him, the only subject that means anything to him, the only subject that really worries him. I don't understand why he is so interested in the Sahara, but as long as he considers the topic of the utmost importance, anything else seems irrelevant. He has great confidence in himself. Sometimes, when he's walking around the palace deep in thought, he'll toss me a question I have no way of knowing the answer to. Still, he expects me to respond even though he won't take what I say seriously. Maybe it helps him focus. In moments such as these, when he is lost in thought, he likes me to walk behind him spewing nonsense, as if he were listening to music or the sound of ocean waves. Maybe it helps. He understands everything from religion to astronomy. He can converse on any topic, bringing religious scholars, exegetes, astrologers, and astronauts from all corners of the globe to his palace. He misses nothing. He knows everything that happens around him, as well as what happens far from him, in the furthest reaches of the kingdom. But ever since the Sahara became his number-one problem, one that he expends great efforts to solve, it has preoccupied him to no end. On its account he invited this important guest and threw him a banquet that lasted for three days, during which time triumphal arches were erected, flags were flown everywhere, parties were held, and singers on the radio and television sang of the glories of the king and his guest. Epics were written praising the deep and ancient connection that binds our two peoples and two countries. Yes, he is very optimistic and he will find an appropriate solution soon.

I don't claim to know everything about His Majesty, for he is truly a mysterious man. One can expect anything from him. For this reason you'll find some people flattering him and others avoiding him entirely, but in the end, everyone goes along with his opinion on every topic. Everyone reveres him and looks to him as a holy figure. However, what I don't understand is why he takes the trouble to discuss with his guest things that are of such critical importance, such as the Sahara. God only knows why.

When he and his guest emerged from the room that contained their secrets, cheers erupted in the great hall as if they had reached a solution. That was what the wide smiles and warm applause that greeted them suggested. General Bouricha met them with a resounding salute, to which His Majesty did not attach any value. Then some ministers and political players from various parties rushed toward them, smoothing and straightening their suits, and bowed with humility as they always do. I was close to His Majesty so he presented me to his guest and I was expected to do something. This was my job, after all, and I was ready for it. I turned around and, finding only the prime minister next to me, I began to enumerate his honorable qualities:

"His Excellency has ten servants—white ones, fair-skinned ones, and brown ones. Once I had complained to him of my widowed status, my financial straits, and my harsh loneliness, so he asked me to accompany him to his house to choose the servant that most appealed to me to take for myself."

The poor man was surprised by my fictional tale and began to pull nervously at his suit as if it were causing him some discomfort. Then I feigned sadness and stopped speaking. His Majesty asked me why I was silent, while His Excellency turned to look at him, gripping the edge of his uniform and waiting helplessly to see what new stories I was going to cook up. He gave a wan smile and waited while the king and his important guest laughed. His Excellency asked me about my experience with the new woman the man had given me as a gift and I feigned embarrassment. I became mute and pretended to run away. I circled around them squealing and swaying while they cracked up. When His Majesty insisted, in on the joke and knowing ahead of time what had been prepared for this scion of political power, I said that I had passed a week with this woman, but had not tasted her fruit. Then I was silent once again. The tears welled up and almost burst from my eyes from the fake pain of it. Fear seized His Excellency as he tried to anticipate the disaster I was preparing for him, readying himself for a harsh, backbreaking blow. He began to shift his eyes around, moistening his lips and curling them in an attempt to recuperate from his dread of what was coming.

His Majesty asked me, "And what was the reason?"

"The . . . the reason?" I stammered.

Then I was silent again, putting on a more exaggerated bashfulness, with a longer hesitation. When His Majesty insisted, I replied, "I myself don't know. Every time I lay down next to her she turned her back to me, laid out on her stomach, and went to sleep. I told myself on that first night that maybe she was tired and just wanted to sleep. On the second night, I said that perhaps we had sat up too late and that her only desire was to go to sleep. On the third night, I began to have doubts. I asked her, 'What's up with you, my girl?' I didn't understand the problem until the night she explained to me that, during the whole time she had lived at His Excellency's house, she had always lain on her belly. This was how His Excellency and his sons who mounted her one after the other taught her the game of love and sexual intercourse."

His Excellency shook as he denied the whole thing. His bald head reddened and he looked around in vain for a hole he could crawl into, but since when had I ever concerned myself with or attached any value to a minister's annoyance? They're the ones who flatter and fawn the most because their positions are the most fragile, and His Majesty can do away with them whenever he pleases. His Majesty exploded in laughter and patted the shoulder of his minister, who didn't know whether he had been spared, or whether there remained other surprises in store for him.

I have been doing this job for fifteen years now and have always wondered what purpose these types of people serve in the king's palace. Haven't I always seen him making decisions about everything on his own? Why doesn't he just ignore them? If I were in his place, I would get rid of them. Why does he even consider them necessary? They are only useful because they distract people during elections and other occasions so he and those who work closely with him are free to get things done.

His Majesty is right that if he doesn't take care of his affairs himself, no one else will, and if he doesn't come up with solutions himself, much could be lost, perhaps even his kingdom. But what do all of these ministers, generals, and politicians who never leave the palace have to lose? Nothing. When they lose their jobs, if they even had jobs to begin with, they'll return to their homes and live off the fortunes they've amassed—fortunes that will make them and their children rich for life. As for His Majesty, if it were to happen, God forbid, that he lose *his* job, he would lose everything along with it, including his head. The others, whether they are politicians or poets, singers or musicians, are nothing but opportunists without loyalty to anything or anyone. The only loyalty they know is to themselves. "My best friend is my pocket," as they say. They'd craft new speeches, compose new poems, and sing new songs as soon as a new victor appears. They would become ministers in a new government, or poets and singers in his new inner circle. They'd be the first to sign the execution papers if his luck turned, God forbid. He is right to ignore them and deal with them like a bunch of corrupt grovelers and shower them with money so that they'll praise him at international events and sing the praises of the model of democracy and social justice we live in. All of this so that they will remain close to him, allowing him to keep watch over them. That's the important thing.

And don't think the tribes will stand with him. The tribes don't stand with or against anyone. The tribes only stand with their own flesh and blood, because, essentially, they love civil strife. They love coups and revolutions and all manner of conspiracies. To their very core, the tribes love war and unrest, and they rejoice at the sight of blood. They love everything bloody, even if they pretend not to. All you have to do is look at them, at their mouths hanging wide open when they see the tragedies and bloodbaths that appear daily on our television screens, to know the extent of their thirst for disaster.

Yes, everyone fears me here. They know well the status I have achieved. They know the freedom with which I behave. I am not silent about things I don't like. I don't fear retribution. I have risen above punishment. I state my thoughts as they come to me without disguising or sugarcoating them. Because of this I say, and I say it repeatedly, that I am similar to His Majesty. Neither of us is afraid of anyone. Both of us do what we please, cultivating a respectable number of enemies as we go. If God allowed us to see into the hearts of those around us, I would be able to see the hatred boiling inside them and the plots they were cooking up for me.

Zerwal hasn't appeared for a while now, long enough for me to know that something has happened. Two full weeks! When I went to his house I found him bedridden. His oldest daughter was moving back and forth between the bedroom and the kitchen. She's the one I found in front of me when I went up the narrow stairs crowded with potted basil plants. I tried to comfort her with a few pleasantries. There was basil everywhere—on the stairs, in the foyer, in the bedroom. His wife was sitting on the edge of the bed, moistening a piece of cloth and dabbing his feverish forehead with it. She didn't turn to me when I tried to comfort her with the same pleasantries. A clear, inexplicable animosity had settled between us, ever since I first set foot in this house a number of months ago. Maybe she thought I was responsible for his chronic immorality. I didn't care about this before and I wasn't going to care now. What had brought me here was to check on Zerwal's illness. I had waited for two full weeks, during which time he had not shown up at the café, or at my house, or even to the palace when His Majesty was present. As one day followed another I became increasingly sure that the plan I had hatched was bearing fruit. Here he was in front of me, just as I had expected, lying on his bed without moving. His eyes were closed. His face had a deep yellow pall. His damp chest rose and fell with his breathing.

What made me even more sure that the sickness had burrowed deep into him was the light fuzz that had grown on his cheeks. Usually he doesn't have a beard. Now I see one spreading over his cheeks, like maggots eating away at what remained of his life. My heart was put at ease.

He was surrounded by bottles of herbal remedies and a number of books. Was he sleeping? I didn't think so. He was trying to listen to his pain. The lethal sickness was deviously doing what it was supposed to be doing. I didn't smell the odor of putrefaction yet; its time would come when the worms will have eaten the better part of his member. The overpoweringly putrid odor I smelled now was coming from the meat and offal cooking in some corner of the house. The hunchback's son-in-law sells sausages in the Djemaa El-Fna and that's what I smelled cooking—an awful, suffocating smell. I wondered how it hadn't yet killed someone in his family. I guess these people are immune to rot. They can eat out of garbage cans and live on waste their whole lives without any harm coming to them. The disgusting smells fatten them up rather than kill them. The potted basil plants fill the stairway and part of the foyer so the smell of rotten meat doesn't make its way to the neighbors.

Zerwal moved in his bed and opened his eyes. I smiled at him, a smile of consolation and encouragement.

I asked him about his health: "Doing all right?"

"Fine, praise be to God."

I asked him about what was ailing him and he repeated, "Praise be to God."

I asked him if he had caught a cold. He didn't respond so I added that all of us are susceptible to catching colds because of the lateness of the rainy season and the microbes that weren't being washed away, and other frivolous things of this nature. His wife was the one who responded to my questions.

"A *good* man, when his gaze strays and he becomes blind, searches for healthy girls. He doesn't collect prostitutes who have caught every disease in the world! A *good* man doesn't bring these prostitutes' diseases shamelessly into his house and close to his children!"

She is a woman whose tongue never tires of censuring her husband. I have never seen her do anything but curse him, his lineage, and his family. She is tall, with light skin and a pretty face, nothing like this hunchback tossed on the bed like a useless rag, and she has nothing in common with her ugly daughter, whose nose is so big that when she tries to stand up straight, she seems to lean forward because of its weight.

The woman was no longer drying her husband's forehead. She pulled away, and I didn't blame her. She seemed out of place in this garden of ugliness. The ugly daughter looked at us, her hands reddened by the bluish ground meat with the disgusting smell, over which floated a halo of flies, and then she fled from the room. When this woman, the hunchback's wife, saw in my eyes that I was interested in her story—even though I knew from the beginning that she held me personally responsible—she burst out, "Now he's paying the price for dubious bad choices! The man no longer knows his own house. He hangs out with libertines, drunks, and whores! He has forgotten that he has a wife and children! He has forgotten his community and his religion! He runs with renegades and sinners! He associates with prostitutes and brings their diseases back to his family! Rather than go to the mosque like his masters, he spends his time in bars with whores and sons of bastards! All the bars of Marrakech and their harlots know him! Why doesn't he leave this house and go live with *them* rather then bring us disgrace with his shamelessness? Everyone points their fingers at us, in the neighborhood and everywhere else! What can I do? I'm just an unlucky woman, and this man wants to kill me!"

She started to sob softly, continuing her complaints. Is there a woman in the world as tortured as she is? Her life with this man is a continuous series of trials. She's paying the price of her attachment to a man without any honorable traits.

And here she is now, taking responsibility for his treatment rather than leaving him to die. Why doesn't she just let him receive the miserable fate God intended for him? She began to sob heavily. She threw down the rag that was in her hand and stood up, holding on to the wall as if she were afraid of fainting. She left the room, crying about her terrible luck. We could still hear her asking herself if all women suffered as she did, as her wailing and moaning rose and fell.

Zerwal stirred in his bed then sat up against some pillows. He wiped his forehead. His illness no longer seemed so critical now that his wife had delivered her lecture. His problem now was that he didn't know which prostitute had given him the disease and he requested my help in figuring it out. I felt kind of sorry for him and it seemed to me that feeling sorry for him in his state was a duty, so we went through them one by one—and there were many—and together we played this adolescent game. We recalled their names, the wonderful nights we spent in their company, and the funny things that happened during this soiree or that. For a few moments Zerwal seemed happy. For a few moments he forgot his pain, but I did my best to remind him of it. I told him that it is called syphilis and that it's a fatal disease if not treated right away. Fatal? Yes, Zerwal knew that. He had read a number of books and knew a lot about it—for example, that the illness was widespread in Ancient Egypt, and that in our country it had taken out whole tribes. I consoled him, and assured him that I would notify His Majesty of what had befallen him so that he could take it upon himself to get him transferred to a private clinic. I told him that those of us in the palace remembered him and his jokes, and that we all loved him and prayed for God to lift his troubles from him. He seemed gladdened by this news and the lines on his face relaxed.

"And has His Majesty asked about me?"

"Oh yes. He has asked about you and how you're doing many times, and he looks forward to you getting better and standing back on your own two feet to return joy to the palace. This is what His Majesty said to me, and to others as well."

The sick man looked cheered by my words. I wondered whether I should continue with this nonsense or stop there. I told him about the important guest and the celebrations that were held in his honor; celebrations the likes of which the country had never seen, and the likes of which would never be seen again.

"The carpets laid out on all the streets with the cars allowed to drive over them so that the guest could see the kindness, generosity, and hospitality for which we are so famous. All we were missing was you, Zerwal."

Should I continue with this nonsense or stop there? I was lost in my thoughts when his son-in-law the sausage seller came in, fat, bald, with a thick beard and no mustache. His forehead shone and there was a spot like a blackened coin in the center of it. His clothes were filthy. His hands were huge. I had never seen such big hands in my life—the perfect hands for preparing disgusting-smelling sausages. He came to look in on Zerwal before setting up in the square to feed the people his poison. It was waiting for him in a large rusty pot by the front door. Who knew how many victims he'd leave behind today. Our conversation revolved for a few moments around how to make sausages.

"What meat do you make them with? Dog meat or cat meat? Surely not beef, in any case! Do some people use donkey meat?"

"Oh yes, it's healthy, and tasty too, like horsemeat. It's sold in many markets in developed countries."

"Is it true that a number of sausage sellers hunt fat dogs in the dumps and cook them in spices and toxic dyes that they buy in drugstores?"

"Yes it's true, but *these* sausages have never killed anyone, as far as I know," he said. "Quite the contrary. Customers flock to them as if they were holiday sweets. If you go to the square at the end of the night you won't find a single one left. The tourists and drunks will have eaten them all."

Chatting about meat is always entertaining, even if it's about the meat of filthy dogs that graze in the municipal dumps. For a little while, our chatter made us forget worrying about the sick man. Jokingly, I said to his son-in-law that when I was crossing the courtyard I heard dogs barking on the roof.

"Aren't those poor dogs waiting their turn to be stuffed into the casings made from the innards of dogs that died before them?"

He strongly and angrily denied this, protesting adamantly: "There are no dogs in this house! We buy our meat from the municipal butcher, meat certified by the veterinarian. They have the proper papers!"

"But then where was the barking coming from?"

"What barking?"

"I'm just kidding," I said, continuing that dogs are clean animals, that their meat is no worse for you than donkey meat, and that they are preferred in China and Vietnam over nobler meats such as lamb. The sausage seller left the room in a huff.

Two tears glistened in Zerwal's eyes. Was he considering his impending death? No, he wasn't. He said, "Your son, Hassan. Now *that's* a man, brave, never mincing his words. I'm happy for him, for what he does. I didn't say it to you at the time but we need people who speak the truth every once in a while in order to maintain our equilibrium."

So the hunchback has become a wise man all of a sudden. Has his approaching end brought wisdom to his tongue? I won't hide the fact that I felt a bit of pride upon hearing these words, but I have to say that his frankness confused me. Was he being truly sincere or was this another of his tricks? There is no way to solve puzzles such as these, and I have neither the time nor the mental wherewithal to plunge into these depths. I left the hunchback's house feeling an optimism I hadn't felt before. Zerwal was on the verge of death, close to joining the line of corpses thrown into the dumps every day.

7

Day Three

NIGHT, HEAT, SWEAT. USING ONLY the light of the moon so the enemy won't see us, we turn our backs to the well and play cards, wiping away our sweat. We sit about a hundred meters from the well so he doesn't smell us. The night cloaks our presence so that no one can see us. There's no wind to hide the smell of our sweat. We, the four conscripts—Brahim, Mohamed Ali, Naafi, and I—play cards. We don't need to turn around to see the well, to know that it's behind us and that we've been guarding it since dawn. We spent the entire day around the well. There's been no cause for alarm. Some travelers came by for water. They hadn't seen an enemy roaming around the well. They hadn't seen an enemy anywhere in the area they had passed through, and that's what we'll say to the captain. "They didn't see an enemy roaming around the well, captain!"

The well is still in its place, along with its stones and its water. We can say exactly where the well is and can see the metal dipper hanging above its opening without turning around, as if we have eyes in the backs of our heads. So we play cards under the light of the full moon, as if it were the sun, providing warmth as well as light. The wind stopped blowing at nightfall. Strange how a person can wait for a little bit of wind as if he were waiting for his life's deepest desire. We breathe with noticeable difficulty. We breathe in hot air, its heat filling our lungs. We sweat and wait for a wind that will never come, because we're in the desert. The sound of bats brushes against my hair. Small black shadows fluttering over my head, arousing no one's attention then disappearing into the desert night. I can't see them, but I feel a thread tying me to them as they pass over my head and greet me like friends do in the train station when they find themselves facing one another on opposite sides of the track.

I say out loud, "So this is how bats sound."

"How did you know there were bats in the desert?"

"I read it somewhere."

No one laughs. We all feel the seriousness of the situation. Nighttime makes a person more serious than he would be during the day. The sound of bats returns, this time without shadows, resembling the screeching of happy children who have just woken up. The moonlight casts strange shadows on the distant sand dunes. A good part of the night has passed. There's no tent for us to take refuge in, so we'll lie down where we are, close to the well we're guarding.

"Play! Put down a card!"

Brahim doesn't put down a card. He shakes his head and remains fixed in place for a moment, then says, "And that sound?"

"What sound?"

"Listen!"

We don't hear a thing, just the sound of the metal dipper swinging and creaking over the well. The well is behind us, close enough for us to hear a dipper made of metal creaking over it.

"Play!"

No one does and we stop playing. "And the creaking sound?"

"It's just the wind making the dipper move above the well a hundred meters away. Play already!"

None of us plays a card. Then, as if it has been decided beforehand, I throw my cards onto the sand, onto the hot sand. Then Mohamed Ali throws *his* cards onto the sand, followed by Brahim, then Naafi. We wait for the sound to return. The sound of the owl's hooting had disappeared just moments before as we entered another part of the night. It sounds as if someone is dipping the pail into the well. We listen closely. Yes, it is as if someone is dipping the pail into the well, but how can we see the well when it's behind us? How can we be sure that someone is dipping the pail into the well? *Creak crak creak crak*. It's the sound of metal. There's no metal in this entire desert except for that damned dipper hanging over the well, but we can't see it. We all wipe away our sweat, all four of us at the same time, as if it had been decided upon beforehand. We are silent. We listen. *Creak crak creak crak*.

I say, "Why don't we poison the well?"

"What will we drink?"

"We have our canteens."

"They have canteens, too! Do you think they're walking around the desert without canteens?"

"Then why are they stealing our water?"

"I already told you, there's no one there."

"And that sound?"

Creak crak creak crak.

"Play!"

I have no cards in my hand for me to play, and I don't turn toward the well. Brahim says that there is no one next to the well moving the metal dipper, that there is nothing making the *creak crak creak crak* sound, and that poisoning the well is an unreasonable idea because we still need the water, here and at the fort. As long as we're in the desert we'll need water.

"Fine." I pick up my cards and brush the sand off of them.

"Why don't we arrest one of them then?"

"One of who?"

"The enemy."

"Which enemy?"

"Who's moving the dipper back there if not the enemy?"

"The wind. It's the wind that moves the sand and the stones. Everything moves in the desert. Why would it not move metal too then?"

"What wind?"

Since sundown we have been waiting for some wind. I moisten my finger and hold it up. There is no wind coming from any direction.

Brahim shouts, "Play!"

But we don't play. We are listening to what is going on behind us.

"And just then! What was that . . . ?"

"Play, Mohamed Ali!"

"Now who's throwing the pail into the well?"

The wind. It's always the wind. We had stopped playing cards a while ago, but we hadn't heard a pail being thrown into the well.

"Why don't we poison the well at dawn before we leave? Then we won't have to wonder who's moving the dipper and throwing the pail in."

But is it the sound of the pail hitting the water in the bottom of the well that we're hearing?

"It could be some Bedouins getting water."

"Bedouins in the middle of the night?"

"Why don't we arrest them?"

"Arrest the Bedouins?"

"No, the others, the ones we can't see. The enemy we've heard about but can't see."

"How can we arrest them if we can't see them?"

Brahim begins to shift back and forth like a horse that senses a snake nearby. We are conscious of a number of things: the desert, the heat, the moonlight, the cards that are in front of us. And there are things that remain mysterious to us, such as what is going on by the well. Now we hear the dipper rising from the filled bucket. We can even hear the water splashing back down into the bottom of the well. We forget about the heat and the sweat. I'm not afraid because we're in the dark, and I'm not sure why I remember that I am hungry. Does hunger have some connection to fear? I lie down on the sand. I can hear its whispering movement, continuous whispering almost like vibrations, grains of sand whispering to one another under the moonlight. Sand speaks in its own special way that you can only fully hear when you're lying on top of it. Brahim, who is still shifting in his place, shakes suddenly as if he has just been stung. It isn't a snake that bit him, though, and there are no bats flying over his head.

"Brahim, what's up?"

He rolls around on the sand like someone possessed and, with terrified eyes, looks toward the well.

"Brahim? What's up? There's no one by the well."

"Yes there is. Look!"

This time we are all looking toward the well—me, Mohamed Ali, and Naafi. As for Brahim, he is far beyond looking. He has left all of that behind him. His cold body is shivering from head to toe and white foam comes out of his mouth and collects on his lips. His eyes seemed to have turned white and his teeth are chattering. Mohamed Ali splashes water on his face and I shake his head and turn it in the direction of the well so he can see the well and the dipper that no one is moving.

"Brahim, look! No one's at the well. It's the wind playing with our imaginations."

Zineb's family came from a coastal city before settling in Marrakech. Whenever I looked at them, I smelled the sea. The month before my departure, I sold my motorbike in order to leave her some money to draw upon until I returned. I recommended she borrow from the doctor and his wife should she need to as well. She looked at me strangely. Zineb had changed. A fatigue resembling boredom had appeared on her face. When I asked her about it she wouldn't respond. She would say that she herself didn't know what had happened to her. I stopped going anywhere, saw no one. My relationships were reduced to almost nothing. I put off my rehearsals. When Aissa would come to rehearse the new show we were preparing, I would say to him, "Another time, Aissa. Another time." I became incapable of thinking about anything that didn't have to do with Zineb. I didn't hear sounds that came from outside. I didn't hear the seven o'clock train passing by the house. She wasn't bedridden yet, but a weakness had stricken her to her very core. I didn't know what this illness was called.

I'd sit in the living room and listen hard. After these four years I was able to distinguish every sound, every movement, and every smell. I knew the smell that would come from the kitchen after a little while. I heard her laugh and knew that she was laughing with the landlord, that she was telling him to come back in a week. I hadn't paid the rent in months, but it didn't matter. We'd pay it later. A visit to the doctor and his wife would return her vigor, and there'd be nothing to worry about. If this was how things were going to be, then it was no big deal. This time, instead of dragging her from them as I had promised myself I would do, I preferred to give in. I would put up with them as long as being with them returned some life to her face. She came and went as if a halo of light encircled the house. Here she was putting the kettle on the stove or pouring a glass of water. Here she was brushing her hair. Here she was opening the kitchen door with her long, delicate fingers. My eyes glistened with tears when I realized that the life flourishing around me could disintegrate at any moment. Tears come easily to me.

The whole month before my departure, I didn't go near her. During long nights I carried hopes of sleeping with her just as any husband sleeps with his wife, but she'd excuse herself. I thought she was pregnant. No, she was just tired. Her mind and body were navigating worlds I had no way of glimpsing. Finally, when I insisted, she took to her bed. Zineb loves breakfast more than any other meal. I prepared her breakfast and carried it to her in bed. I kissed her forehead. It was cool. What was wrong with her then? Zineb was sick, but I didn't know whether her illness had a name. Because of my longing to kiss her all over her body, I didn't notice her illness.

I don't think she yearned for nights at the Shahrazade. I don't think she yearned for singing.

The day I left home, I looked at her, beautiful as she slept. The tranquility of sleep brought a translucent rosiness to her cheeks, so I left, carrying my desire and heartbreak with me.

Just before dawn, as we are returning to the fort, the question just hangs there, Brahim can't get it out of his head: "The ones who were throwing the pail into the well, did they come by horse or did they come on foot?"

8

THE IMPORTANT GUEST LEFT, BUT the celebrations continued for a number of days. The whole country is in nonstop celebration. I have never seen people in such a state of joy and happiness. Everything has gone well and everyone is optimistic and wishing each other the best. Crystal chandeliers sparkle above us, casting pure light over the vast palace hall. It is a great day that no one will ever forget. Invited guests hover around tables and are served a variety of food and drink—pigeons stuffed with almonds, plates of gazelle and ostrich meat. The guests stuff themselves as if they are starving, and they squirrel away pieces of meat in their pockets as good-luck charms from the royal dinner. Afterward they'll hang them in their homes as amulets and precious souvenirs. Some of them speak with long pieces of meat dangling from their mouths that resemble tongues. Their talking in the great hall is like a roar as jaws and teeth tear at their prey. You can hear bones snapping. Then the national orchestra occupies the podium in their solemn black clothing and the singers begin to sing anthems praising the dams that have been built, the sugar refineries that have been erected, and the rugs that have been manufactured.

His Majesty appears in the small window that looks out over the hall, and calls of "Long live the king!" rise up. He greets everyone and begins to throw coins. The singing stops and an indescribable chaos ensues. Some of the adulators throw themselves on the coins, exaggerating their movements so His

Majesty can see what they're doing. Others, when they grab a coin, turn toward him and kiss it with tears in their eyes. The king comes down from his perch, approaches the singer, and throws his coat over his shoulders. There isn't a dry eye in the place. The singer shakes with fear. Perhaps he is remembering what had happened to his colleague when he had his shoes taken from him in front of the important guest. Trembling, he grabs his oud and begins to sing a song they say the king himself had stayed up all night writing the words and music to.

Ministers in their fancy suits walk in and out of the great hall drinking tea and loudly exchanging news as if they were the ones staying up all night planning our next victory. No doubt they are completely ignorant of His Majesty's intentions, and this is for the best. Why should they be privy to the secrets they haven't participated in planning? The officers also don't know a thing. As a result they are relaxed, in their somber suits and with their official manner of standing. His Majesty decided all by himself to bring this affair to a definitive end. He's a genius and doesn't need anyone. They say that the important guest encouraged him to follow his plan, that the guest's encouragement for his initiative gave him a new momentum. Everyone expects that the problem will soon be solved, although they don't know exactly how. Perhaps General Bouricha knows the details of the plan, or at least some of them, but he doesn't reveal a thing. This, too, is good.

I hadn't seen the Sahara before, nor had I ever seen someone from the Sahara—a Sahrawi—in my life. I was picturing it as an endless expanse of sand, with snakes and turtles and a lingering sun capable of melting rocks. There's no doubt that the days are longer and that stones have been melting there for ages, and there's no such thing as a desert without sand. This is why there would be no battle. If there even is an enemy, the poor guy will only have his own shadow to hide behind. I hope to accompany His Majesty there to see the sunsets that the foreigners talk about with such enthusiasm. They say that the world stops for a few minutes at that moment because it's so close to the sun. I'll see it for myself when I go there with His Majesty. I'll also see the enemy's final evacuation from our land. Unfortunately, Zerwal won't accompany us on our trip because his illness has crippled him.

His Majesty remained in the palace for a few more weeks. General Bouricha is the one now shuttling between Marrakech and the capital where the military headquarters are. For a number of days now he has seemed extremely energetic, as if additional hands and legs had been added to his body. The general's face is thin and harsh, with eyes that are always concealed behind his dark glasses. I've never seen him without his uniform. I imagine that he doesn't take it off except to sleep. This has caused me to change my opinion of him. Is this to say that I was wrong about what I had thought of him? Yes it is. The general is an important man. Weeks ago he was transferred to the theater of operations and soon he will bring to light all that he learned in French military schools. For the first time since his participation in the Indochina War, since which he has been unemployed, the opportunity to display his talents had arrived. For this reason his enthusiasm was redoubled. Like anyone else, he doesn't want to dash the hopes that have been placed in him. The mission that he was charged with brought back his previous seriousness. He became distracted, like someone who could think of nothing else, like someone about to undertake the greatest mission of his life. What could he possibly be thinking about so much if not the Sahara crisis? Surely he's thinking about the Sahara the same way the king is. He puts his head on his right hand and looks grave for a while, exactly as the king does.

The important guest returned to his country and the preparations for war were completed quite a while ago now. The army moved in with its ordnance and deadly weapons and the people cheered because they wished to migrate there after the end of the war, to acquire apartments and stores there in order to live easier lives.

In the month of January Marrakech is flooded with light, but it doesn't seem like a lot of light. It's as if it has passed through a sieve. As I like to say, there are mornings when the light heals. The general has left for the Sahara. From there we receive nothing but good news. All the newspapers talk about him and his victories. Here in the palace, the slaves circulate this news and even exaggerate it a little. This makes sense, considering he is a man they had known only as someone living in the shadows—whether out of shyness or fear nobody knows—and whose star rose so suddenly and resoundingly.

The general's status has improved considerably. The king shares his table with him between deployments, and this has never happened before. They talk nonstop, and when he returns to the battlefield, the king continues to talk about him and his life. I don't understand this surprising passion His Majesty shows toward his general. Here in the palace they say that a previous general had had the same status and inspired the same awe, and he met *his* end when the king strangled him with his own two hands. I wasn't there at the time so I can't compare the two men. All I can say is that they both carried the same name, an ordinary name that doesn't betray any superhuman gifts. I don't read into people's names. I'm waiting to see what happens for myself, but I can say that I don't trust him, that I don't trust people in general. Based on my experience, when someone sits down next to you, the first thought that comes to his mind is how he can take your place. Ask anyone out there in the street. Ask any rookie cop or aimless beggar and they'll tell you the same thing. Perhaps I'm wrong, in which case I'll need to reassess how good my intuition is in the upcoming days.

The general has three daughters and two sons. The oldest daughter is unmarried. She lives in Paris and says she won't be a slave to any man. The other daughter, after having been married to a lawyer from Marrakech for two months, left him and joined her sister. The two sons are continuing their education in America. As for Joumana, the youngest of his daughters, they say that he spoils her rotten. He gives her a new BMW every month because he's the one who markets these cars here in this country, and also because whenever she gets drunk she slams into the first wall blocking her way, or she hits the first man not paying attention to her passing by. Then, usually what happens is that the family of the crushed man comes to apologize to the general.

She has a dog that sleeps with her in bed and bathes with her in the same tub. These aren't just stories or exaggerations. This Joumana is never seen without her dog. A lowly little black dog whose eyes, nose, ears, and mouth are indistinguishable. A mass of black wool between her hands as she strokes it tenderly with her slender fingers, even when she's behind the wheel, not paying attention to the road. They say that when the accidents began to add up, and the apologies from victims' families who had died under her car's wheels began to multiply, the general told her that he would take her to the Sahara. They also say that it was her decision to accompany him to the desert so she could take pictures of the sunset that the foreigners talk so much about. So far, though, all this is just hearsay.

She's not ugly or wicked, but she is a bit dim. I notice that in her laugh and in the way she walks. She drinks a lot—she's eighteen years old—and it may be that spending all of her time with her dog has affected her behavior. I don't like dogs, especially this little puny type she carries in her arms, never separating herself from it day or night. There's no doubt that the general plans to get rid of her the first chance he gets. No matter how high a rank he holds in the army, and no matter how many victories he has achieved, he is a human being before anything else, and seeing that his two older daughters aren't married, how could he leave his youngest daughter to remain unmarried too? This subject doesn't concern me, but this is my opinion on it. And I don't like dogs, any dogs. They're dirty and forbidden from entering heaven. When they enter a house, the angels leave. This is why Joumana is so flighty.

The general is someone who, in my opinion, is of no importance, even if the consensus these days suggests the opposite. I have said this before and I still hold it to be true: the general is a person of no consequence, and any interest His Majesty shows in him is merely a temporary strategy adopted in a time of war. He has no choice but to flatter him pending the end of this matter. In reality, the king pays him no mind at all. He's just holding on to him because he inherited him from his father.

They chat for a long time with the map between them. His Majesty finds the time to think about and plan for the next and final step to disperse the enemy and root out traitors. His Majesty explains his plan in detail to his officer. I have never seen him ask his opinion on anything before. Has he been waiting for the general's approval for this campaign? I don't believe so. Then why does he invite him to come in alone, and why does he deal with him differently than he did before? Now, all of a sudden he is interested in his opinions and nods approvingly at his suggestions. There is no doubt that General Bouricha is an important person and that he understands matters of war, so I see why His Majesty has changed his behavior toward him so suddenly. However, all of this is temporary, as I explained before.

So, the critical hour has struck. The crowds who rushed toward the gates of the Sahara in order to occupy an apartment or a store or to get a job will gain their booty after this lightning-quick attack. For this reason he needs a general who is an expert in military planning to lead his campaign in the best possible way. Bouricha is, after all, the king's officer, and what is an officer's role? What is his role if he is incapable of leading a campaign as simple as this?

When the secret discussions are done, the map disappears under the general's jacket and the two of them approach me. I know what it means when His Majesty approaches me—the time for seriousness has ended and the time for joking has begun. This time is necessary for providing comfort and relaxation to His Majesty after a day weighted with the worries of planning for war. After the tiresome business of thinking and planning, the time for diversion has come.

9

Day Four

WE FOUND THE FORT TURNED completely upside down. They were waiting for General Bouricha to arrive. The Sahara is *his* Sahara, and the war is *his* war, as the soldiers who came before us said, and as those who come after us will say. We busied ourselves laying barbed wire around the fort as soon as we arrived in the heat of the morning. We began to unfurl the barbed wire. Did this mean that the war was coming to the fort, then? "No," said the captain, "but as in all other parts of the world, all military buildings must be surrounded by barbed wire, war or no war. This is the rule."

Our bodies came undone in the heat, but what could we do? Hundreds of meters of wire and not the slightest breeze to push away the blaze of this summer inferno. We listened for the sound of the turning waterwheel for some hint that a breeze was blowing on us, but we couldn't hear it . . . then we could! We raised our heads and turned toward the wheel. We expected to feel the breeze that moved the wheel. Nothing. Then we waited for it again. Not a thing. The waterwheel mocked us. Nothing but heat and protective wire.

Brahim wasn't with us. The captain had sent him out to the pasture, where he was herding the captain's goats, far from the fort. Captain Hammouda, the one in charge of the fort, ate nothing but goat meat to avoid high cholesterol, and he had six goats that Brahim was grazing in order to bring his anxiety level back down. We said to ourselves, "Right now he's under a palm tree, far from the heat and the wires. What do we need barbed wire for in the middle of the desert? The desert is our barbed wire." We were almost jealous of our friend Brahim, smoking his cigarette in the shade of the palm tree, unconcerned with stringing up the barbed wire. Mohamed Ali, Naafi, and I wished that *we* were under the palm tree smoking like Brahim rather than stringing up barbed wire in the heat. The other soldiers sang their monotonous song, running back and forth in a display of exaggerated zeal.

Brahim hadn't suffered any harm last night, except for the moments of fear that frazzled his nerves. And we had forgotten all about it, as if there had never been a metal dipper creaking all night long, as if it had been our imaginations that formed the image of people repeatedly throwing their pail deep into the well. But for Brahim the metal dipper continued to turn in his mind. Then he disappeared. At around ten in the morning, when the sun extended its rays to focus their flames onto the vast wilderness, Haris Sahrawi, the guard, came yelling, "Brahim has disappeared!" Brahim, whom we thought had cast his fear aside at the well, disappeared at about ten in the morning while the six goats remained, grazing by themselves around the palm tree. He had packed up his fear and fled.

The search for him, with the help of a team of trained dogs from Agadir, lasted for the better part of the day. Twelve men wearing khaki djellabas instead of military uniforms, and sneakers instead of heavy boots, finally found him in one of the caves. They turned over every grain of sand and every stone in their path, and even climbed to the tops of the palm trees to look out over the sprawling desert horizon. At the beginning of the afternoon, the boss ordered them, "Search in the east where we don't expect him to be!" They jumped into a dilapidated truck that, to look at, you'd swear couldn't go a hundred meters before falling to pieces. But it drove over the rocks—dancing and shaking and driving nonetheless—well suited to such a task, with the special team from Agadir riding on top of it and flanked by their exhausted dogs, eyes wandering, unsatisfied with themselves.

Neither the dogs nor the team members—both with the same viciousness and the same roving eyes—wanted to eat or drink until they found the runaway, Brahim, the one who had stuffed himself into one of the caves to the east where the boss pointed, where it wasn't expected he would be found. Brahim was listening to his heart pound and quiver, and to the dogs approach his cave, so close he could almost hear their wild panting. All this time we were in the fort, ready for anything short of finding Brahim between the dogs' teeth, hoping that he would be saved, but betting that he wouldn't be. We were wondering what Captain Hammouda would do with Brahim in the event that he found him. Would he skewer him and roast him in place of one of his goats? Would he throw him to the dogs? Would he place him in front of a firing squad? A general languor prevailed over the fort for the whole day. We took a break from the barbed wire. Captain Hammouda, the one in charge of the fort, didn't leave his office. He remained standing in the doorway, shooting glances this way and that, chewing on his moustache. Then he climbed to the top of the watchtower and swept the area in a complete circle with his binoculars. What did the captain see? The runaway conscript or the goats who no longer had anyone to herd them?

He came back down to the office doorway and we said to ourselves, somewhat relieved, "He's forgotten us. He's forgotten all about the wire. His brain cells are burning up because of what has happened with Brahim. Or is he thinking about his goats that had come back without Brahim? It's a miracle they didn't flee from this hellhole just as the conscript Brahim did, lucky guy. The captain won't die anytime soon of high cholesterol as long as his goats are nearby, in the sights of his binoculars. He'll continue to slaughter them one by one until they're gone." We were also saying to ourselves, while watching him fixed in his spot, "The captain is thinking of Brahim and how he'll receive him in the event that they find him."

We didn't do any work that whole day. We completely forgot about the barbed wire. We left it burning in the sun, hoping it would melt so we wouldn't have to return to it. We pretended to sweep the courtyard, we sang the national anthem, or we did guard duty on the roof of the fort with our eyes fixed on the wasteland extending out from it. We pretended to do drills or eat or sleep, but we were listening to every noise coming from outside the fort. We became nothing more than eyes and ears. We saw ghosts dashing by that no one else saw. We heard distant barking that no one else heard. We bet that Brahim had been saved from all of this, and we also bet that he hadn't been. We heard the dogs howl as if they were wailing, as if the echo of their disappointment repeated itself, and we said to ourselves, "Brahim has been saved from their tyranny today!"

Toward the end of the afternoon they found him to the east, where no one had expected him to be, just as the captain had indicated. His face had disappeared into the dark rings of his two terrified eyes and he seemed emaciated from the excessive fear that had gnawed at his body, poisoned by thoughts of his fate. We, soldiers and conscripts alike, were also thinking about his fate, just as the special team and its dogs that were hunting him were thinking about it, just as the captain who was awaiting the arrival of General Bouricha to decide on the matter was thinking about it too. We wondered whether they would skewer and roast him or string him up in front of a firing squad. And the vicious band of twelve? They were thinking about Brahim just as we were, but in their own way, polishing their rifles and waiting for the general who would come in the evening. Everybody here talks about his viciousness, about how blood freezes in the veins at the mere mention of his name. Our fear for Brahim doubled. We approached the cell to have a look at him. We saw the fear in our own hearts in there with him. We looked at him and saw him even more emaciated and fearful, and we said to ourselves, "He knows. News of the general's arrival has reached him." We saw him change over the next hour: his clothes became torn, his hands cut up, and his lips chapped, as if he had spent days living in a thicket—but it was only the result of one day's fear. Then, after we had seen enough of him, we went out to the courtyard in a stupor, not playing cards or going to Fifi's tavern—not because of the heat buzzing in the fort's courtyard, but because of the other heat roasting our insides.

Then, before sunset, we stood in the courtyard on the general's orders, all of us, including the captain and the special team, but without the trained dogs and without the goats because the captain had sent them to the mountains out of fear that the general would devour them. We waited in the courtyard under the hot sun until the general had eaten his meal. Then he appeared in front of the office wearing his flak jacket that shone in the rays of the setting sun. They brought out the conscript Brahim, handcuffed, blindfolded, dragging his bound feet in the dust. The full regiment lined up facing the fort's door and gave a military salute. A heavy silence prevailed.

"Why did you run away, private Brahim?"

"I don't know."

"You don't know why you ran away?"

"I don't know. I don't know why I ran away, or why I'm here, or why I'm fighting. The Sahrawis are my brothers and they've done nothing to me, so why am I fighting them?"

We froze in place, fixed there by fear and the boldness of what he'd said, as if Brahim was trying to commit suicide by jumping from the tenth floor, and we were jumping with him.

"Brahim? What's with you? Has fear garbled your words?"

No, Brahim is lucky because he isn't thinking about what he's saying or what he's doing, like the day he stole Fifi's turtle.

The general remained looking at him, trying to read what was inside him, and the silence became deafening. Even the water-wheel stopped squeaking.

"What do you want, Brahim?" the general was asking calmly.

"I want to return to my mother." His mother, at that moment, was looking for a bride for him.

"Okay. Get your things and go."

No one could believe it. Brahim was luckier than he knew. Captain Hammouda came forward, took off the shackles, and walked away, dragging behind him his dashed hopes of a punishment that would have taught a lesson to the others. Brahim asked me to help him collect his things. I walked beside him. In the barracks he gathered up his stash of cans—sardines, cheese, powdered milk. He had bought them from the general's store along with some pieces of bread.

He asked me, "Do you know where the captain gets the cigarettes he sells us? Ask any soldier and he'll tell you."

"I don't know anything about that," I replied.

"Don't you know that he reveals our locations to the enemy in exchange for boxes of tobacco that he sells in his store? Did you know that?"

"No."

"Did you know that in the capital they pay you until they receive word of your death? Because of this, many soldiers prefer to surrender rather than die so that their families will continue to receive their pay. I don't want to do as the others do, surrender in order to keep my pay. I don't have a wife or children to worry about and I'm not brave enough to be taken into the enemy's prison cells. That's why I ran away. But, as you can see, things turned out differently than I had expected. That is, if the general is really serious.

"But I feel sorry for you. Take this. Here are some of my rations. They'll be enough for a month, before the sand swallows you up or the snakes eat you, if you don't surrender yourself because, as you said, your wife is sick. You'll have enough time to run away or surrender."

He put his box down on the ground and walked out carrying a light rucksack, and I walked out behind him.

He stopped for a moment, gazing out in every direction. Then he began to cross the courtyard. We watched Brahim, who we thought would stand before the firing squad, cross the courtyard toward the gate. We waited for the squad to open fire. But no, Brahim walked toward his victory one step at a time. He took one step out of the fort and turned around, bidding each of us farewell without a nod or a wave. Then he left the fort—with no special team following him or dogs following his scent—toward the last rays of daylight that shone in the distance, and he headed west, toward other villages, big cities, and the sea. Not toward the east, where the boss had indicated when they arrested him.

10

ALL I CAN SAY IS THAT mysterious things are happening. No news comes to us from the desert, neither bad nor not bad. It is June. Communications have been severed and the general is not responding to His Majesty, who had decided that he would personally bestow the medals that would decorate the chest of his great general, but he never showed up. His Majesty remained in his palace waiting for him for days, but nothing came except a telex saying that he and his army were tied up in the desert, forced to hold their positions. His Majesty was extremely angry. Usually he only put his wig on in the afternoon, but after receiving this unfortunate news he started putting it on as soon as he woke up. Perhaps it is his new way of receiving bad news. Now he spends his time walking around the palace gardens waiting for the general to appear. He has begun to reveal his true nature, and this is what I have been saying the whole time. My prediction concerning this dog had come true. I can read people better than anyone else can.

I consider the bird that smashed into my window during the night to be a bad omen. A general unease spreads over the palace, and over the city as well. The streets are empty, as if everyone's hopes for a staggering victory have been dashed. Hatred seethes in the eyes of the few people out walking. There are burned and overturned buses that some protesters had attacked the previous night, stores whose doors have been bashed in, and smoke rising from the tires that the rioters had put in the middle of the street and lit on fire. For the first time, I see the square completely empty. From between the ribbons of rising smoke, an old man comes out carrying a sack on his back, searching for something among the fires. He picks up a babouche from the middle of the pile and proceeds to try it on for size, smiling.

It is true that people have been grumbling about the rise in prices for some time, and strange stories have reached the palace, of protest marches where villagers carry huge loaves of bread, but rather than complain of their hunger and their children's hunger, they are shouting, "Long live the king!" and, "Freedom for the Sahara!" When have people ever complained of the rising cost of living like this? I don't understand this form of protest. Surely it's a trick by the politicians. This is generally what politicians do—they whip people into a frenzy from time to time so that it seems they bear no responsibility for the situation. What I like about His Majesty is that he considers what they do to be completely useless. Even though the politicians take advantage of every protest to present themselves as spokesmen in his name and saviors of His Majesty's regime from peoples' wickedness, when has a politician ever been interested in other peoples' fates, especially those ambiguous multinational types of wealthy politicians who hang foreign flags inside their own palaces?

A dreary atmosphere falls over the palace, the streets, and the whole country. The king doesn't leave his palace. He doesn't receive anyone. His face is pale and lately he has neglected to put on his wig, after he had been wearing it on his head all day long, as I mentioned before. He seems almost entirely isolated. He doesn't want to see anyone or hear so much as a word. The palace is silent. Is he comfortable with this state of affairs? You can no longer tell if he is happy or sad, as if he wears a mask that hides his true face from the few visitors he has. He no longer gives any indication of what he is feeling so

I am unable to ascertain what's going on inside his head. No doubt there are scary thoughts. He goes to the clock repairman's workshop and watches him repair the thousands of clocks of different sizes and types that adorn every corner of the palace. Maybe he is starting to see that he has gone down the wrong path, but is there another one? I believe that every road is the wrong road. Why? Because you don't know where you'll end up when you start out. To me, this just seems to be how it is. I only wonder whether he feels some sort of regret because he let his general get away from him. His punishment will fit the crime, that much I hope.

A new guest came to stay at the palace. He was a French engineer who had come to plan a project to build a mosque overlooking the ocean. Although it was a fabulous idea, I didn't understand how His Majesty could put aside the subject that was currently occupying him and direct his attention toward something else, such as the mosque. He was poring over the plans when the French engineer pointed to the highest part of the minaret and explained that sailors would be guided by the laser light affixed to the top, which would be visible from a distance of forty kilometers. His Majesty appeared to be convinced by the Frenchman's explanation, if only to be done with the matter as quickly as possible. For the first time I saw him showing not the least concern, as if he had lost all interest. Out of politeness to the engineer, he nodded twice, but after the engineer left he fell silent again. He valued the engineer, which was why he was nice to him.

Many soldiers have fallen in the Sahara, and twice as many have been taken prisoner, yet the general is nowhere to be found. The time for fun and games has ended. Not more than two years ago, the atmosphere in the palace was cheerful. Now it is tense. There's no comfort or relief. His Majesty's health has deteriorated a great deal in the last few months. He takes his binoculars and focuses them in every direction. I don't know what he's looking at. Perhaps he is looking at the slaves frolicking in the Mechouar square without a care in the world, as if he were saying to himself, "Now that the house has fallen, is it possible to save the furniture?" One of his ministers came to him with a rug made of lion skin. He paid no attention to it and the man left disappointed. The soldiers quartered in the barracks haven't received their pay in months and now they're selling their uniforms and furniture in order to find the means to save themselves. And the ministers? Some of them have gone abroad claiming they needed medical treatment, while the ones who remain stopped going to meetings, where anything could happen, so as not to have to meet the gaze of His Majesty. If His Majesty did get angry at someone, it would be of no use to slaughter a lamb at his feet or appeal to a holy man for help. All of them know about the terrifying secret prisons he has recently built. For this reason they stay home, and the majority of them have, in fact, traveled abroad for medical treatment.

His interior minister was unable to escape. I had never seen such anger on the face of His Majesty as I saw that morning when he received him.

The interior minister entered with a downcast gaze as he usually did and said, "I have learned that Your Majesty is angry with me, but you must know that you won't find a man more sincere than I in the entire kingdom."

Even though this was not the time for joking around, he took the opportunity to add, "It's true. In the entire kingdom you won't find a man better at lying to its citizens than your minister of the interior."

Finally, the king laughed. It was a short laugh, but it brought back a bit of his optimism. However, it didn't take long for his depression to return.

He turned to his minister and said, "Tell me. You're the one who gathers information on the rabble. What are they saying? Are there more seeds of rebellion?" Then he added, "Is building the mosque a good idea? Something to entertain the people and make them forget the difficulties we're facing?"

The minister didn't know how to respond, as if he had swallowed his tongue.

The king continued: "You're the expert in these types of ruses. What do you suggest I do to divert peoples' minds? Do you have a better idea than the mosque?"

I was dumbstruck. His Majesty was no longer sure of anything. I had never seen him ask anyone about anything, but now he was asking about everything and seeking counsel on every issue, as if the compass he had been using to guide himself all these years had broken. Nothing was as it once was, may God preserve him.

When I returned to the palace, His Majesty didn't recognize me. He was in the middle of the palace courtyard bent over a small clock, fiddling with its insides. He asked what my job was, which took me completely by surprise. The king didn't recognize me! I told him that I was Balloute, the court jester.

"Jester?"

"Yes, I make Your Majesty laugh."

He gazed at me with a look of contempt, and said, "Shame on you! A man of your age laughing! Don't you fear God? Satan is the one who laughs. He's the one who invented laughter to fulfill one of his missions—to seduce the sons of Adam in this world so as to laugh at them in the next. Does God laugh? Have you ever heard of God laughing? Have you heard of angels laughing? There's nothing uglier than when the sons of Adam lose their composure. What do you find so pleasing about a face that distorts what the Almighty has created, and who brays like a donkey?"

Then he headed for the clock repairman's workshop.

11

The Fourth Day (Conclusion)

FOR THE WHOLE DAY, SINCE beginning the search for Brahim, we see a cloud of dust rising in the distance. It's General Bouricha. The Sahara is *his* Sahara. Ever since it became his affair, say the soldiers, he has moved around it as he pleases, on foot and by plane. From time to time we raise our heads and say to ourselves, "Look, it's the general's convoy passing by. Those are his flags and that's his convoy."

But we don't actually see him at all. The sand is his sand, and the desert wind is his wind, taking him from one place to another. Every place is his, to the east and to the west. He's really busy. For five years the war has moved from one place to another. These difficult days are still upon us, now as before. This became clearer with the general's arrival. He has always been out there somewhere in the desert, but now he's here. We don't see him with our eyes, but we *do* see him in the panic that has seized Captain Hammouda and Brigadier Omar who have left Fifi's tavern, and Sergeant Bouzide who has hidden the playing cards under his bed. His existence hadn't taken a clear form before today. After Brahim's flight, it was as if he had come here to fix a mistake we had all made together. Since he became the one holding the keys to the war in the Sahara, we hadn't heard any name besides his. He had been an undistinguished officer, but became a star when he took it upon himself to take control of the war.

The war has been going on here for years. They say that the king tried to get him on the telephone, but he didn't answer. It was the first time I had heard of someone not responding to the king. Rather, he just sent a telex saying that the king's messages hadn't reached him because the enemy had destroyed our telephone lines with their advanced weaponry, and as long as the king remained unable to travel to the battlefield himself, there was no more to be said. The general is an intelligent man. He said that the enemy had destroyed our lines and that their weaponry was so advanced that the king should remain where he was. In the telex he said that the enemy possessed the latest in Soviet technology. Meanwhile, we haven't seen any enemy. We haven't seen Russian-made weapons, Your Majesty, nor would we be able to say with one-hundred-percent certainty if weapons were Russian, or modern, or deadly. The general is forced to resist with the little ammunition he has, with *no power nor strength save for in God*. God willing, we will be victorious. Then His Majesty sent him another message saying that he wanted to hang another medal on him to honor the great services he has rendered during this war. He responded by telling the king that he is a soldier, and that a soldier doesn't leave his post. So, what could the king do besides send the medal to the desert where it would find its own way to the general's chest carrying the king's gratitude? And with that, the line went dead, as did the thread of communication. The lines of communication disintegrated and disappeared completely. The king sent messages summoning him, insisting, and promising to bestow every medal available in the kingdom on him, but the general remained in his desert, on his farm, pressing olives and keeping track of the foodstuffs he would sell to his soldiers.

We stopped stringing up barbed wire. We prepared a special wing for the general at the fort's entrance. It had three spacious rooms that we covered in rugs, drapes, and chests. There was also an air conditioner, water, electricity, and rare fruits, all because the general was coming with his young-est daughter, Joumana. While she played with her dog, the general was in the courtyard selling drinks and donuts to the soldiers. That's right—he had come dragging carts full of goods behind him and he was selling them himself! There was sugar, raisins, salt, and cigarettes, as well as all sorts of drinks and sandwiches. As for the fresh olive oil whose press-ing he had personally overseen at his farm, he sold that to his officers. That was why he always had the smell of oil on him. After he was done with the Brahim affair, he returned to finish selling what remained of his wares. Every once in a while he would go to his apartment for a few glasses of whiskey while he watched his daughter Joumana play with her dog, or to change the rags he had draped over himself as clothing. He rubbed her shoulders with some satisfaction. Between one good deal and another, the general looked at his daughter and asked her, "Everything all right, Marjana, my dear?" He calls her Marjana instead of Joumana. When he's drunk, he thinks about his wife Marjana, who was a servant in the royal palace. "Everything's fine, Papa. The desert is beautiful, as is the heat, and the soldiers are good men. Everything is wonderful here, Papa." Then she waits for him to leave so she can gulp down what's left in the bottle.

His face is gaunt, harsh. He neither laughs nor smiles and his eyes remain hidden behind dark glasses. No one has ever seen him without his glasses or uniform. They say that he only takes them off when he goes to bed. It's impossible to tell where the person ends and the uniform begins; it is stuck to him like a second skin. He walks along dusting off the arms and legs, tugging on his sleeves, and smoothing down the collar as if there were two people struggling with one another, two lives occupying the same body—his life, and that of his uniform.

For one reason or another I spent the afternoon thinking about Zineb and the nerve-wracking state I had left her in. Whenever I tried to turn my thoughts to something else it proved impossible. One week would be enough for me to see Zineb and to feel the throbs of longing in her that have only gotten louder during my absence. Just one week, but how would I get this time off? There are spring days during which the heart becomes light and restless, wanting, if only it could, to flee its cage and soar through space or roll in the dirt like a child on the morning of a holiday, or to shake its wings like a bird that has finally landed close to a pool of water. The heart is prepared for a first whisper, for the most distant memory, for the first snatch of breeze, as if God has grasped it between His palms with all possible gentleness, out of fear that it might break or dissolve because of its excessive fragility and trembling, the trembling of a man consumed by deprivation, thirst, the desert, and longing for Zineb.

Three years ago Zineb decided to put an end to her pregnancy. We went to bed late, after our evening with the doctor and his wife. A viscous liquid in the bed woke me up. It was past midnight when I carried her, covered in blood, to the hospital. She remained unconscious for a long time. The hospital was empty and silent while I stared at Zineb's face as she lay on the bed. I watched her pulse. Every once in a while some patients stopped at the door. They didn't make a sound as they passed through the hall, nor did they make a sound when they crossed through the doorway. They passed over the edge of her consciousness like shadows, like passing shadows. They cast a glance at the bed then disappeared into the darkened hallway, the smell of their breath lingering, mixed with medication and camphor, as well as the smell of disturbed sleep. No one else was in the room; no one except for us, Zineb and I. Zineb was sleeping on the bed. A yellow pall covered her face. Drops of sweat on her forehead glistened under the light's depressing glow. "A Corpse in the Moonlight." A good title for a story, but this wasn't the time for stories or for titles. Zineb didn't die that night, but she wasn't all there in the hospital either. Rather, she was traversing the swirl of another life, while I wondered how to cross over into it.

The hospital was silent except for the patients' shadows that passed without a sound. The echo of distant footsteps. A door closing, or opening. It's all the same. I wasn't too interested in the difference. I was only interested in when Zineb would wake up so that we could go home.

It was past midnight when I carried her, covered in her own blood, to the hospital. It was the blood of another life that she had in her womb that had flowed onto the bed. I woke when my fingers touched the viscous liquid. I sat up and pulled the cover away. Zineb was swimming in a pool of blood, completely awake and looking at me with eyes free of fear, surprise, or wonder. In fact, she was smiling as if she had spent the night waiting for something like this to happen. The look on her face was saying one thing and her smile was saying another. She remained smiling for a few moments before she fainted.

I had been expecting to dream of her laughing, because she had spent the evening before laughing constantly. When I went to sleep next to her I was looking forward to waking up early to prepare her coffee black and strong, just as she likes it. I wasn't expecting a disaster like this when I went to sleep next to her, or when we were at the house of the doctor and his wife that evening, despite the atmosphere that was fraught with conspiracy.

"Zineb." She couldn't hear me. She was smiling to another person, to another life that had been inside her, but had disappeared. Nevertheless, she was Zineb now.

"Zineb. Can you hear me?"

We were at the house of the doctor and his wife, sitting around the light of a red candle in the large sitting room furnished in a European style. A red rug was in the middle of the sitting room and the atmosphere was charged with secrecy. Zineb was curiously exuberant as she accompanied the doctor's wife around the house. When the first signs of pregnancy appeared, Zineb hadn't seemed happy. Now, in the doctor's house, she seemed quite cheerful all of a sudden. She accompanied his wife to the kitchen, as they whispered to one another. Then, when they came out of the kitchen, they whispered or laughed, sitting with smiles on their faces that hid more than they revealed. All the while the doctor leaned on a pillow in a state of relaxation, smoking a Cuban Davidoff cigar. He raised it high, studying it closely, blowing smoke on it and smiling like a child at play. Meanwhile, I could hear them laughing in the kitchen. Their laughter echoed throughout the house. I should have known that a plan was being hatched. That night they didn't speak at all about children, even though that was their favorite topic: "Children? What use are children in a backward society?" That night they didn't argue about their socialist views, even though they'd never had a meal without this, their favorite dish. This was a night completely and unusually devoted to levity, exchanging jokes, laughing in the kitchen, and cigar smoking. I should have known that a plan was being hatched, but no, I didn't see anything that would cause one to be nervous or suspicious or to wonder what was going on. Zineb was happy. The cigar smoke made her laugh. The doctor's wife's walk made her laugh. Everything made her laugh. It was as if they had decided that tonight was the night before her birthday, or something like that. How was I to know that she had decided to abort the fetus and that they were secretly congratulating her, celebrating secretly among themselves? And all the while I was sitting there like a piece of decor to furnish the scene, a boring husband that they begrudgingly tolerated. Decor, like this candle or that rug. And it wouldn't have hurt me at all if only she had asked me. But she didn't ask. She acted as if the matter concerned only her and her socialist friends who had convinced her to do it. She didn't say a thing. It was up to me to figure it out and to see that she didn't want it, because the socialist doctor and his wife had convinced her of the uselessness of children.

In the hospital, I was intent first and foremost that the doctor and his wife not visit her. I was prepared to do anything, even to fight tooth and nail if I had to. We were done with the doctor and his wife. I would insist on that myself if I wanted to protect Zineb. I didn't know why she trusted them so much. I couldn't bear them from the get-go. I couldn't take their artificial and superior airs. I couldn't stand the way they talked about everything with the same enthusiasm and abandon. They competed and tried to outdo one another when they talked as if we were on a playing field. Whether it had to do with Freud or the market price of potatoes, they spoke with the same enthusiasm, exchanging knowing glances as if they were saying something brilliant.

Zineb's sister, Leila, and her husband, Abdelilah the taxi driver, came with their three demon children in tow. My sister, Fadila, came and cried a little over her rotten luck. But the doctor and his wife didn't show up the entire time Zineb was in the hospital. It was as if they had realized what they had done; as if they realized that we had no desire to see them, not in the hospital or at home or anywhere else.

The patients passed by again. Were they passing by the whole time? They looked at the bed and shook their heads regretfully, then disappeared into the dark hallway while the smell of their regret remained floating in my head. The body lay on the bed showing no visible signs of life. Her hands remained on her stomach as though she were scared the fetus she had just aborted would return. It was now swimming in a jar of formaldehyde arranged on one of the hospital shelves among other jars in which swam fetuses of other mothers convinced of the uselessness of children. She moved her toes, which stuck out from under the cover. I recognized the toes. They were Zineb's toes, all right. Her toes are slim and beautiful. Her body was beautiful under the cover, even without a bulge. The cover was white with no blood on it. Zineb didn't die that night. That's what was important.

The nurse's shadow appeared for a moment.

Before she disappeared, I asked her, "Is she in pain?"

She didn't understand my question. I asked again, pointing to Zineb, "Is she is pain?"

"Yes. And she'll be in even more pain when she wakes up."

"Must she be in pain? Isn't there a magic injection that can get rid of the pain?"

"The magic injections are at the pharmacy, and the pharmacies are closed at this time of night. Zineb will be in pain when she wakes up, believe me."

After that, the nurse disappeared. Then other specters began to pass by as if the talk of pain had attracted them. They looked at Zineb, shook their heads, and disappeared.

When the first signs of pregnancy appeared, Zineb didn't seem happy like a woman preparing to become a mother for the first time. Before she made the decision to induce an abortion, I asked her why she didn't like children. I'm also not that interested in children, but I wouldn't go so far as to say I don't like them. I didn't understand Zineb's behavior. I suggested to her that we go to another city like El Jadida or Essaouira. I'd be able to get some unpaid gigs at the youth center. I arranged it with my friend Aissa, who helps me put together my performances. What was most important to me was a change of scenery and getting away from the ideas of the doctor and his wife, who had begun to get on my nerves. As for her nerves, they were steady, but at that point she hadn't yet settled on a decision.

My desire to protect Zineb came before everything else. The influence of the doctor and his wife had really begun to frazzle me. I didn't understand their thinking about children. They didn't have children, and they were trying to convince Zineb of the uselessness of having them in a hierarchical society where poor children have no future besides poverty and ignorance and so on. How would they know without having had children themselves?

Zineb seemed interested in the idea of travel and said that she would seriously consider it. Aissa began to gather the set pieces and clothing that a modest show such as mine would need. Aissa has been my friend for years. We worked together in an amateur theater troupe. He joined me when I decided to establish my own troupe. Aissa loves the theater and he loves my shows. His father left him two houses, for which he receives rent at the end of every month, so he helps me with my shows and doesn't think to take his cut afterward. After two weeks of thinking, Zineb decided that first we had to say good-bye to our socialist friends, the doctor and his wife—her dear friends. So I found myself in their house, in the European sitting room, a halo of red candlelight and Cuban cigar smoke hovering around me, along with the smell of conspiracy.

The doctor and his wife are friends of Zineb. They weren't socialists when I first met them. They were like everyone else, with the same problems as everyone else, notwithstanding the fortune they were sitting on. The wife was also a doctor, specializing in venereal diseases. They were heading toward divorce when Zineb introduced me to them. At that time, they were trying to agree on how to distribute their wealth in a civilized manner, both the money that they had inherited from their parents and that they had saved during their twenty years of practicing medicine. Because they were a modern couple, their discussions were civilized. Zineb invited them to our place so they could come to an agreement. To create an atmosphere of trust, I brought out a bottle of champagne, which we finished without them having agreed on anything.

Each time they broached the subject, the level of tension between them rose so high that it seemed certain they would stay caught up in this endless fight.

She's forty-five but looks like a woman of no more than thirty. Slim and elegant, she struts proudly like a constellation of stars, something between walking and floating, as if she were not walking on the ground at all. Her smile is beautiful and when she talks it's almost a whisper. He is the same age, but bald and fat and ugly. He has bulging eyes and couldn't possibly appeal to any woman with normal tastes.

Late that night, very late, they reached a level of drunkenness that took the edge off of the tension. They drank two more glasses then went into one of the bedrooms and slept until noon. This became their habit at least twice a week, the same scenario, as if they only derived pleasure doing their deed chez nous, in our house. Zineb and I would tell ourselves that this time they would arrive at some sort of a solution, but they wouldn't arrive at anything of the kind. The doctor's wife would drink numerous glasses of champagne until her cheeks reddened. After that, she would burst out crying, apologizing to her ugly husband, pleading for him to forgive her. She would kiss his face and hands as she cried. On one occasion, she went into the kitchen and prepared a piece of fish that Zineb had set aside for the following day, and served it to him. She didn't invite us to share it with her ugly husband. For his part, he didn't exert any effort other than that necessary to devour the fish. After that, they'd finish up at dawn in our bedroom, always in our room, and always until one or two in the afternoon while we were in the reception room, forced to listen to their giggles and cries of pleasure while they did their thing, like any two beasts, like two cats at the peak of their pleasure.

Zineb would leave the house and I'd sit there wondering when the doctor and his wife, who, as I said, specializes in venereal diseases, would wake up so that I could take my turn to sleep. Once I said to Zineb, "There needs to be some other solution," and she looked as if it was of no concern to her, or as if what they were doing was not outside the realm of normalcy. I started buying cheap wine instead of champagne. At first, they both looked at it in disgust. The doctor took the bottle in his hands and turned it over, reading every letter written on the label, sticking his nose in it, and then returning it to the table with lips pursed in rejection. All the while he and his wife discussed how they could distribute their wealth in order to split up for good. His wife did the same thing, only without pursing her lips. She looked at me with her beautiful eyes, picking the bottle up and then putting it down. Her sweet eyes glistened. Her eyes are beautiful and always laughing, except when she and the doctor are trading insults. No more than half an hour passed before the wine took the same path as the champagne had before. We discovered that she was a bona fide drunk. She drank twice as much as the ugly man, running her hand over her flowing red hair while draining the last drop from her glass, then heading for the kitchen to get another bottle and any food she could lay her hands on.

Finally, they made up. When they came to the realization that the masquerade had gone on long enough, they decided to patch things up and became socialists just like that. When they realized that we had taken all that we could bear, they ended this habit and took up another. They agreed that there were more important issues, and for the sake of those issues, they were prepared to set aside their petty problems. Yes, overnight they became socialists, struggling with organizations and attending meetings, and this is something that resonated with Zineb. They had put an end to taking over our bedroom, but Zineb started spending time in their company while they discussed socialist issues and talked about class struggle. Perhaps they were expecting that I would join in their discussions or that I would join their party, but I didn't. Neither their party nor any other party. I'll never join—not because of a dislike for these particular organizations, but because I shun *all* organizations, whatever they may be. I don't see myself as a part of the herd, whatever it is—militants or Sufis or the rank and file of extremist groups. I don't need a pretext of any kind, and I'm not expecting a reward from anyone, whoever they may be. I love my sketches, I try to live off of 'them, and I believe to the depths of my soul that my criticisms of society and the state are much more important than those leveled by politicians and their parties, by "movements" and their lab rats, whose echoes reverberate in all sorts of places.

People are who they are, socialist or not socialist. People are who they are, regardless of appearance, thinking, or position. People are like a bunch of children—if you take them separately, they play in a reasonable way, their devilish natures seem cute, and their stupidity is loveable. However, when they're in a group, disaster strikes. No sooner do they become part of a group than their blood begins to flow in a different way: it becomes clannish, that of a wild herd, conspiratorial. In a group, children attack stray cats and dogs, pelting them with stones. They light small fires. Adults stone people. They slaughter. They tear their victims to pieces and eat them while the blood of malice continues to flow hot in their veins.

There's nothing easier than convincing a young woman of the uselessness of bearing children in a hierarchical society. The doctor and his wife are friends of Zineb. They're socialists now, and don't have any children. They rent a spacious apartment in Gueliz and they don't think about owning one. They're not so petit bourgeois as to think about owning an apartment for themselves. They're not so selfish as to think only of themselves. In fact, they are against all forms of ownership, which teaches the individual about selfishness and self-love, despite the fortune they inherited from their parents and the size of their bank accounts. When discussion between them and Zineb heats up, the doctor is quick to point out to her that the doors to the houses in the old neighborhood are always open to everyone, young and old, from near and far. When his mother needs salt or bread, all she has to do is knock on the closest door. Everyone gives to everyone and everyone takes from everyone. There's no difference in wealth, rank, or status. There's no system closer to socialism than the traditional life of our forefathers. And what is socialism in the end? "To each according to his need, and from each according to his ability," right? So I wonder why they don't distribute *their* wealth among the neighbors and the needy who are constantly passing by in front of their clinic?

Her foot moved and the cover fell a little to one side. I recognized the leg. It was Zineb's leg, life shimmering from it under the depressing light. The ghosts won't pass by anymore. No one will pass by. They've carried their death far away. Here, the water of life flows through her body and illuminates it. Her body was beautiful under the cover, even without the bulge. It's not important that the fetus has disappeared into a jar of formaldehyde. Zineb had returned, and this was the most important thing. I love Zineb. I don't love anyone but her.

I don't love my father because I have forgotten what his face looks like. Perhaps I'd love him if any memory remained. I was young. For a while after he left us my mother would say that she had seen him in his circle in the Djemaa El-Fna. She would say it casually while crossing the house's courtyard, as if she were speaking about a passing acquaintance, as if it had been *her* who had left *him*. So why did she insist on walking through the square? When she returned in the evening from the traditional arts collective where she was working, carrying potatoes and oil, loaded down with the charitable donations that would fill our bellies for a while, and would say to no one in particular that he was there, in his regular corner, telling jokes, I wasn't picturing an actual being with a face and eyes. I wasn't picturing anything at all. My sister Fadila's descriptions of him remained contradictory. She would say that he's a tall man with a thick beard who recited poetry in his circle and that people would head toward his space from every neighborhood to listen to his poems. Other times she would say that he sold herbs that cured all illnesses; that he brought them from the desert to treat incurable diseases. Then, in her distracted way, my mother said that he had disappeared from the square. Still, she continued to walk that way. She didn't admit until years later that a fat woman selling amulets and remedies had taken him away in the Mercedes that she wouldn't drive without her black sunglasses on. Maybe she didn't know about them at first.

She continued to cross the square every evening and my sister Fadila continued to imagine him and wait for him on the doorstep, expecting that he would rush through the door one day wearing his wide white djellaba. We would say to her, "Fadila, come inside," but she wouldn't. She would sit on the doorstep waiting for him and his thick white beard, maybe even imagining him coming on a white horse.

The person who did appear one afternoon was the neighborhood pharmacist who came to propose to her, without a beard or a djellaba. At that moment we were all reminded that she had grown up. She was older than fifteen. She had become a woman. Her chest was swelling. That young man had walked by her dozens of times and she had never noticed him. For that matter, no one had noticed him when he opened his pharmacy close to our house, or when he settled down nearby, or when he prowled around us. We noticed nothing of him, her first fiancé, until he appeared one day inside our house bearing gifts and candles, some sugar and tea. Before him came Dada, the old matchmaker without whom no engagement is done and who introduced him to my mother.

"The young man is an orphan raised in an orphanage where he studied and learned everything that a young man who wants to become a pharmacist can possibly learn."

My mother replied, "How lucky. You've given us exactly what we've been waiting for. God has granted us this gift at just the right moment!"

Her back was stooped from sitting so much at the loom weaving the rugs that the tourists buy from the traditional arts collective. From then on she wouldn't have to go to the collective to weave those rugs in exchange for a bag of potatoes. Her joints ached, as did her eyes. The pharmacist was parentless, and he had come to deliver us from the fried potatoes we ate every evening when my mother returned from the collective. He had come to fill the house with the manly smell and respect we had been missing. She said that he would take care of all of us. As for my sister Fadila, she secluded herself deep inside the house, running her hand over her chest, wondering what the pharmacist wanted, what he wanted from her and her chest.

When the pharmacist came to our house with his modest presents, Fadila wasn't there. We looked for her but could not find her. As long as the pharmacist remained in the house, she remained hidden in some deep dark corner. Where had that devil disappeared to? Was she in the corner of some darkened room? Could she be on the roof or at the neighbors' house? She wouldn't appear until the pharmacist had left the house, having waited a long time for her. He had left the pharmacy empty and had come to say hello to his fiancée, but instead of exchanging greetings with her, he would spend an hour or two exchanging words with my mother about the weather. And Fadila? She would disappear, just like the day before. Why? She just wasn't ready. Her chest hurt and her head was spinning.

"But she'll rally with God's help," said my mother. Then she said, "It's the evil eye, God forbid! The women living around us envy us because God has bestowed his mercy upon us." Then she said "It's magic. The girl is bewitched."

So one day my mother took her to the tomb of Sidi Bou Amr close to the house. She burned incense, waving it all around, and leaned her head on the wood of the coffin for a whole night in order to get rid of the effects of the cursed magic that was messing with her mind, but Fadila continued to disappear whenever she caught wind of the pharmacist's approach. Every time she smelled him coming, she would be stricken with real trembling and would begin to run about like a chicken with its head cut off. Yes, Fadila had grown up all of a sudden. Her breasts had swelled to alarming proportions, but my mother's alarm was even greater. What would she say to the pharmacist when he came, his gifts having preceded him, counting on him to give us something other than potatoes swimming in oil to chew on, counting on him to allow her to stop going to the collective? Her joints ached, as did her eyes and fingers. Every part of her body tingled with pain. When she thought about waking up at six in the morning and spending the day bent over the loom, she was overtaken with a desire to drag the girl by her hair and shove her under the pharmacist in order to be done with this nightmare.

It seemed that the pharmacist was in no hurry. He took up residence in our house, going to his pharmacy in the morning and returning home right after work. His room was cleaned every day. His food was prepared on time. He left early and when he came home he would head straight to his room, as if he were in a hotel. He no longer sat with my mother to talk about the weather. Then we all went to visit Saint Moulay Brahim, without the pharmacist, of course, because he no longer asked about Fadila. Marriage no longer concerned him. My mother lit candles and circled the tomb with Fadila for three days straight so that God would open her heart to the pharmacist, but it remained closed despite all of our supplications and prayers. Even though my mother sprinkled her body with water that flowed from under the tomb's dome, the effects of the magic and the evil eye did not go away. Fadila's pains got worse and the pharmacist stopped asking for her.

He would cross the patio and cloister himself in the room that had become his, as if he had settled there permanently. He bought a new bed, a dresser, and linens. He bought soap, toothpaste, a brush, and cologne as if he were in a hotel, albeit a free one.

Then my mother no longer saw him crossing the patio. She only smelled the scent of his cologne that he left trailing behind him as he walked by quickly on tiptoes. Then he began to lock his room—*his* room—just like in a hotel. The only thing missing was a number on the door! And my mother kept wondering what had happened to the pharmacist. When she asked him to at least pay her rent, he refused, saying that he had rented another room in another house, and just like that, the pharmacist disappeared along with my mother's faith and hope that the burdens of life would be lifted for her and for us.

Fadila returned to her previous life and nothing much changed at home. The matter of my sister Fadila's marriage and its failure became a familiar story. I can't think of her without recalling all her subsequent engagements. As if there was little more to her, my mother viewed it as a duty to mention the stories every chance she got. Anyone entering our house would hear her complaining about the ruin of her daughter to whom God had forgotten to grant His mercy, and whoever left the house would have the same disgrace ringing in their ears. Then my mother began to complain all the time and about everything, from the heat to the cold, from over salted food to a forgotten spoon on the table to an unwashed glass. And along with all of this complaining she wouldn't miss an opportunity to launch into endless formulaic expressions such as "God forgot her in His mercy!" or "What can we do? She has followed the path that God laid out for her."

And the old neighborhood matchmaker, Dada, would keep coming by with news of a possible new fiancé.

12

I KNOCKED ON THE PALACE door at ten in the morning, as I usually do, and the guard simply gestured for me to go away.

"No one is expecting me today? How strange. Have I become deaf without noticing? I heard of His Majesty's arrival, which is why I came."

The guard didn't notice my joke and repeated the gesture, indicating I should go away. My problems with Aziza and her mother diminished a bit beneath the crush of black thoughts that were now descending on me. Those problems paled in comparison and more pressing questions took their place, eventually transforming into a single question: What's going on inside the guard's head? Did he really not recognize me? Does he want a bribe? Did the king not ask for me yet? For days I have been hearing on the radio about His Majesty's inauguration of this or that school, and I've seen on television that His Majesty visited this orphanage, or that he welcomed some guest to his palace in Marrakech. I told myself that His Majesty was busy and when his tasks were all done, he'd call for me. I calmed myself with the notion that his mood would have improved since the last time, lulling myself to sleep with these comforting thoughts and waiting, but no one knocked on my door. And that morning, when I stood in front of the palace door, the guard shooed me away.

Aziza and her problems faded into the background. Her mother had taken up residence in our house weeks ago. She brought along her son, who had just gotten out of prison. New problems, to be sure, but they were obscured completely behind the clouds of much more serious concerns. The question hung above my head like a sword: Does he not need me anymore? This would be extremely unlikely. First of all, why would he not need me anymore? Zerwal has been away for a long time now. He might even have died, and no one cares about him, even enough to know the cause of his death. Second, I don't recall ever hearing of a jester who was not needed. He remains sitting on his chair jesting and making a fool of himself and of all those around him until he dies. Third, is there another jester in this whole country so much better than I am that His Majesty would no longer need me? I look around me and count the faces that appear on TV—all types of faces, all types of expressions, all forms of eloquence that pass across the screen—and I don't see anyone as gifted as I am. All of the images that go by and all of the words that are said don't equal one iota of my silly antics that make even those in mourning laugh. If Zerwal were alive, I would have said that a trick was being played on me, but Zerwal is lying in his grave with his hump underneath him.

At the Café les Négociants, I sit watching the street. My mind is there, my whole being is there at the palace, or, rather, at its door. I wait for the person to appear who will take me by the hand and lead me there. People walk by in front of me, but I don't see the person I'm waiting for. I don't see anyone. I thought about Aziza's mother. What would she say now? She's mocking me deep down inside, I know it, or maybe she's crying to herself now that she no longer has a son-in-law working in the palace. I'm sitting on the café's terrace like an overly anxious adolescent. No one is coming today. I think of Aziza's mom until I'm no longer thinking about the palace's locked door. Something has gone terribly wrong. I don't drink my coffee.

I can't stand the atmosphere at home. There are too many of them now: the mother, her sons, her daughters. And Aziza has become silent. Her mother is the one who has decided on everything since settling into my house, since even before that.

I spent the evening and half the night in the garçonnière lying down, not moving at all. Will anyone knock on my door to deliver me from my thoughts? I go through all of the funny stories I've told and I think of others, but I don't laugh. The king has forgotten me. After a week this has become all but certain. They have forgotten me and I don't know why. Did I do or say something that angered His Majesty? I remember my last soiree at the palace as having gone well, although His Majesty was not present and all I gained from it was a suit that one of the businessmen gave to me as a present. What happened then? Did someone whisper some sort of scandalous words about me into His Majesty's ear? What a black night, like being in a forest in the middle of the night, with all of its ghosts and nightmares.

The following morning I got on my bicycle and headed to the palace. This has been my place of work for more than fifteen years. Not counting the times I went to this wealthy person's house or that politician's or high-ranking officer's place, I haven't known another safe place. I have no refuge or calm, except for right here. It is my home and my Kaaba and I won't leave it. I'm a jester, and the king himself is the one who made me a jester!

I had never considered becoming a jester before, and it only happened with the king's intervention and divine providence, but where were they now? This was when I needed them most. The jester is allowed to do anything, even head to the palace in the morning unannounced. The proof of this was the bicycle parked in the square facing the large gate, waiting for an order to enter that would surely come at any moment now. But the gate remained closed. After waiting for a while I approached the guard like any other citizen requesting an interview with the king. The guard was new on the job and didn't know me. It wasn't the same guard who had been standing there a few days before. It was a guard who never in his life had heard that there were jesters in the palace. He was baffled as he looked through the small opening in the door and saw a man in full possession of his faculties submitting such a strange request. I imagined him thinking, "Is this man *really* asking for the king, or is he kidding?" The guard replied sarcastically, "Sure," then retreated behind the gate and closed the little window. Perhaps he was smiling to himself and shaking his head, and perhaps he continued to laugh once he reached his little hiding spot behind the door.

What am I going to do at home? I won't be able to face my loneliness, or my questions that don't have clear answers. I no longer have the desire to see anyone. The only people I run into seem to be gloating. What will the barber say? Will he satisfy himself by laughing at me? I took a taxi and went to my unfinished house on the outskirts of the city. I would rather spend my time surrounded by plaster and concrete, isolated and not seeing or hearing about anyone. I won't open my door to anyone who knocks, even if it's someone the king has sent personally. Everyone has disappointed me, and from now on I don't want to have any human contact. I'm just fine in my unfinished house. I'll finish it when I'm done with all of this trouble, with Aziza and her mother, with the palace and its problems. I'm done with everyone. I have everything I need here and I no longer need anything else. I never needed anyone. On the contrary, they're the ones who were following *me* around, seeking *my* company.

The guy digging the well on the plot of land that was to become my garden was more important than anyone else at that point, a simple man who knows what men are worth. I sat not too far from the well to exchange a few words with him while he was down in the hole swinging his pickax. I looked at him every once in a while, watching his sweaty back and his strong hands powerfully striking the dirt. Down below, four meters underground, he didn't complain about anything. He knew neither king nor minister, and that didn't concern him at all. With the same pickax and the same digging motion, he dug deeper into the depths of the earth, resigned to his fate. Six meters, then ten meters, he kept on digging, and after a little while, or after a few days, a spring would burst forth here. Yes, water would gush underfoot, as if it were a miracle. And what did the well digger hope for? His only hope was to finish his work early so he could attend a friend's wedding where he'd eat, drink, sing, and dance until morning. Then the next day he'd return to his digging. His friend was marrying a co-worker of his from the olive-processing plant.

It was Saturday. Not so long ago all days were the same to me, to the point where I couldn't distinguish Saturday from the other days. I listened for the digging, but didn't hear him striking the earth anymore. I could no longer stand the silence. I asked the digger what he was doing. Had he reached the water? This digger is a better man than me. What am *I* doing? What's *my* role? What useful work have *I* done other than make the king and his entourage laugh? And for what? Tomorrow I'd stand in front of the palace door, only to see the guard gesture for me to go away. I didn't know what I was waiting for. The digger dug. He was waiting for the water that would flow out from under his sandals, whereas I was waiting for one person to remember me. I'd left his inner thoughts and there was no way to return. The digger was waiting for water to gush out from under him. His friend in the olive-processing plant moved olives from one barrel to another, waiting to take his bride, while his bride, for her part, had spent years in the plant next door, separating the olives from their pits and dreaming of the young man who would deflower her tonight. They would marry tonight. No one would be satisfied with them or dissatisfied with them. They were all happy and content. They'd sing and dance until morning, whereas I was truly the most miserable creature on the face of the earth. I don't make water burst forth from the earth, nor do I remove the pits from olives. I'm just a jester, and what's the use of a jester without his master?

I saw clearly how far I'd fallen when the digger came out of his hole, wiped off his sweat, washed his hands, and invited me to go with him to the wedding of his friend who worked in the olive-processing plant. This digger didn't know me. He didn't know anything about my recent past, nor did he know anything about the people I'd associated with. Perhaps it wouldn't interest him at all that I was the king's private jester. I found myself smiling as I thought about performing for the digger. This invitation showed me perfectly clearly how far I had fallen, in a way that no longer needed any explanation— from the palace to the wedding of an olive worker. Was there a downfall any greater than this?

I headed off to the house of Si Hussein the barber. Si Hussein was a childhood friend. I knew him and the cobbler he shared a house with. Two bachelors hanging out together singing, smoking kif, and laughing. This was what I was lacking. My gloomy face had a positive effect on them. They found my sullenness, which resembled the anger of a child who refuses to accompany his father to the hammam, hilarious and didn't stop laughing until I got up and headed toward the door. What had gotten into them? I'd thought I would be able to relax in my friend the barber's house. It was the kif smoke that finally refreshed me, not the laughter of Si Hussein or his friend the cobbler. I got up without fanfare so as not to give them another reason to laugh. I went down the stairs and listened. They hadn't noticed that I had left. They were completely stoned. Well, they wouldn't spend any more of their evening at my expense, these two dogs laughing inappropriately and for no reason.

I waited for a taxi but none came, so I walked home. I found it locked and my keys wouldn't open it. The door finally opened and Aziza's mother appeared. Next to her stood her son, the one who had just gotten out of prison two days before.

She informed me that Aziza did not wish to see me. She disappeared for a moment behind the door and reappeared with my suitcase. She threw it at my feet and stood there waiting for my response. There was nothing on the woman's face or on the face of her criminal son to indicate that she was kidding. The first thought that crossed my mind was that news of my supposed dismissal had reached her. I became aware of my profuse sweating, so I wiped my face with the sleeve of my djellaba. What am I to do with all of this nonsense? Am I to wipe *it* away too? And does my dear mother-in-law know where I'm supposed to go? No. No one is interested in this. I remained standing there staring at the door, half expecting Aziza to peer out from it.

"*I take refuge in God from the accursed Satan.*" I said these words as if to lessen the bad thoughts that had overwhelmed me, as if to find my way once again.

13

Day Five

I ASKED JOUMANA WHY HER father the general doesn't laugh. She said that he's always been like that, that she'd never seen him laugh, not even once. He has a cold disposition and a dry temperament. Perhaps that is why he covers his face with black sunglasses, and has requested that they be buried with him. Then she showed me some x-rays. His heart is as small and shrunken as a piece of burned rubber. Doctors have advised him multiple times that he should laugh more in order to prevent further shrinkage and hardening, but despite this advice his lips rarely part in a smile. When he settled in the Sahara he tried bringing along a number of jesters and deformed freaks, but he got rid of them after less than a week. She also said that he has an excess of bile in his spleen, and that this is what causes the aggression and bouts of fury he's known for and that worsen in the winter months, and for this too there is no treatment other than laughter. "The bile is infected too," said the doctors, "and no medicine will be of any use to him except for laughter." But what can be done if the body doesn't comply? The doctors advised him to start doing laughing exercises, little by little, like a medication taken in small doses until one becomes accustomed to it, because sudden laughter can also kill. This is why he brought the jesters and the freaks to his farm.

I said to Joumana, "He has to keep practicing, especially someone like him who's trying to find laughter for the first time."

His Excellency thought that the matter was this simple? But how many years does it take a man to regenerate his blood? An entire lifetime perhaps, and that's how it is with laughter too. A disposition that is closed and hard requires a lifetime to transform itself into one that is open to the world and to people in all their seriousness and silliness, harshness and levity, intelligence and stupidity. He didn't get this, but tried to enter a new world: the world of satire. What did he expect? What exactly was His Excellency expecting? That his heart would just open up to laughter, free of charge, for nothing? I understand perfectly well why the general doesn't laugh. It's because of the uniform. Once you put a uniform on in order to become another person, the person who was there just moments before is hardly recognizable, as if a demon takes you over, whips you into a frenzy, and pushes you to kill the first man you run into.

His youngest daughter settled into the room that was intended for her father. His daughter Joumana, after wandering from one void to another, decided that she was going to become a professional photographer, so she came to photograph the Sahara, to capture what her father had never been able to see during his quick tours of duty. She saw it in her dreams—spaces overflowing with femininity, a sea of pain and desire, shadows like eternal bodies, an unspoiled expanse extending out into infinity, all the way to her empty heart, shadows secretly sleeping and dreaming of the girl who will immortalize them with her camera. The captain ordered me to stay up all night at her service. I watch her going in and out of her room carrying her small dog in a dreamlike state. She's a skinny, ugly girl, and where her breasts should be there's a camera hanging from a strap around her neck that swings back and forth with the rhythm of her uneven steps.

Captain Hammouda said to her, "I present to you the conscript Hassan. He is an artist just like you, miss. He appeared on television once and presented a sketch entitled 'The Butcher.' Did you see it?"

"No."

"Did you hear about it?"

"No."

She went back to playing with her dog.

The general has three daughters. The middle one got divorced after having been married for two months to a lawyer from Marrakech. The oldest one went abroad without marrying. She lives in Paris. As for Joumana, since becoming a quasi-orphan, she hadn't done anything except play with her dog from the time she gets up in the morning, until she hit upon the idea of photography. She really seems like an orphan. No one cares about her. In fact, she's like a shadow or a piece of furniture, and I found that she was even uglier than I had previously noticed. At twenty-eight years old she resembled the dog she carried around. She was so ugly, in fact, that it made one want to turn away so as not to have to look at her, and she was dumb too. She spent her time in the company of dogs, thinking about taking pictures of rooms and doors and the crumbling walls of the fort, and here she was today, waking up with the idea of photographing gazelles. Where were we going to find these gazelles?

Four of us set off in the car, before sunrise, going to hunt gazelles. In addition to the idiot Joumana, the general's daughter, there was Naafi and Mohamed Ali. I told them that we were going to be tortured by this creature. From the beginning, I felt no affection toward her but they just felt they were on vacation, with the general's daughter no less, happy with their luck. Joumana scanned the horizon with Captain Hammouda's binoculars—binoculars that no one else was allowed to get close to but that he had handed to her, practically melting with happiness. Naafi had been polishing his rifle since we left the fort. He wore a taraza made of palm leaves and, having gotten rid of the military cap, he did look as if he was on vacation. Mohamed Ali was smiling. He was still happy because he had been delivered from at least one unfortunate day of stringing up barbed wire. The others—conscripts and non-conscripts alike—saw no end to their labors and were bent over the wire, stretching and stringing it up, all to remind them that they were at war while they burned a little bit in its false hell.

We were going to hunt gazelles.

I was like the attaché to the general's daughter, as if that were a new, high military rank. I was also an artist like her, an artist who wrote sketches and performed them on TV, while Naafi and Mohamed Ali were the specialists in gazelle hunting. I wasn't sure who exactly had told her that the area was filled with gazelles, but I had added, "And for hunting them, you won't find anyone better than my friends Naafi and Mohamed Ali. We have barely been apart since we were brought together by accident, by the barracks, by this strange war."

She's really an idiot, this girl. She had never seen a gazelle in her life, living or dead. She squawked every time one of us turned our head. Every time one of us moved, she thought he'd seen a gazelle, so she let out a squawk and stopped in her tracks. She wouldn't stop squawking or standing up and sitting back down. She was expecting a gazelle to appear at every turn, even under the car's wheels, as if it were cats we were hunting. The idea of seeing a live gazelle and taking its picture had lodged itself in her head. I would have preferred being in the tavern with Fifi, angry over the disappearance of her turtle, watching her come and go, just as Brahim used to do, instead of running after this spoiled brat. Where was Brahim now? In some other tavern. In front of another turtle, or in front of a bride his mother was able to find from among the young women of some village. Brahim didn't want to marry a city girl because he was afraid she'd laugh at him. I hoped he found what he wanted.

And us? We scampered over rocks like monkeys. Two strong slaps on the idiot Joumana's face. That was all that would be needed to return her to her senses, but instead we went along with her because she was the general's daughter, allowed to ruin our day. We crossed over rivers looking for a gazelle that refused to appear, that threatened to thwart her adolescent plans, and that left us wandering in these wastelands. All around us, as far as the eye could see, there were extremely high mountains. We moved slowly forward, following narrow, dry riverbeds. The silence was absolute, savage, and we moved along to its rhythm. Naafi sang a Sahrawi song because he had Sahrawi roots. He once told us that his grandfather came from the Sahara to Marrakech with nothing but his sword. Naafi swept the mountains with his eagle eyes, humming a song that never ended.

We stopped when the rising sun shone on our backs. No sign of a gazelle. Mohamed Ali lit a fire and Naafi said, "I'll take a look around." He jumped without a sound onto the rocks, lightly, doing away with anything that would weigh him down except for the rifle that he raised up in front of him like an Indian getting ready to pounce on a White Man. He walked away with quick steps, jumping carefully from rock to rock without a sound. Naafi knows the desert. No one knows it like he does, which was why he walked as if he were in his own garden. After a little while, we heard a gunshot. Mohamed Ali said that Naafi had found a gazelle, whereupon Joumana jumped up from where she was sitting and screamed—baffled, happy, and frightened all at the same time. She said that she wanted her gazelle alive. I wasn't interested in what she said. She remained standing and gazing at some distant spot where the gazelle was going to appear, coming toward her in surrender. Mohamed Ali said that Naafi hadn't fired another shot because he had wounded it, and began to prepare the cooking pot and get the fire ready. Joumana calmed down a little and waited like us, sitting on the ground wrapped in a blue cloak, watching Mohamed Ali's every move with mesmerized eyes. Everything mesmerized her—the dust, the turbid water we drank, the car as it rocked and almost turned over, day, night, the wind, the emptiness, sleeping in the emptiness, the fire, and Mohamed Ali as he lit the fire. Naafi came back without prey. He had wrapped a covering around his head to keep the burning sun off. He put his rifle down. He lit his Mauritanian pipe after filling it with tobacco, and sat smoking.

He said, "The wind changed the bullet's trajectory."

"You didn't get it?"

"Nope. I found no trace of blood."

"Should we go back to the base, then?"

"No!" yelled Joumana.

All of us understood the meaning of the "no" that had shot out from this childish girl's mouth—until we got her gazelle for her, there was no use in even thinking about going back.

I was the one who said it from the get-go: This girl wouldn't allow us a minute of peace and comfort until we found her animal. Where was this damned gazelle? Why wouldn't it show itself and deliver us from a night or even longer in the wild? And it might all end badly. Our hides could be roasted if the enemy were to come upon us. We hadn't seen an enemy up till now, but they were out there. However, it was the general who would roast us if anything bad should happen to his daughter. Nonetheless, I spent some of the afternoon hoping something bad happen to her. For example, a scorpion could sting her, or a snake could bite her, or the enemy could show up and take her to their camps in the heart of the desert, thus ridding us of her forever. Otherwise, being stuck in this labyrinth with this creature would know no end.

But the enemy didn't appear, just as the gazelle didn't either. We were not worth observing, as we were when they ruined our night at the well. I spent the afternoon repeating, "This is when it will appear," but it didn't appear. All I heard was the sound of Naafi singing or the sound of Joumana dreaming of the gazelle. Wasn't there an enemy out there reasonable enough to appear when we need them? Wasn't there an enemy who could rid us of this girl who dragged us across the desert waste, dreaming of gazelles night and day?

We spent the afternoon as we had spent the morning, driving through dry riverbeds and narrow ravines, and over bumpy roads. The car rose and fell as we bounced from side to side with its unsettling rhythm. Our meager rations were close to gone, and this pleased and excited Joumana's capricious mind even more. After having tasted being lost in the empty desert she wanted to know the taste of hunger too. She refused to drink in preparation for this festival of famine. Naafi and Mohamed Ali got out of the car. They would go around the mountain and we'd meet up with them on the other side, maybe after they'd found their rare animal. The girl had begun to get on their nerves. The whole affair had begun to irritate them. That was why they had gone off. The car chugged along and it seemed to me that we would never get to the other side. It had been a while since Mohamed Ali and Naafi had disappeared. After half an hour they came up to the car, but without results, while the sun rose high in the sky, burning above us.

Then, totally unexpectedly, a gazelle appeared in front of us, a little to our right, grazing contentedly. We stopped, frozen where we were. It lifted its head. The gazelle raised its head and looked at us with its black, calm eyes that were not expecting anything bad to happen. There was no trace in them of what was about to occur. We froze, the gazelle and us, exchanging curious looks. There was a silence among us, a sense of surprise, the idea that death could arrive at any moment. When Joumana let out a squawk, the gazelle jumped up and fled. Naafi immediately knew what to do and hit the car's horn. The gazelle stopped. It went back to guardedly watching us and the car, which it took for an animal like itself, a little bigger but with the same two eyes. The gazelle approached the car. Its initial tranquility returned and the same inquisitive look remained in its eyes. At that moment a gunshot rang out and the gazelle fell to the ground, dead. Joumana screamed like someone who had lost her mind. She jumped out of the car and went over to where the animal lay on the ground. She circled it in disbelief. She sat down then stood back up again. She took some pictures of it—pictures of the gazelle, pictures of its dead eyes that it had seen us with, just moments earlier. Joumana said that life continues in a gazelle's eyes after it dies, but we didn't understand what she was talking about. She was delirious and we were walking along beside her in her delirium. As Mohamed Ali busied himself with skinning the gazelle, his arms covered in blood up to the elbows, Naafi sat on a rock, smoking his Mauritanian pipe and singing.

14

I DIDN'T ADVANCE ONE STEP. There was no way of knowing that they didn't need me at all; no way of being absolutely sure of anything. I think about leaving the city for the citadel, or for any unnamed village just as Rahhali did. When he fell out of favor he packed up his bags and went to Settat, but I don't have the same conviction as he did, nor do I feel the same despair, and no one is angry with me. I haven't done anything that would harm anyone influential. I'm nothing but a jester, and no one has anything against a jester. Oh God, but what about what I said about the minister of the interior? I'm still hopeful, though. A mere misunderstanding that will pass. They might call for me at any moment so I must remain where I am, close to the palace. Things will be much worse if His Majesty asks for me and I'm nowhere to be found, neither at home nor at the barber's house. Then, it would look suspicious. I mustn't give anyone a pretext. There are so many evil people. I must be careful, extremely careful.

The last time I stood in front of the palace door, the guard assured me that God would do what was best, and that for his part he'd try to get my messages and gifts through, one way or another. But I don't need someone to reassure me or prove his good intentions to me. All I want is for someone to remind His Majesty, to tell him that there's someone at the door, or to say to him, "It's been so long since Your Majesty laughed, since we've seen your face break into a smile, all because of the problems in the damned Sahara," or "I can't remember a day when we laughed like we did when Balloute threw himself naked into the swimming pool," or "Does Your Majesty remember the day when Minister So-and-so came before us in a bad way complaining to you that he was late for a government meeting because he was suffering from severe intestinal pains, and you asked your jester Balloute whether he had any medication to treat him? 'Yes,' replied Balloute immediately. We laughed and your brilliant jester added, 'There's an easily taken, quick-acting cure. It'll be enough for your minister to stick one finger in his mouth and another finger up his ass, after which he should proceed to switch and alternate them. After half an hour he'll see how the wind whistles out of both of his holes. He'll feel completely better and will be able to devote himself entirely to the venerable government meeting.'" Just a few words is all I ask. At that moment, His Majesty would wonder, "Where did that weasel who used to delight us with his sense of humor, his anecdotes, and his different types of laughter disappear to? Every laugh was stranger than the last. What was his name? Hold on, I remember it now. Why, his name was Balloute!"

Is this too much to ask? Isn't there anyone who can perform this good deed for heaven's sake, or for a rare wall clock?

Another time, the guard told me, "Since I started working here, all sorts of people have passed by, and all of them have said that they work in the palace. There was even someone who said he was the king's uncle! Am I supposed to believe everything everyone says?" Your words push one to despair, guard, but I won't despair, even though all this really does make me lose hope.

Two weeks have now passed. No sign has come from behind the locked palace walls. His Majesty is devoting all of his thoughts to the Sahara, and specifically to General Bouricha, who isn't responding to him. This general, he's the reason. He's the one who has so ruined his mood. Damn him!

It doesn't seem that he'll respond to him anytime soon, which is what I said from the beginning. I said to His Majesty, "Don't give him your finger because he'll devour the whole arm!" This man was once a mere shadow. Now look at him. No one knows what's going on in the Sahara or what's going on in the general's head, not even His Majesty!

The ideal way to find out what's going on and to put my mind at ease once and for all is to write a letter begging his forgiveness, but I don't even know what grave error I've committed that I could possibly try to explain and justify. Perhaps I'll just write something with no connection to what has happened. No, all of this would be of no use. Gifts are the way to reach the hearts of these sorts of people. Yes, gifts. A gift for the guard to soften his heart, and another for the servant. A gift for the cook and another for the gardener. Once the gifts are distributed around the palace, I will have taken the first step. My goal is for my gifts to reach the king so that he'll remember me. That's the important thing. I'm sure that with just a passing mention of me, he'll remember me, and he'll remember that he loves to laugh. The king needs to laugh, especially now in these tense times.

Aziza and her mother discovered the right time to form an alliance against me. Their collusion has gone as far as it can go. I had lost control over the household some time ago, and had begun to scream endlessly. Those two damned women would let my yelling just float there in the air, in the open space of the courtyard, as if it didn't concern them, while they continued scheming against me. They would whisper to one another, deliberately cloaking their gestures in obscurity as they plotted away. All the while I would say to myself, "Soon I'll find the wind whistling through this house that has been emptied of everything. If things go on this way, the furniture, the dishes, and everything large and small will disappear." And Aziza, of course, said that she cannot rein in her dear mother. But even after having had the door closed in my face,

I still clung to the notion that a thirst for goodness has not disappeared completely from people's hearts. I reassured myself with the hope that things would return to the way they were, but unfortunately, little by little, things only got worse. The mother had set her daughter against me. She had delivered her and her children from misery and beggary, and then she rewarded herself by throwing me out of my own house.

The house is off-limits to me now, but their plan won't succeed for long. I have friends in high places, lawyers and judges, although I don't see this as the most opportune moment to cause a fuss. There's no point in bringing about another scandal that might play against me during this tense time. I have always been a skillful and intelligent player. I need to act with the utmost discretion. "Seek help in meeting your needs silently." I've always lived by that hadith. It's not the first time I've faced such adversities. Everything passes. I must not give the enemy additional ammunition; I mustn't give the impression of weakness or despair. Plus, the house had been emptied of its contents some time ago. The rugs had disappeared ages ago, and her son had sold what remained of the dishes at the flea market. Nothing remained except for the walls standing witness to the vileness of Aziza and her mother.

I passed by Sidi Slimane and thought of the family I once had there. Should I visit them? I should at least go see that son who writes the off-color sketches. Maybe he was right in insulting the government as Zerwal, may God have mercy on him, had informed me that day. I don't like the government. And the king? I don't know what to think of him after what has happened recently. During the past week I sent numerous gifts—some of which cost me a pretty penny—and the guard reassured me that they would arrive. The following day he reassured me that they had indeed arrived, and he confirmed that the king would receive me in a few days' time, but there's no way of knowing whether he was being truthful, or whether he was lying. He said to me, "No doubt *this* time you'll receive the honor of appearing before His Majesty. His Majesty seemed energetic this morning. He woke up whistling a merry tune, his face shining, and he had his wig on. His face had a look that said he would summon you soon. I've spoken to him about it, and although he didn't respond verbally, he appeared to be seriously considering the matter. All indications show that your request has entered his heart and mind."

There's no way of being sure of anything with these uncivilized brutes. I know them all too well. I've spent more than my share of time with them and I know their tricks. They're all cast from the same mold. He said that the king had gone away, then he said that he had returned, so I presented more gifts to mark the occasion, with no way of knowing whether they reached him or not. These gifts are what will result in me reclaiming my position, my work, my honor, but there's no way to be sure of anything. I don't know where my gifts go once they leave my hands.

So, Balloute the jester is almost sixty years old, and happy with the luck he has been destined to receive. He ate his bread cold for almost fifteen years. He doesn't give a thought to the day he was born, or to the day he will die. He has only one care in the world: how to return to what he was—a jester in a chorus of jesters. This is his past and his future. I can't picture another future outside of His Majesty's shadow. I make him laugh and provide diversions for him so that his mind remains alert.

And Aziza? Has her heart shut me out completely, and with such speed? Not even two years have passed since our first meeting. I've become a bit confused and I don't know which weighs heavier on my heart. Yes, sixty years old and still my heart flutters and my fingers shake whenever I recall that day when she called out my name. The memory of our intimate nights plays over and over in my head while Aziza remains in my house harboring nothing but hatred for me. No, she doesn't hate me. Her mother is behind it all. Two eccentric women living in my house, eating my bread, and thinking little of me. They take my money and my gifts, they take my heart and my mind, and they give only hatred in return. Pleasant words had flowed from Aziza's mouth that day two years ago when we met. Sure, many pleasant words came out of her mouth, but the words seemed as if they flowed like water into the sand; they disappeared quickly. Couldn't that be considered a form of hatred? Would you expect a woman to whom you've given your money and your heart to pay you back in such a cruel way? I gave her everything. For two years I had been promising her that I would buy her a luxury apartment in Gueliz, which was what her mother wanted so as to be rid of me as quickly as possible. But Aziza didn't seem very enthusiastic about the idea, saying neither yes or no. Whenever I would talk to her about the apartment she would purse her lips in a grimace somewhere between a smile and a scowl. Maybe that was her way of hiding her true intentions.

What does this girl want? A truly eccentric girl. She doesn't ask for anything or refuse anything. She doesn't see any difference between dining in the finest restaurant or going to bed hungry. She only sees what her mother sees. Her face doesn't show that she has been granted special distinction for sitting at my table. She doesn't betray any hint that she values my efforts. If this isn't hatred I don't know what it is. It's true that she hates me more than anything else. The only thing on her mind is revenge for my having come along to marry her just when she needed to marry in order to escape her family. All of these ideas occur to me in an attempt to understand, to come to terms with, to comprehend this contempt. It should be the opposite—that she think of *me* night and day, and that she wait longingly for *me*. It should be that my presence makes *her* swoon and that my absence tortures *her*. She should thank me for my kindness toward her and the generous gestures I show her. But it is not like this at all. It's as if I'm only doing what

I'm supposed to do. It seems like sometimes she doesn't possess the same intellect that other people do. As for her heart, it is fragile, quickly damaged. She tried committing suicide once, days before I married her. I remember I went to see her in the hospital, and to justify or hide what she had done she held her bandaged wrists up in front of me, saying that she had used a dull razor, as if she wanted to say that she wasn't serious about it.

Who can understand women? Sometimes I say to myself, "Maybe she did it because of me; maybe she secretly loves me, and that was the natural thing to do. Her hands were covered with white bandages, and underneath the bandages there were minor cuts, signs of her love and her hardness." Sometimes jealousy eats away at me when I think of other possible reasons for her suicide attempt that are no less sound. Might her love for someone else have pushed her to it? This is also possible—more than possible. Other times it is enough for me to shake my head and repeat, "Who can understand women?" She completely occupied my thoughts. With what she had done, she put me entirely at her mercy and had taken the upper hand. I no longer thought about anything but marrying her. Her wish was my command. My only desire, my last desire, was to spend what was left of my life at her side.

I'm nothing but a stupid old man, without the least bit of dignity, and with the smell of decay seeping from my pores. No one will save me. I think about staging an open-ended protest in front of the palace door, or in front of the government headquarters, or in front of the parliament, so that passersby will know what injustice has been done to me. Sometimes I want to throw open the windows and scream at the top of my lungs so that people near and far will hear that I have been wronged. I take the cap that I wore on many occasions because His Majesty used to love it. I kiss it repeatedly. I turn it lovingly in my hands. I pass my fingers gently over it as if I were asking it for help. I think about the injustice that has been done to me, about how I am a person whose rights have been violated. I pick up old issues of *Paris Match* and look at the pictures of me accompanying His Majesty on the Champs-Élysées, or on the deck of the *Ibn Battouta* ship, smiling, a glass of champagne in my hand. I cut out the numerous pictures and put them up on the bare walls. I sit and study the color pictures. I am just fine with my pictures. I haven't felt this sort of calm in a while. My eyes overflow with tears of happiness as I look at my past laid out before me in such riotous colors.

I am just fine at home, in the company of His Majesty on my bedroom wall. I won't go to see Fatima, my old wife. For the past two days I had sent my friend Si Hussein the barber to gather news of the old house and who was there. He told me that Fadila was to marry. And the boy? He'd been drafted into the army. Why was I interested in them? I wasn't going to go to see them. My own worries are enough for me. I have no desire to lay eyes on a son who insulted the government. What would they say there in the palace? I won't fall into that trap. Maybe that's what they're waiting for—for my fall from grace to be complete.

The garçonnière is empty as well. The wall clocks and silver dishes have disappeared. They were taken by the building's caretaker, or the cook, or some other person I have no way of knowing. It's impossible to know where my gifts have disappeared to. The caretaker said that they had been returned to those who sent them, with nothing remaining except for the glass aquarium on the shelf with the fish swimming in it. Gone are the gifts I had received on special occasions, and for no occasion at all. Gone are the Persian rugs. But there still remains the little red and black fishes swimming up and down, imprisoned in a basin of water half a meter high, and these pictures—His Majesty and I on the Champs-Élysées, His Majesty and I on the deck of the *Ibn Battouta*, His Majesty and I on a hunting trip, each of us holding a rifle and smiling for the camera, aiming the barrels of our rifles at the photographer and laughing, and this lump as a big as a ball stuck in my throat, making it all but impossible to breathe.

The walls begin to close in on me, so I leave the garçon-nière. It is evening. Suspended time. I drag my feet along the streets for half an hour before heading to the house of the barber and the cobbler. I have a pleasant time in their company. The kif smoke calms my nerves. The barber picks up the oud. My mind is set free by the smoke and by the melody flowing from the fingers of my friend the barber. As I float for a while in another realm, the clamor of the world lightens. I thank him silently. I am relaxed. I'm not sure how much time passes while I'm in this state.

As I'm going down the stairs I stumble and fall. That's what I remember. The barber and the cobbler say that I fell down the stairs and didn't stop until I got to the front of the house. I don't remember any of this. They also say that I lost consciousness and didn't open my eyes for some time. Where am I now? In my old house, with them at my bedside watching over me. They take the opportunity to tell me that that they brought me to my old house because that's what I wanted. Did I say that to them? Together, they indicate yes, and then they leave. Perhaps it really did happen like that.

I turn to look around. In my old house, on my old bed, breathing in old smells I had forgotten, coming to me only from memory. I leave the bedroom, limping. My foot hurts. I stop in the middle of the courtyard. My wife Fatima doesn't get up to greet me, and to give the appearance that she's busy with something of the utmost importance she raises her dough-filled hands. She is preparing gazelle-horn cookies, which the guests will devour next week. Fadila is done with her dough. She has shed many tears as she welcomes me into her arms. Her mother Fatima also cries, but from a distance. Her crying isn't as convincing as Fadila's. Fadila loves me. I'm moved and place my hand on my thigh to compose myself.

My wrist has swollen a little. I go back to the bedroom and see that the swelling has increased and the skin is bruised. The pain has gotten worse. Being in this house increases my pain and misery. I send Fatima to summon the mosque's imam, who also works taking care of the hammam. The faqih rubs my foot with hot oil and wraps it in a bandage. The following day I discover that my limp attracts the curiosity of the people around me, and as a result they stop asking me embarrassing and malicious questions. As long as the bandage remains on my leg, no one questions me too far or shows too much malice toward me. I can walk around my old streets and buy my bread in peace. I hope that my limp will continue indefinitely so that they won't pay attention to my other handicap—how long that will last I don't know.

Every once in a while, my foot hurts. Not the same foot that was in pain a few days before as a result of falling down the barber Si Hussein's stairs. No, the other foot, or maybe it is the same foot. I can no longer distinguish between the two. I can no longer tell. My head hurts too.

15

Day Six

THE STORY OF OUR FRIEND Naafi is neither entertaining nor pleasant, especially the part where he went raving mad and began to dig around the fort trying to find his missing leg. When his raging madness calmed down a little, he continued to sit at the gate under the shadow of the wall asking about his vanished leg, or he wandered around the fort, hopping on the crutches we made out of boards from the destroyed supply store, as if expecting to see the man who had opened fire on him.

I didn't see his leg, and neither did Mohamed Ali, just as we didn't see the bullets. When Naafi was wounded, I wasn't there to hear the shots or see the Kalashnikov bullets tearing through his leg. I was getting some sun in the far corner of the courtyard waiting for Joumana, the general's daughter, to wake up so I could tell her I wouldn't be taking her to her father General Bouricha's farm for him to bless our marriage. I had already told her I was married, that I had a wife who was sick and who cared a great deal for me. After the miserable hunting trip it seemed that she was interested in me and that she had decided all on her own—as General Bouricha and all wealthy people do—that she would marry me for a period of time, as if I were a doll she could play with for a little bit. I would rather have found myself on the front lines than in bed with this worm. I was thinking about this and, in fact, was so preoccupied by it that I didn't even hear the gunshots. I was busy thinking about the matter of Joumana and her father when I saw four soldiers leave Sergeant Bouzide's office and run out of the fort, and then return carrying Naafi on their blood-soaked shoulders.

His leg was torn apart, its bone sticking out and shattered like glass. The thigh was enormous because of the quantity of shredded cloth wrapped around it. The blackened dried blood on the rags that covered what remained of his leg, as well as on the soldiers' shirts, shoulders, and hair, made them look like they had been playing in the mud. Naafi is quite fragile. In fact, his body is so thin that even without bullets, the wind could knock him over. He appeared even tinier and slimmer as he shrank into himself, teeth chattering. They placed him in the middle of the courtyard. And the bullets? They were still lodged in Naafi's splintered leg. We wondered whether we should leave them where they were. Many soldiers have sustained injuries with the bullets left lodged in their thighs, legs, and heads. With time the pain goes away, while the bullets remain behind as a reminder. Wounds heal, scars form, and memories shine like a defunct lighthouse illuminating a future no one else will see.

They set him down in the middle of the courtyard and went back to playing cards with the sergeant. What else were we supposed to do with the summer heat blazing? As we rushed toward him, Mohamed Ali and I asked him whether we should leave the bullets where they were or remove them. Naafi was almost completely withdrawn from us, swallowing his pain as he looked in the direction of the bar and wondered whether Fifi, the bar's owner, could see him in this miserable condition. The bar was on the other side of the fort, behind the walls, and thus difficult to see. Nonetheless, Naafi could see it at that moment and wondered whether Fifi was looking at him from the window and saying to herself that he no longer resembled Alain Delon. What could we do except wait for the doctor to come from Agadir? He would know the best course of action.

This whole time, Naafi was silent, lying in the middle of the courtyard staring in the direction of the bar with a look of disappointment in his eyes. His smile was sad. Naafi loved to laugh. He would even laugh at the story of his father's death. Naafi loved to laugh and eat gazelle meat, and he loved Fifi. He used to say that he would never leave this place. He would marry her and they would run the bar together, selling drinks to soldiers under the table, just as Fifi does now, and we would go along with him just to prolong the dream. Now Naafi said nothing. He waited for the doctor who wasn't in his office. We took him to an adjoining room because of the heat, staying close to the gate, to the bar, and to his thoughts about Fifi, which came to him between moments of fitful sleep and periodic stretches of unconsciousness. Naafi had not yet begun his state of delirium. The lights were still on in many parts of his brain, but his leg was shattered, and the pain had reached an intolerable level. No one was bold enough to remove the rag it was wrapped in. And what would be the use of removing it? We would find a leg like any of the other legs pierced by the bullets of an enemy whose whereabouts we didn't know, and whose distance from us we were unable to measure.

When he's around, the general sometimes gives us the impression that he knows who the enemy is, but at other times he gives us an entirely different impression. In any case, he's now busy at his farm pressing olives. The general loves to see the oil flow between his fingers, but at times like this, when the enemy opens fire on us, we don't know how to respond to it because the general hasn't yet told us what to do.

The enemy wears the same clothes as we do, they speak the same language, they sing the same songs, and they dream the same dreams that inspire all of us, but they aren't visible to us as we are to them. It's enough that they open fire on us and whether we're at the well or on the ramparts of the fort, their bullets reach us. At that very moment, their bullets were still lodged in Naafi's leg awaiting the doctor's arrival. After a morning spent on the beach getting some sun, he finally came. He told us that he had been attending a soccer match between doctors and nurses at the hospital's playing field that had lasted for the entire hot morning. The leg had swollen and the pain had sapped all of Naafi's strength. The sun had burned the doctor's skin after a morning spent officiating a soccer match.

"I'm a referee," he said, "and a referee, like an officer, does not leave the field in mid-battle."

He's not a man who lies. He has never told a lie in his life. He had come straight from the hospital's playing field, directly from Agadir in a state-issued jeep. He examined Naafi and didn't say a thing. He ate with us and played cards with the adjutant and the sergeant and drank to Fifi's health while he checked her out, telling her that her blood pressure was very normal. Then he examined Naafi again and smiled at him, but didn't say a thing. He gave him some shots in different parts of his body until he was sedated, and asked us to leave him with the patient. Half an hour later, Naafi was still lying down in the same place in the same room, but without the leg, while we were in the courtyard making crutches for him out of the rusty nails and boards we found tossed behind Fifi's tavern.

So that's his story, or some of it anyway. Naafi was the youngest of us, not yet nineteen years old. The thinnest too, as if his numerous dreams had squeezed him and sucked him dry. Between becoming a professional soccer player and a history professor, other dreams forked off from there. He had finished his first year of university when the call came. Like the rest of us, it never occurred to him that he would go one day to enlist, and like the rest of us he didn't possess the knowledge necessary to find a way to be excused or to avoid military service by the circuitous means that the rich use. At the general headquarters they told him what they told each of the four of us: "Service is compulsory!"

His father was of the opinion that the call came at a bad time because of his university studies and all of the hopes he had pinned on them. Carpentry was his profession, and so he made a table to give to an officer as a gift, as well as an armoire for his wife, but he died on the way, crushed by a truck. His father's death is a funny story, actually. He was riding his motorbike and on the handlebars he had balanced the table he had made with his own two hands, carving it beautifully so as to make it suitable as a gift. But it was big, this table. When we wanted to be entertained we'd ask, "How did your father die, Naafi?" and he'd tell us that his university future so preoccupied his father that he didn't realize the table he had put on his motorbike's handlebars obscured his view of the road, and so he didn't see the truck coming toward him.

Then there were the other dreams that had made their way into Naafi's head during his abruptly curtailed university studies. These included marrying a student who shared his interest in history. He told us that he had actually met a student at the university at the end of the year and that he was preparing to woo her at the start of the next year, but the damned call up came at the wrong time, just as his father the carpenter had said. Mohamed Ali and I are both married, which, when we saw how attached he had become to Fifi, was what prompted us to say in unison that Fifi was the first woman in his short life. That was why he had become so attached to her, just as a child becomes attached to his mother. In the bar, drunk, we'd ask Naafi, "What do you see in that buffalo, Naafi? Her flesh is tough and difficult to chew." Naafi would laugh and say that that was how he liked it. This way he didn't have to share it with anyone. He would also say that Fifi's flesh was just right for him, just as everything about her was just right for him.

He spent the rest of the day in silence, staring at the empty space his amputated limb left underneath the cover, and at the empty space left by the successive questions of someone on the verge of imminent collapse. The bullets hit him just outside the fort, not while he was guarding the well, nor while he was on reconnaissance patrol in the far desert wastes. They came to him here, while he was taking a piss against the fort's wall, and the bullets remained lodged in his bone for the whole morning because the doctor wasn't in his office, or at home, or at his usual café. He was at the public hospital refereeing a soccer match between doctors and nurses. The missing leg was what bothered him now and when he ran his hand over it, the space left behind became even greater, and that was when the questions came:

"Where did the bullets come from?"

"We aren't sure, Naafi. We looked all around the fort, leaving no stone unturned, but we didn't find anyone carrying a Kalashnikov or any other rifle."

"And Fifi?"

"She's at the bar asking about you."

"And what does she have to say about this whole thing?"

"She doesn't say anything. She doesn't know anything about the leg."

"And the doctor? Why didn't he come during the first hour after it happened? Or the second? Why did he leave it to swell up so much?"

"Like you, Naafi, we don't have a clue."

"And the enemy?"

"We didn't see an enemy. The general says that he's on the other side of the sand barrier."

"Then who opened fire?"

"We don't know, Naafi."

A little before evening, he heard a crow outside cawing. He crept up to the window and saw it flying around, spreading its blackness above the fort. The black crow came closer this time and landed on the window's edge, letting out another "Caw, caw!" Naafi remained looking at it, dazed. He said it could smell the leg that was buried someplace outside the fort. Then the black bird flew high up, and landed on the wall. This time, he heard it say, "Walk, walk!" Naafi gathered up his pain and left his room, hopping on his ridiculous crutches. Then he saw it outside the walls, pecking at the ground, and he said, "This crow knows where it is!" That was the moment the idea of finding his severed limb lodged itself in his brain, an idea that seem to mock him, causing him to lose his mind.

The doctor had thrown a piece of his human body into the trash, or into some damned hole, rather than treat the poor limb as a part of a human being. Wasn't it a part of him? Why deal with it this way, as if it were a chicken leg? Naafi protested strongly, saying, "They need to bury my leg humanely, like any other human leg, at least."

Naafi hopped around on his crutches as if the severed leg had made him lighter, clenching his jaw in pain and anger, and went everywhere the bird placed its claws. He followed the crow. Naafi dug a hole here and a hole there, asking, "Where's my leg, you son of a bitch? Is it buried inside or outside the fort? And the doctor, has he left, or is he still sunning himself somewhere around here? Has he taken the leg with him to display in the War Museum as a testament to our heroic steadfastness in a war we know nothing about? No. It's been buried without a funeral or ceremony or farewell speech. It's been tossed into a strange hole as if it were a chicken or dog leg, not part of a human being deserving respect."

This was why the missing leg was still bothering him. It was in pain and was waiting for someone to recover it from its hole.

Naafi did not venture as far as the tavern. He stopped digging, temporarily. He thought Fifi was watching him. He waited for nightfall before resuming his digging. Naafi was no longer the same as he was before. We begged him to calm down, to relax. Mohamed Ali and I told him that Fifi was waiting for him and that she'd open her bedroom to him, just as she had that one night. "Do you remember? She still feels the same love." Then he looked at us, smiling, and reminded us that this was a secret between the two of them. He sat at the gate of the fort singing, as if he were rocking his orphaned leg to sleep and consoling its loneliness. He imagined that he would return to the way he had been when his leg returned to him. He dreamed of nightfall, which would allow him to continue digging before the crow made off with it.

Evening had fallen a while ago. Mohamed Ali and I are sitting in the room waiting for our appointment with death to arrive. We had been four, Brahim disappeared and now Naafi raves in the other corner of the fort, and we no longer consider ourselves to have been saved. At dawn, Captain Hammouda is going to send us to the front lines to die, just Mohamed Ali and me. The others are luckier than us. I'm being sent because I disobeyed the orders of my superiors, and Mohamed Ali is being sent because he's my friend. I had told the captain that I would prefer to find myself in the line of fire, or if possible, at a line even farther away, rather than marry this damned worm.

The room is spacious now because there are two empty beds and at daybreak it will become even emptier. That's what the general's spoiled daughter had decided.

This is always how it has been for me. My relationships have always been intermittent and fleeting. I'm not sure if it's the result of shyness, or of fear. In the corner of my house's courtyard, there was a well. When I was young, my mother couldn't be bothered to look for me and so she left me crouched down at the bottom of the well, exchanging words with the frogs. The frogs disappeared from my life, and Zineb took their place. And my father disappeared when I was five or six, or maybe I was ten—not that there's any use in dwelling on what age I was. Dad disappeared, and good riddance. Zineb took his place too and she alone is enough. My relationships have always been limited. This has never been one of my favorite subjects. After the frogs, I formed a relationship with a cat I found meowing under my window. I wouldn't even have been that interested in it had it not insisted on rubbing against my leg whenever I stopped in front of the door, and had it not truly wanted to get to know me. I'm not exactly a lover of cats. I'm not one of those people who loves animals more than God's other creatures, but I realized that I understand them. More than once I have wondered why animals are so affected when they see me. Is it because of how I look, or because of the way I get them, or is it something else I don't understand?

Zineb came along like a raincloud after a long drought, like a gift, like an oasis at the edge of the desert. At the Shahrazade Cabaret I told her, "You're the gift I wasn't expecting." In our small house in Riad Laarous I never got bored of watching her come and go. I spent strange days with Zineb in our modest home, like a tightrope walker, light, walking on air, with just the right balance, neither a hair too heavy nor a hair too light. She did everything I desired, like the ideal wife one reads about in fashion magazines. Suddenly we had become conventional, and this was a beautiful thing after so many years of wandering aimlessly.

At home, she forgot her leftist tendencies, spending the day between the kitchen and the bedroom. She folded the sheets while singing "Far from You, My Life Is Torture," while I would think of ways to make her happy. I borrowed some money from Aissa so she wouldn't lack for anything. What could I have bought her otherwise with the little money I had that would have made her happy, so that she wouldn't feel that she had made a mistake, so that she would feel she had chosen the right man? Sometimes I would get on my motorbike and join her at the Shahrazade Cabaret, where I'd spend a pleasant evening watching her sing her favorite Oum Kulthum song, "Far from You, My Life Is Torture." I would wait for her until she finished, late at night, after which she would ride behind me, filling me with warmth—I'd feel her arms around my waist and her breasts on my back like two amulets protecting me from all of the world's evils. After a quarter of an hour we would find ourselves back in Gueliz eating a plate of fava beans with cumin and olive oil or drinking a pot of tea made with wormwood leaves or mint.

I love Zineb, and I love the house that shelters Zineb. If I was away for a performance I'd rush home to prepare something for her to eat when she returned from the cabaret. I believe that this life suited her as well, at least during our first year, before the abortion, and then again after we had gotten rid of the doctor and his wife, having put behind us the ordeal of the abortion that practically tore us apart.

I presented my comedy acts at private parties, and while I only did a few and what they paid wouldn't make you fat or rich, it was just the beginning. Not long ago, I presented a sketch entitled "At the Butcher's Shop," which got the attention of audiences as well as praise from some journalists. "So I go into the butcher's shop and ask the owner, the butcher, for some bones for my dinner, but he doesn't pay any attention to me because right then a très chic woman enters, wanting three kilos of meat for the poodle she's holding in her arms." I play three roles at the same time: the poor guy asking for bones; the très chic woman who's only interested in her clothes, the way she walks, and the handbag she recently purchased in a fancy shop in Paris; and finally, the dog who feels sorry for me and who says consolingly at the end that he'll give me some meat the first chance he gets.

Zineb's brother-in-law, the taxi driver, says that my work focuses too much on politics. I had never thought about it before. Most of the time I come up with my stories while I'm walking down the street or in the hammam. I like to think while I'm in the hot room lying down in the middle of a cloud of steam. How is this related to politics? It's just about a woman who buys three kilos of meat for her dog that doesn't weigh more than half a kilo! Is that politics?

Abdelilah likes to spew words larger than he is in order to obscure the label of "taxi driver," which really annoys him because he studied up until the baccalaureate and used to believe, still believes, that he's going to become an important person in the business world. He says that when the opportunity presents itself he'll enroll in a school of informatics—intensive evening classes. After that he'll start a company in Casablanca that will provide services for the largest national and multinational corporations. His ambitions will carry him far—very far—and so in order to appear important, he always argues with me. He says that my works are political, leftist, and extremist, and when I try to engage him in a discussion about his opinions he stops talking in protest. In general he opposes everything I say or am about to say. Even when he agrees with me he begins speaking with a "no"—a long "nooooooo." Sort of like that.

My relationships were limited, whereas Zineb's were many and varied. She never said that she had leftist tendencies, but the way she acted spoke for itself. In addition to singing at the Shahrazade Cabaret, she also liked cultural associations, cinema clubs, and political demonstrations. I'm not sure why. Her family isn't interested in politics, having no connection whatsoever to it, neither up close nor from a distance. They're simple people. Her father is a cobbler who spends his days repairing shoes at the door of the municipal market and her four brothers are still in middle school trying to perfect the best ways to drive their teachers mad. As for her, she's the way she is and that's all there is to it. She likes these things. They aren't inherited and a person isn't born with them. One day they just appear, like symptoms of a disease, like leprosy. Can you be cured of leprosy? Or maybe she caught her illness from prolonged exposure to the doctor and his wife. Same difference.

On Sunday mornings I'd take her on my motorbike to quench her thirst for discussions about class differences. I had

never before joined any party. I didn't lean toward monarchists or socialists. The mere thought of it had never even
occurred to me. I am an individualist. I love Zineb and on
Sunday mornings I'd take her wherever she wanted to go on
my motorbike. Zineb was the one who introduced me to the
doctor and his wife and she was the one who introduced me to
the group of socialists. I attended some of their meetings with
her. Not a meeting would pass without them talking about
Che Guevara, Lin Biao, and the revolution of the workers and
peasants. And as if this weren't enough for them, just when
you'd think that they were tired from talking, they'd break out
into song: "We will ignite it, a revolution in the mountains /
The mountain will burn, but it doesn't bother me at all."

The majority of those in attendance were refined and well
intentioned, but some of them would sit next to Zineb and
rub up against her while explaining the meaning of dialec-
tics. This annoyed me, even if it was funny. Thus, instead of
explaining their theories to peasants, they'd explain them to
Zineb as they rubbed up against her. Instead of focusing on
the workers they focused on a singer named Zineb, and then
worked earnestly on grabbing her from me as I looked on
without embarrassment.

One night I went with Zineb to one of their soirees at a
conference in a chic villa in the city. Zineb presented me to
one of the higher-ups in the party. He was smoking a fat cigar.

After giving me the once-over with piercing eyes, he said,
"Wonderful, wonderful. *A one-man show,*"—this last statement
was in English—"wonderful. Maybe we'll need you to give
one of your performances in the future. Our youth brigade
needs these committed performances."

I asked him about the pay I would receive for my committed performance and he looked as if I had hit him on the head
with a hammer.

I asked him again, "How much will I receive for the performance I give to your youth brigade?"

He continued to look at me as if in shock. "You're asking to be paid? Our young people sacrifice their time and money. They sacrifice their lives and you ask to be paid?"

His anger at me was indescribable. For a moment I thought he was going to slap me. Instead, he bit down on his cigar and blew smoke in my face. And where was the youth brigade at that moment? No doubt eating sardines in small dorm rooms in high schools, lying on dirty bedrolls singing, "We will ignite a revolution in the mountains," while the party official, having satisfied himself with grilled meat, blew his cigar smoke in my face. Maybe I was wrong to have asked to be paid. When the socialists ask you to give a performance, you must always assume that you'll do it for free, and you must always be prepared for and happy with this honor, as if it were a holy duty. You must say, "Yes sir." You must be happy and proud of the good fortune that has come your way, and for the honor that you have received as you stand before their youth brigade— sweaty and hoarse—in order to reach their hearts, whereas *they* are in the air-conditioned villa eating caviar and blowing Cuban cigar smoke in your face.

That official looked at me with searching eyes and said, "Wonderful, wonderful." The second time he said it, it was with a tinge of contempt. As if he were saying, "Never mind, one more reactionary in our ranks. We'll execute him when we take over." He shrugged in open derision as if he were informing me that their youth brigade didn't need the likes of me. Then he chewed on his Davidoff until it crumbled and repeated, "Wonderful."

I reminded him that he hadn't yet named a price. This time I said it to annoy him. His eyes glowed viciously. He took a violent drag on the cigar, blew the smoke off to the side, threw Zineb a look of reproach, and walked off.

That's how it goes. They praise you for an hour, saying in front of everyone that you perform committed sketches, but as soon as the issue of compensation comes up, everyone goes silent. "What's that guy saying? He wants to be paid a fee?" They open their eyes wide and are amazed that you've requested compensation, as if you had asked one of them to strip naked. As if Zineb and I didn't eat anything but bread and didn't drink anything but water, as if we didn't have expenses like everyone else. Zineb doesn't smoke or drink, and I don't smoke Davidoffs, but I do pay the rent and the electricity and water bills, and I buy medicine for the headaches caused by people like this official. It is true that sometimes we eat eggs and tomatoes for lunch, but that doesn't mean we can be belittled when we ask for payment for services rendered.

Sometimes, especially on Sundays when Zineb doesn't go to the cinema club and when there isn't a communist or socialist conference, we are struck with the desire to buy some veal or lamb cutlets just like everyone else (we haven't yet gotten to gazelle or ostrich meat). As for the monarchists, I haven't attended any of their conferences, but I don't think things would be that different there. Perhaps they'd be worse. The monarchy isn't a person or a group of people. It's a system, like a dragon that knows neither friends nor enemies, with a large belly that is never satisfied, never full. It devours everything and then demands more—men and rocks, the sickly and the fat, those who possess something and those who don't. It devours everything—the present and the past, the ancient and the modern. It leaves nothing behind—neither distance nor space. As long as it continues to devour everything, all is fine. As long as it continues to devour, you just have to wait until it has eaten its fill. But can a dragon ever be satisfied?

16

I BEGAN MY WORK IN the Djemaa El-Fna with an old basket made of straw and a small teapot. When I stood out in the square, there was nothing but the djellaba on my back, a basket made of straw, and a small teapot. After meeting Drissiya, the fat woman who sold amulets and herbs that she said she had brought from the Hijaz, I married her and went around the country with her in her Mercedes-Benz that she wouldn't drive without her black sunglasses. I learned a lot during that year with her, and then with her husband as well, whose sudden appearance hadn't surprised her at all. After that, I began to wander around the markets and set up shop at the gates of military barracks on my own dime. I told people I had brought the herbs I was selling from the Hijaz, just like Drissiya did, and they snatched them up. At least the year I spent with her wasn't for nothing, thank God. But the commander of one of the barracks had me arrested because I (with my made-up recipes) had allegedly caused the death of three of his soldiers who were looking for something to enhance their virility before going to the bordello.

"Three soldiers at the same time!" The commander walked around me screaming, "Three soldiers at the same time, you infidel!"

His neck muscles tightened and his thin moustache quivered. I didn't know how to respond. He seemed to be overplaying how agitated he was, as if to prevent me from getting worked up too. He circled me, threatening to shoot me without a trial. In the end, his soldiers threw me safe and sound into a narrow cell, but the firing squad was waiting for me, or I was waiting for it—no difference, really. I was not at all expecting to wind up where I was. I was over forty, and rather than God decreeing a happy ending for me, I found myself closer to nothing at all—no money, no family, and my final home a dark cell deep inside a military barracks in the middle of nowhere. Every once in a while the guard (a man with a thick moustache) would look in on me and say he would have been the fourth victim. He said it sarcastically and sometimes with an angry fire burning in his eyes. The soldier with the thick moustache had not yet gotten over his surprise, was still amazed at his luck. He would have been the fourth victim had he not decided, at the last moment, to stay in the barracks, for no clear reason. He hadn't taken those herbs because he had chosen to stay in the barracks rather than go with his friends to the bordello.

"That's all there is to it, you heathen!" Then, peering at me through a little window in the door, he said, "You thought you'd be able to do it again, you son of a bitch?" As if to remind me of the bullets waiting to pierce my trembling heart in the barracks courtyard at some soon-to-arrive dawn. In my head my entire wasted life spooled out before me. I was hoping for a fate other than this one. My friend Si Hussein the barber had once predicted fame and fortune for me. How funny his prediction seemed then, as I looked around my foul-smelling cell. I thought about crying but pulled myself together. I remembered that I was alone in my cell and thought to myself, "What's the use of crying when there are no witnesses to my tears?"

It just so happened that the king was taking a tour of the provinces to inspect his troops, and while passing through Marrakech he heard about the crimes of a person named Balloute who had been tossed into a prison cell in one of the barracks. When His Majesty arrived, the commander told him that yes, within the walls of his barracks he had imprisoned a dangerous criminal who had killed three of his best soldiers in a single swoop and that he was waiting for permission from His Majesty to fill the perpetrator with bullets. The king ordered that I be brought before him.

I asked the soldier with the thick moustache, "What does your king want with me?"

"Either the day of your death has arrived, or the day of your deliverance, you wretch. He'll either strangle you with his own hands, or he'll release you. It all depends on his mood. He's the king. Do you know what that means, you infidel? The king does what he wishes in his dominion."

But the king was in a good mood that day.

The king stood there examining my face for a long time, while I wondered how my face looked to him. I left the king to study my unflattering form at his leisure: a round face with two small eyes, two flared nostrils, and a small mouth resembling a hole. Si Hussein the barber always said that my face had the look of someone who was permanently shell-shocked, or like someone expecting the roof to fall in on him at any moment. Did the king see the same thing as the barber? Yes he did, and in order to hide the urge to laugh that suddenly struck him, His Majesty put his hand over his mouth and addressed me with false sternness.

"You criminal! It seems that you have killed more of my soldiers than you have treated."

I answered him right away, as if I were responding to the local grocer. "Has even one of them complained of a fever or headache? Does Your Majesty not see that I have treated them completely and definitively?"

If one of his officers had responded to him with such impudence he would have met a very bad ending, but I was created to be funny—with my words, with my silence, with my body, with my whole being—and I was absolutely certain that this was my chance.

His Majesty asked me, "Do you realize that the commander wishes to put you in front of the firing squad?"

I replied that most people in this day and age are dying, and most of the time without any reason whatsoever. Then I added that this man's soldiers died because they didn't follow the medication's instructions, and that they would have died of syphilis in any case because they frequented Oum Habiba's bordello in the Ursa part of town. The word "bordello" made the king laugh. Of course he knew it in French, but coming off my tongue in Arabic, the word acquired a new strangeness, an original peculiarity. The king continued to stroke his chin while studying this creature standing before him.

"What's your name?"

"Balloute."

It was that he was still hesitating and had not yet decided what to do. Would he send me to the barracks courtyard so one of the firing squad's bullets could pierce my heart, or would he leave me to continue liquidating his soldiers?

The king asked me, "Do you have a story to tell us?"

The commander was disgusted by this whole circus, angry with the attention His Majesty was giving me and the time he was wasting on me. He chewed on his upper lip and his thin moustache, waiting. As for the king, he hadn't yet decided whether he was going to send me to be executed or wait for the end of the story that I was about to narrate to His Majesty.

I told the fart story, that always gets people to like me:

"There once was a king who was hopelessly sick. He was a devout and religious man. One day, his private physician visited him and, after examining him, told him that one fart would be all it took to get rid of his illness. The king appealed to God to consider his condition and grant him the fart that would save his life, but God did not answer his prayers. When the king's entourage and servants saw his condition deteriorate and became sure that the king's cure was all but impossible, they grabbed what they could from the palace and fled. No one remained at his side except for his companion and jester, Messoud. He cared for him and consoled him, but with no hope of a cure. One day, on the edge of death, the king appealed to God to grant him a seat in heaven, to which Messoud said, 'How can you ask God to grant you a seat in heaven when he doesn't even deign to grant you one small fart?' The king exploded in laughter—a loud laugh that filled his mouth, his eyes and veins and every part of his body, and with it, his belly exploded with a resounding fart that restored him immediately to health. The end."

I stood staring at His Majesty, waiting. Then I said, "Okay, so let me laugh first," and I did, and the king followed suit.

I knew very well why I was laughing. I had been saved in spite of the commander. As for the king, no one knew if he was laughing because of the joke or because of the happy ending with the king or because of my laughter. Or was he laughing on account of the fact that God heard the much-repeated prayers of the sick and responded to them? The commander, who had not yet swallowed his disappointment, did not say a word. He was seething inside, marveling to himself that His Majesty had pitied a trickster such as me. When the king asked me to honor him in his palace and to entertain him, I responded immediately, as I always do. I earned almost nothing from my work as a serious and responsible doctor, so why not try my luck as a jester in the king's court?

Rather than being imprisoned in a military barracks for the rest of my life, rather than a firing squad riddling my chest with bullets in the barracks courtyard, I spent close to fifteen years in the king's palace as a jester. I came and went as I pleased. I sat next to His Majesty. I ate at his table. I even entered his bedroom. People in the street bowed when I passed by, moving to the side and begging my pardon for being there in the first place. They'd kiss my hand, apologizing for not being able to do more. They'd send me letters that included their complaints, desires, and buried passions. In the market they filled my basket free of charge, and in the shops of the bazaar they begged me to honor them by receiving their humble gifts. Wearing a short djellaba and a red tarboosh, I'd sit in the Renaissance Café looking down over Marrakech, as the waiter whispered into the ear of someone going up the stairs that *he* was sitting upstairs. "Who?" "Balloute, the king's private jester."

And what does Balloute say now? This requires no comment. God destines wealth and he destines poverty. He destines greatness and he destines lowliness. He destines that you appear before the firing squad, and here you are in the sultan's palace. He destines what He pleases. He destines that you to go in and out of the palace as if it were your own home, and He destines you to find the door closed in your face with no one remembering who you are. He destines greatness for whomever He pleases, and He destines lowliness for whomever He pleases.

I am nothing but a jester, but what's the difference between a jester and a minister or a general when you're in the shadow of His Majesty? All of them pray behind His Majesty and pray to God to prolong their time there for as long as possible. They all walk in the same entourage and together they fear the day that they will be thrown from it. "Last stop. Everybody off!" This is the nightmare scenario. To them that day seems far off, but they think about it nonetheless. Nothing else preoccupies them. They are kept awake at night and during the day their bodies are stricken with a weakness that makes them unable to do anything. Their minds are stricken with something resembling paralysis, where not even the smallest thought can enter their heads, as if they came here only to be tortured as they wait for the day when they'll leave the king's retinue. God is all powerful. He destines greatness and He destines lowliness to whomever He pleases. He alone determines who He wants in the palace, and here you are outside of it. Here you are wondering what other end awaits you. But you haven't got to the worst of it yet. This is just the beginning.

17

Day Seven

WE SET OFF INTO THE arid and wild expanse spread out before us. We left for the desert, Mohamed Ali and I, to explore a location that Captain Hammouda said the enemy was thinking about taking from us if we didn't beat them to it. Brigadier Omar was the third man in our party, something we never would have foreseen. He hadn't yet come round from his drunken stupor as he stood in the fort's yard waiting for us. He wasn't laughing. We walked into absolute desert, the purity of which was unsullied by mountain, gorge, or hill. Brigadier Omar was behind us. We walked without expecting anything in particular. We didn't know what we were supposed to expect. Brigadier Omar was behind us, and from time to time he spoke into the radio to receive orders from the general himself. Did he know why we were here? Did he know that his precious daughter was punishing us? Was there any doubt? The general guided our procession from his farm, and at the same time he pressed olives, surrounded by a group of his officers. He explained to them the benefits of olives against constipation.

From time to time we saw Bedouin tents in the distance, with camels and small bunches of goats around them. That was how it was in the beginning, but after two hours of marching, the tents and camels had disappeared. In fact, all life had disappeared except for that of the sand and the rocks and the pebbles, and our threatened lives. I didn't know which direction we were walking in—perhaps toward Las Palmas, where the houses that Mohamed Ali's friend built were?—and I didn't know why we were silent. A sort of premonition told me that silence wasn't suitable in these sorts of circumstances. Should I remind him of the builders of Las Palmas just to make him laugh a little bit?

We talked about Naafi, whom we had left digging in search of his leg, and about Brahim and his potential wife. After that, we talked about the Sahrawis. Mohamed Ali knew a lot about them because he was from Zagoura. As for me, I had never seen a single Sahrawi in my life and had no idea why I was fighting them. Mohamed Ali said that the eyes of the Sahrawis were wide and black and weren't suited to the desert's heat, sand, and mirages.

"But why are we fighting them, Mohamed Ali?"

"They're big, those eyes, despite the fact that nothing but sand fills them."

"But, Mohamed Ali, answer my question. Why are we fighting the Sahrawis?"

"They're big, those eyes, and wide, shining because of the copious light. Instead of blinding them, the light fills their eyes and they become wide and bright white. Their eyes are always happy, proud, never accepting darkness . . ."

Then we heard Brigadier Omar behind us start to narrate this story out of the blue: "There was a teacher in our neighborhood who wanted to see what war was like, and when they sent him to enlist, the first bullet shot at him lodged in his head. When they took him to the hospital, upon seeing his condition the doctor said, 'If the bullet comes out, taking some of his brain with it, he'll die.' The teacher replied, 'May God bring you good tidings, doctor, remove it and don't be afraid. I don't have a single brain cell in my head, for if I did, I wouldn't be here in the first place.'"

The day before yesterday, after our return from the hunting trip, Joumana, who was happy with her outing and happy with the pictures of the gazelle that she had taken, said that after we got married I would become a beacon of civilian life because the general, her father, would take the necessary measures to end my deployment in the desert to allow his dear daughter and me to have beautiful children with black eyes. His exceptional offspring would enrich the military establishment. She delivered this happy news joyfully and cheerfully, dancing around me like a butterfly. No, that isn't right. Rather, she danced around me like Satan dancing around someone sentenced to death with the noose tied around his neck.

Her dog had a black wool covering on his back and around his neck was a red leather collar that ended in a golden clasp. She was rubbing her eyes because she was tired and wanted to sleep, but before rushing off to bed she wanted to deliver the good news to me. Yesterday evening, after she had rested from her hunting trip, I remained a good distance away from her so she couldn't pounce on me and dig her fingernails into my face. She petted the dog in her arms and ordered me, with an air of indifference, to get ready because we were going to visit the general on his farm to watch him press olives by hand. I told her, "I'm not going anywhere, not to see the general or his uncle!" It was as if she hadn't heard what I had said, as if nothing but air had come out of my mouth. The creature paid no attention to my refusal to go. She continued to pet her worthless little dog. I continued, "I would rather commit suicide in the line of fire than go with you." Then I headed to the tavern to say good-bye to my friends.

The tavern was practically empty. Our numbers had dwindled without us realizing it, both inside and outside the bar. Fifi was not optimistic. In the fort we had been one hundred and thirty conscripts and soldiers, but our numbers dwindled to half that in the space of a year, but who's counting? The tavern was as it was before, except for the number of soldiers. Many of them had fled or died, or been thrown into prison, with no one expressing any heartbreak or sorrow over them.

155

I have no desire for the civilian life that the general's spoiled daughter proposes. I'm already married. I have a wife who is sick and whose name is Zineb. More than two months had passed since I'd seen her face. I spoke to her on the telephone once and she said she was resting with the doctor and his wife, who were taking good care of her. Joumana, however, had told me that, God willing, the general would divorce me from Zineb so that I would be fully available for his daughter who had so attached herself to me. I'd rather engage in a pitched battle from which I'd never emerge. I would prefer to face a hundred enemy soldiers armed to the teeth. There's nothing but the enemy in the Sahara, not to mention the burning sand and sun, and other things of that sort. I'd rather be sent to the front lines to die in an ambush.

Brigadier Omar had no idea that he would find himself in the same boat as us. In the tavern he whispered in my ear, "There's another option, but it's not for you. Some pay an amount of money to the general for the enemy to purchase them. This allows the general to maintain his list of prisoners. Get it? There are two lists, and if you reject the ugly and spoiled Joumana you'll be on the list of soldiers who'll be killed."

I'd rather die than be in a relationship with that imbecile! She resembles the cig she holds between her fingers and her voice is thin and offensive—I can't stand even a single minute of it, so just imagine how it would be if you had to hear it for the rest of your life. I'd rather go into exile or throw myself headlong into any losing battle.

Then silence prevailed once again. We don't hear a sound in this stretch save for the crunching of stones under our shoes. We don't expect to hear a sound coming from either human or animal. We don't have Naafi with us to scan the distant mountaintops with his sharp vision, looking for a quarry. If there were an enemy there, Naafi would have at least helped us figure out where we were. We began to walk along a stone path with dirt and sand extending out on either side. There was no trace of a single plant to mark this stretch, and in the distance there were gray mounds obscured by the fog of distance that lay between them and us. The country became something else. Brigadier Omar now only spoke into the radio in whispers, as if to alert us to the imminent danger. From time to time, a burned-out tank frame rose into view, the remains of a forgotten battle we hadn't heard about. The tanks resembled calcified boats anchored on a sea of sand from which almost all life had receded, now inhabited only by snakes and lizards, with the wind and the dust of the desert sands whistling in the hollows, along with the souls of the soldiers who had passed through toward the unknown.

Fear began to creep in little by little. I recalled Brahim. Not one of us had been hit while we were guarding the well. Except for a few moments of nerve-wrenching terror, nothing memorable had happened. We forgot everything about that day. The following day Brahim ran away, and then was released from service by what seemed like a miracle. The day after *that* we saw Naafi being carried on soldiers' shoulders, looking sadly in the direction of the tavern. What was he doing now? He was leaning up against the fort wall combing his hair, waiting for his leg to rise up from the dirt. We tried to forget the fear that was gradually creeping in. In the tavern, we heard the remaining soldiers tell stories of the hallucinations, of things they had seen such as swarms of locusts that pierced the skin, or mirages you took for water and that you couldn't help but head toward as they beckoned you to them—as soon as you saw one it would call out to you and seize you, your mouth watering, and you would have no choice but to go toward it. Then I tried to forget, to sleep, to remember beautiful things like Fifi's turtle, for example, or the small cat that used to rub up against my leg whenever I stood in the doorway, and that came wherever I went for a while, before a runaway taxicab ran it over.

I tried to forget, and then the burned tank frames appeared. I looked at Mohamed Ali, who was walking in front of me. What was he thinking about right now? About his French wife who loved the desert? I saw his sweaty back rising and falling as he stumbled between the soldiers' helmets and shoes strewn over the obscured road. We saw the remains of war right in front of us, and they threatened us at every moment. There was no metal dipper swinging nearby, but nonetheless, my imagination continued to conjure up a distant creaking and people moving on the horizon, to the right and the left, like those who kept throwing their bucket into the depths of the well.

We approached a small hut erected on a bare stone hillock with a cannon on top of it, its barrel aimed in our direction. Above the hut, next to the cannon, a flag with faded colors fluttered. In front of it was a short wall made of stones piled up haphazardly. The structure appeared to be a primitive fortification. We stopped, first Mohamed Ali, then me, then Brigadier Omar, who was attached to his radio. Silence prevailed. All of us were waiting. Every once in a while the brigadier lifted his head in our direction to indicate that we should move forward, but we didn't move. He made to shoo us with his hands as if we were two chickens, but we still didn't move, like two stubborn horses. Then the brigadier returned to the radio, asking questions and talking. The general on the other end of the line ordered him to push us in the direction of the hut. We sensed that something was not right here; that the cannon was a *real* cannon, and that it hadn't just fallen from the sky. The brigadier continued to insist that the cannon was made of rubber, but one would have had to be blind not to see that the cannon was real. Nonetheless, the brigadier thought otherwise, and the general on his farm thought otherwise as well.

As we faced the hut's door the cannon let loose a shot that went right over us, just a few paces away from us. After that came the roar of bullets. Should we flee? What should we do? Should we protect ourselves with the wall? What wall? The wall had been blown away and dust covered everything. I couldn't see Mohamed Ali in the middle of the dusty whirlwind. I heard the brigadier yelling from far away, "Stay where you are!" Brigadier Omar couldn't see that I was crawling in the dust trying to save myself, just as he had. He ordered us to not leave our posts, but where was Mohamed Ali?

The sand enveloped the sky. Mohamed Ali and I were surrounded by sand; we were deep in the sand, and it felt like needles in our eyes. We ate sand and breathed sand. There was sand in our lungs, noses, and mouths. The brigadier's voice grew distant. Sand filled my mouth, and it didn't matter whether I tried to spit it out, swallow it, or just leave it there. I guessed that Mohamed Ali was not far away. I crawled through the dust. I felt the sand. Then I found him. His body was covered with blood, flowing copiously out of him. In place of a head there was a big hole with blood bubbling from it like a fountain. I called for Brigadier Omar but his response never came. I could make out a shadow passing through the wall of sand, fleeing. I saw him but he didn't see me. I called out nonetheless. No sound came out of my mouth. My voice had become sand and Mohamed Ali's body was just a trunk and a hole with blood gushing out of it.

What's the use of war? Bullets, knife wounds penetrating through to the bone, injuries that would inevitably come, sooner or later, killing, death here or there. What is death other than a commodity that people carry in their blood? In times of war and times of peace people learn how to stay alive, but is it possible to do so without also killing in one way or another? All roads lead to killing. All plans are laid with devilish care to promote the commodity of death. Perhaps people invented war so as not to die alone. The soldier draws a small heart on his grenade before throwing it at his enemy, or he might write "Good morning, friend" on both sides of it.

Soldiers celebrate their collective death like children. "Hello, death, and welcome!" Damn you, death! All of those who fled were right. They threw down their rifles and gave themselves up to their enemies willingly, in order to keep their salaries flowing, and in order to preserve the hope of returning to their loved ones alive.

If I were asked about my position concerning this war, I don't know how I would respond. I don't have a position. I've never had a position on any issue, nor has anyone ever asked me for one. Ask Captain Hammouda, who raises goats so as not to die of high cholesterol. Ask Brigadier Omar, who flees toward Fifi's tavern where his stinking drink awaits him. Ask General Bouricha, who knows better than any of us; this is why he sits on his farm pressing olives without responding to the king. However, I *do* know that I don't want to die. Moreover, I don't want to defend anything except for the stories I invent lying down in the steam room of the hammam, and Zineb, whom I love as no one else could possibly love a woman.

18

GOD IS THE ONE WHO takes and the One who gives, and getting worked up about it is nothing but a waste of time. I have my health and what remains of my fortune. I have my family, and if God decreed that I take leave of them for all these years then He had His reasons. A man is a man wherever he goes and wherever he settles down. Fadila's marriage is what concerns me right now. The scent of henna and lemon and rosewater wafts through every corner of the house. I'm not the sentimental type. I'm not the type who reveals his feelings and emotions by what he says and does, and from the look in his eyes, with or without reason, like a woman does. No. Never. I wasn't concerned with Fadila's hands, which were covered with dough, or with her mother's glances, which, despite all of these years, still overflow with desire, or with the looks of the neighbors who harbor an overblown grudge because they weren't expecting me to appear in the middle of "their" wedding celebration. Despite all of this, my emotions got the better of me and I shed two tears, two rare creatures. Fadila loves me, that much is clear. As for her mother, Fatima, after the initial shock, my presence in the house clearly makes her very happy. The day after my arrival she went to the hammam and came back seeming younger. She put on perfume and painted her cheeks with rouge, perhaps so that I would feel some regret for all that I had lost.

Fadila's groom is a teacher. His father is unemployed, his mother is sick, and he has six brothers and sisters. He may have been thinking about moving them all into this house, but now that I am here, his calculations have been thrown off. When I sit on the house's patio watching them come and go as if they were walking around their own courtyard, I'm seized with the desire to throw them all out. The teacher tries to get close to me because he heard that I work in the palace and he thinks he can count on me to support them. He doesn't know anything about my unenviable situation. This is what I read in his eyes, and it's for the best. He thinks he can find his way into my heart just by throwing himself at me, kissing my hands, and yelling, "Welcome, Hajj!" This teacher thinks he'll dazzle me when he sits down to debate matters of religion with me. They had told him that I am learned in the religious sciences and he contrives this blunt way of getting close to me. His most recent idea was to let his beard grow long so as to appear respectable and so that his talk about what God and the Prophet said would be convincing.

Fadila attached herself to him as a drowning person desperately grabs onto the last piece of floating wood. I saw how she looked at him, her will stolen from her, and he looked at her the same way, with the same idiotic eyes. All lovers have this stupid look that distinguishes morons and fools, and that reminds you of patients in a mental hospital. I always wonder why lovers look like such idiots with their sick stares. I never asked Aziza to fall in love with me, only to marry me. It was her chance to think about her future, as well as the future of her mother, her ex-con criminal brother, and the rest of the family. She found a husband easily. It was the only way for her to reach a decent social status. That's what I used to say. I was wrong.

"A teacher," she said. You can never tell with this type of person which leg he's dancing on—one leg is with God and the other with Satan. Fadila is happy, unlike her mother Fatima. She waits impatiently for the celebration that will conduct her to the house of the man she has chosen. Fadila loves me in her own way and I hope she has an agreeable marriage, but a man is a man no matter what, and when he lets his emotions show in front of everyone, with no sense of shame, it is inappropriate even when it comes to his own daughter. I'm against this sort of manufactured overflow of emotions. Showing emotion during these sorts of affairs is a waste of time. Tomorrow she'll get married and after two months she will have forgotten us. The same thing goes for me; in two months time I won't even remember the color of her eyes.

My new life preoccupies me and makes me forget my problems. Most of the time I get up before ten. Fadila is washing the courtyard, singing the song of her coming happiness. Once I've left my bed, completely refreshed, her mother prepares bread and country butter for me, along with a glass of tea, as if for the first time. The teacher passes by wishing me a nice day and leaves for work. I won't go to the palace door today. I'll give them more time to think. I continue to linger in bed, studying the room's walls. I see that I am at home, with my people, and I think about how when I return to the palace, I'll pay them back for all that has been lost, because they deserve the best.

Then I put on a short white djellaba, my yellow babouche, and my red tarboosh, the national hat. I go up the street to Si Hussein's barbershop. I try to walk with a serious gait, the way I used to walk, as if I were still employed at the palace. I hurry my steps to look like I'm rushing to take care of something, not in an exaggerated way, but just enough to garner the respect of those I meet and to put sufficient distance between them and me. I also do this to avoid the abundance of hellos and hellos-to-you and the kisses on this cheek and then the other cheek, two or three times depending on what the kisser wants, sometimes even four times. I don't know where they got this baffling custom from. Three or more kisses? What's with us? And you'd think that I could avoid them if I took this extremely long and winding alley I haven't set foot in for quite some time. Oh no! There are always three or four people waiting to ambush me at any time of the night or day. This one wants a job for his son who has been unemployed for years (he doesn't know that I'm now unemployed just like him), that one wants a permit of one sort or another. This one hands me a piece of paper requesting a taxi license, that one wants me to intervene in a legal case, and this last one heard quite by accident about my return and wants only to see my dear face, to say hi to me, and to inquire about my health. But they're always there, wherever I happen to be passing, always lurking and waiting to pounce, night or day, even if I walk by at three in the morning, as if they spend their time sitting on their doorsteps or in front of their shops waiting for me.

In the barber's living room I tell stories to the customers about some of the different phases of my long life in the palace. They enjoy that a lot and it only increases their curiosity and enthusiasm. They crowd around me to bask in a little bit of the warmth of absolute power. The barber's customers consider themselves lucky to be listening to my wonderful stories, the likes of which they have never heard before. Stories about when I would sit with His Majesty, about when I would tell jokes about this or that minister, when I would travel with him abroad or accompany him on a hunting trip, what food His Majesty likes to eat and what drinks he enjoys, how he sits and how he sleeps. They are awestruck when I tell them that I'm the only one allowed to enter His Majesty's bedroom. I never thought the effect I would have on them would be so great. I describe His Majesty's laugh for them, the different types of laughter, the meaning of each, the extent of each, and the wisdom hidden behind each of his different movements. Usually I spend my afternoons this way, happy in my role, and the day passes without bringing anything new.

Before the wedding and all the commotion that goes along with it, with the approach of the fateful night, strange symptoms began to show on Fadila. Her breasts grew like two water skins filled to the brim and she began to give off a foul smell like a lion in heat. We watched her as she crossed the courtyard and entered the bedrooms shaking her two full water skins, trailed by the strong smell coming out of every pore in her body. The teacher never grumbled or complained as she walked in front of him, which was understandable, considering he was the type of person who, on occasions such as these, was completely preoccupied with the profits he was going to reap after the wedding. He'd get rid of the smell later. But the others? I wasn't sure why they hadn't noticed anything. They hadn't complained or betrayed any reaction, however small, as if they were of the same species as her, or as if they were her accomplices. And her? She didn't utter a word. It was as if the penetrating smell spoke for her and the others didn't exist. The smell of henna mixed with rosewater no longer had any effect. Fadila's smell had completely conquered it. It obscured every other smell—lemon and clove and henna—all of which had disappeared under the smell of sex. The more her mind tried to flee from it, the more it tyrannized her body, surrounding and squeezing it until its repressed desires were secreted. Then, when the teacher and his family showed an exaggerated enthusiasm as the wedding day grew near and the feverish race toward the rewards they would reap overtook them, Fadila began to complain of pain in her head and in all her joints. Fatima said it was just a temporary illness. But no, this was not a simple cold or headache. The pain settled in her knees. This made me secretly laugh. The poor teacher's hopes were dashed. He wouldn't get a thing and his family wouldn't know any of the comfort or luxury they had been counting on after divvying up my fortune because my daughter Fadila was no longer strong enough to walk. She was confined to her bed and didn't get up even when the teacher and his large entourage left the house never to return.

Dada, an expert in these matters, said that it was an oppressive jinn that was in love with her. He had taken her over and inhabited her body. Every time he saw another human being he fought it. It might even be the King of the Jinn, may God protect her, and for these cases, no treatment would work. The only treatment was to wait. One day they'd decide to leave her body on their own accord. I said before that jinn kings are like human kings—they have their whims and we can't do anything about it, for *there is no power nor strength, save for in God*.

19

Day Eight

I SNUCK INTO MY HOUSE, tired, completely exhausted, but I made it, at dawn, after walking day and night. Fear and worry haunted me. Dogs didn't follow me as they had done with Brahim. My clothing was torn, but I made it. I avoided villages, places where there'd be people, and patrols of gendarmes. No one was home. Zineb was out. As soon as I stepped through the door I really wanted to take a bath. I was out of luck, though, since the water and electricity had been cut off. The refrigerator was turned off and empty, and the smell of rotten vegetables wafted from it. The house had been abandoned for days. I didn't understand why.

I sat in the living room thinking. Where had Zineb gone? The closet was empty, no trace of her clothes, no trace of her perfume, no trace of anything that would establish that she had stayed in the house while I was gone. Where had she gone? I returned to the living room. I was unable to sit, imagining something horrible had happened to Zineb. Maybe her health had taken a turn for the worse. I had three hundred dirhams in my pocket and what remained of my money was in a shared savings account, but the passbook had disappeared too. At least it wasn't a lot of money—enough for one month at the most. I didn't need it as much as I needed to know where Zineb had gone. I would ask her sister, Leila. Maybe she had changed her mind about staying at home and gone to her house. Or maybe she'd gone to her mother's house. I wondered if she had thought about staying at the house of the doctor and his wife. I couldn't visit anyone right now, while everyone was sleeping. I'd wait until daybreak. Desert days break quickly because they don't carry any surprises (except for that one that was waiting for us near the old hut). The city, however, is pregnant with all sorts of surprises. I wasn't expecting a surprise here, though. All I was expecting was for Zineb to throw herself into my arms. I heard a knock at the door and rushed to it. It was the neighbor, but she had no news of Zineb. All she said was that the landlord had been knocking on my door every day in order to collect the back rent. "He thinks you've left the place for good." Another disaster. I hadn't paid the rent for a year and a half. For a whole year I was indifferent to it, a combination of lack of funds, neglect, and procrastination. Day broke late and I left the house. Zineb remained in my thoughts. She was the spark that lit the dark night of the desert I had crossed. I cut across the Djemaa El-Fna and entered an alley that resembled a hallway. It was covered by a roof made of dried straw, hemp, and the remains of vines whose leaves had yellowed—a shady place pierced by scattered shafts of sunlight, scarcely lit, a familiar place providing much-needed serenity for the soul.

I had left Mohamed Ali in the desert, emptied of blood, and fled. I had already gone some distance when a second shot rang out from the cannon that Brigadier Omar insisted was made of rubber. It didn't hit me because of the thick dust. I left Mohamed Ali laid out near the wall with neither head nor blood. By now, he will have been completely drained. No one will be able to recognize him. Maybe his wife will be able to identify him from the dreams that he used to put down on paper and that might have been spread out next to him, mocking him under the short stone wall. He wouldn't see her again, his French wife who was awaiting his return to Zagoura. Before meeting her he would draw only one picture: the desert road leading to Timbuktu, with a tent on the horizon, an expanse of yellow with a few date palms, and a road sign in the foreground that said "Timbuktu fifty kilometers." His life changed completely after he met Françoise. He no longer drew the road to Timbuktu. He began to draw a black cat that would regularly come and sit at the door of his shop. Then Françoise asked him to draw her. For the next two years he drew nothing but her, in all positions—sitting, lying down, standing looking at the desert from the window—and nude, always nude. He filled dozens of canvases and frames and sheets of cardboard. Nude pictures of her filled the house until he no longer knew where to put them, whereas the shop was empty. A picture of the black cat guarded it. No one saw or heard of those pictures. I was the first one to look at them and catch a glimpse of his last dream, which was to go to Paris and exhibit them there. Once, Mohamed Ali suggested that we do what the officers do: buy tea on the black market and resell it, or sell camels in Algeria, so as not to leave the marketplace that was this war empty-handed. He never stopped thinking about ways to make some money to fund his travels to Paris with Françoise because nothing was waiting for him in Zagoura, due in no small part to the fact that his shop was empty, with nothing there but a picture of a black cat sitting on a chair made of straw.

I didn't find the doctor and his wife at home or at their clinic. It wasn't Saturday, so they couldn't have traveled to their farm for the weekend. Nonetheless, suspicion had lodged itself in my mind. She was always here. When I asked them both to visit Zineb they said they would come every day to keep her company since they didn't have any children waiting for them at home. I hadn't heard them speak of an expected absence or an upcoming trip. I'm not saying that they have to inform me of all of their plans, but my thoughts are always filled with distrust when it comes to the doctor and his wife. My relationship with them has never been good. A few months after Zineb's abortion, the waters of friendship flowed between us once again, yet I always felt an aversion to them deep inside me. If it weren't for Zineb I wouldn't have been able to bear sitting with them ever again. But it was Zineb who insisted. She said that they had completely changed, that they were no longer socialists. They had joined a new party whose slogan was "Restoring trust to the citizen." They were extremely enthusiastic about the new party and its slogan and saw it as an opportunity to exact revenge on socialists and capitalists alike. The leader of the party had been a socialist himself, but God had enlightened him at just the right moment. She also said that they were preparing to perform the Hajj. Sure enough, we saw them go and come back and we sat listening to what they had to say about that holy site, and about how a person's only desire after returning from the Hajj is to do it again and to settle in Mecca for the rest of his life. While the doctor was telling me about the benefits of the Hajj, his wife was telling Zineb that she had become quite attached to the party's new leader; that he was the greatest man in the world because he loved all Moroccans and was working on getting all of them to join his party. That was his plan and it was up to us to help him.

It was the end of one era and the beginning of another. Once again I was no longer free in my own home despite my silent protests. No one cared. They didn't consider my presence necessary or worthy of note; they didn't think it should be taken seriously. When I returned home I would find Zineb and the doctor's wife exchanging whispers. They whispered to one another on purpose to deepen my suspicions and so that the wife could dig another ditch between us that this time I wouldn't be able to fill in. I came to long for the months that Zineb and I had spent alone together, just as one longs for a beach vacation.

After a period of total despair, I lost interest in what was going on around me. For their part, they no longer spoke in whispers. The doctor and his wife discussed the policies of the new party completely freely while Zineb listened to them with interest. Sometimes the doctor reproached his wife for the love she harbored for the party leader. Other times he encouraged her because it was the path to our collective salvation. Then their intimate sessions would be brought to a close by expressions of praise and thanks to God who had finally opened their minds. During this time I remained silent, following their fiery enthusiasm and wondering what they had in store for me.

In this state of desperation I go to Aissa's house and he asks me about the new performance I'm preparing. "Where does it stand right now and when will we pick up rehearsals again?" I don't tell him that I'm not preparing anything, and that I'm not rehearsing anything.

It's almost noon. I turn toward my mother's house. I couldn't have been more surprised to see her addressing me in sign language until I finally realize that she is speaking to me about my father, and that she's asking me to lower my voice because he is sleeping in the bedroom. Despite her best efforts, a bashful joy slips out. Yes, I notice the transformation. Her eyes are made up with kohl, the siwak has polished her teeth, and from under the headscarf with the decorative fringes that holds her hair up, a single braid slips out. Hanging in the air between us is a scent I don't recognize. Is it the smell of perfume? Herbs? Some other fresh secretion? Or is the smell coming from him? At first I can't clearly make out the features of that man lying on the bed in my mother's room. She sits me down without my noticing as I am still dumbfounded, and my sister Fadila offers me a glass of tea with some odd herbs in it. My mother says that my father had brought them with him, and was taking them with his meals. Her cheeks are tinged with a disgraceful blush. To hide her embarrassment she says that he's sick. A frightening silence looms over us. The man's snoring rises up in the bedroom. I cast a glance at him lying there on his back. He seems short. His face is smooth, with no trace of pleasure or pain on it.

When I return to my mother's side, she says, "Having a man in the house is preferable to not having him here. His job at the palace is done. He thinks we don't know. Nevertheless, it's better that he's here."

He came back at the same time that I went to the front. God had responded to her prayers and compensated her for her loss.

Fadila says sarcastically, "He's no longer needed, and all of a sudden he remembers he has a family. Even his other wife threw him out and took over his house."

I say, "Maybe he finally figured out that he needs to take care of those who care for him in order to wipe away his sins, now that he's stooped over before the looming grave."

My mother scolds me and then, after a long silence, she says, "What can we do? He's here, and that's what's important. However things were before, the man is done flying around and has returned to his original nest."

And here he is, settling in at home and spending his days going up and down Sidi Slimane Street so that everyone in the neighborhood can see him. Right then I feel hatred toward him, which becomes even greater when I hear him start snoring again. I don't ask about Zineb. Nothing has indicated that she passed by the house, and there is no reason to expect happy news.

I pass through a maze of archways, and then houses piled on top of one another outside the old city walls. Piles of garbage everywhere you turn and people walking along rubbing against the walls so as not to fall into the deep, muddy puddles. Leila and her three children live in this filthy neighborhood. It's the filthiest place I've seen in my life. From right under the villas of the wealthy this shantytown extends outward. These shacks are as depressing as the palaces of the wealthy are gleaming, as if the sun shines only on *their* buildings. I picture them sitting and sunning themselves on their soft green lawns, the women rubbing almond oil on their bodies, stretching out on the pure, green grass as their husbands grill gazelle meat, preparing for a regular banquet—just a normal day for them. Meanwhile, just a stone's throw away, there are low houses made of sheet metal where an army of have-nots lives. The women, nearly all of them pregnant, hang their blankets, damp from the humidity, next to the railroad tracks, and there they sit casting out the cold that lives in their bones year round. I have noticed that wherever there are wealthy people's palaces, there are always shacks right next to them. I'm not sure what wisdom dictates this. Perhaps they are choosing the most appropriate place to put their poverty on display so that they appear more naked and more starved. This is why they seem more miserable and dirty in the harsh sunlight. Gentle sun, good health, and abundance are to be found on the other side.

The door to the house where Leila is cooking is wide open. Her three children are half naked, jumping in a pool of water in front of the house. Three dogs bark from a black patch of mud that shines like oil. The dogs quiet as soon as I appear in front of them. A mixture of dirt, stones, water, wires, vegetable peels, and dead rats. Her kids' heads are infested with ringworm and lice. They're bleary-eyed and their skin is filthy, yet they are somehow cheerful surrounded by this strange mixture of broken pots and pans, split-open furniture, and the smell of piss and whatever was vomited up from dinner the night before. The dogs wag their tails as they approach to greet me, rubbing up against my leg. Leila greets me while moving her cooking utensils inside. I follow her in. The interior of the house is more or less a large square; this is the whole house—the kitchen, the sitting room, and the bedroom. As for the matter of bodily functions, that's done outside, in the dump. The middle of the house floats in a dirty gloom. Rays of sunlight seep in through small holes at the top of the wall. The eye grows weary searching for a trace, however small it might be, of something clean—just a tiny trace of some human cleanliness to pay the eye back for its efforts, to give the soul a bit of brightness; some hint of optimism that could be planted in the mind of someone sitting there. But there's nothing of the sort. Whether it's the clothing or fruit or bread or a candle or a piece of wood or a stone or a whoosh of air, everything is marked with misery, filth, and humiliation. Even the sun is filthy here.

Her husband, Abdelilah, sits in the corner smoking a dirty cigarette. His clothes are tattered, his face in a frown. He remains as I had left him, angry for the most trivial reasons and in disagreement with every viewpoint he hears, whatever it may be. He sold his taxicab because it had started to make a whistling sound that bothered him. "Like a locomotive passing through my chest," he says, letting out a long sigh.

Then he becomes obscene. I'm not interested in the foul words that come out of his mouth, nor in his children who look over at us laughing, nor in the embarrassed blushing of their mother's cheeks. All of my thoughts are on Zineb, but Zineb is nowhere to be found here. As if Leila's husband had guessed what thoughts were swirling around in my head he began to narrate, loud enough for me to hear, something about the simple life he leads and the harmony that exists among his family members, as if I were the one responsible for Zineb's disappearance. As if being here with his wife and his three little demons gives him the right not only to give me advice, but also to forbid me from responding to him. Then he proceeds to attack me, saying that I don't understand the meaning of family life, love, and commitment. After that he gets up and hits the table violently, yelling out more of his obscenities. The table wobbles on its legs and falls on its side. He begins to move about haughtily, heaping more insults upon me. He crosses the room, proud of his misery, overflowing with it in fact. And to emphasize his animosity toward me, he punches the door violently and leaves his miserable den.

Leila indicates that she's sorry for what Abdelilah said. Her face is sad. I ask her for a glass of water. She puts the table back up on its legs in order to put the glass on it. She says that this table and those dishes are the last things remaining in the house. Abdelilah sold the taxicab, and now he's selling the furniture, piece by piece.

"Yes, he's a failure, I already knew that, just as I knew that his dream of conquering the business world was never serious."

To stop her from continuing to display her misery, I ask her about Zineb. That's what has brought me here. She doesn't know where her sister is. She tells me that she had visited her right after I left, and that there was something wrong with her. Zineb had said to her that she didn't know what to do with her life; that she was following the wrong path. For some time she had been grappling with a decision that she hadn't been able to make until recently. I say that maybe she was thinking about returning to singing. She had tried to return to singing after the abortion. The attempt failed and her confidence in herself was shaken. Leila shrugs, but I don't understand what this gesture means. Leila had told her that it was up to her, to do whatever it was she wanted, but Zineb never came back to the house after that.

Leila says, "I think she was staying at the doctor's house. When I spoke to her on the phone and asked her how she was doing, she said that she was feeling better and that she was more relaxed now. On the phone she seemed happy to me. She found the light that showed her the way. She had begun to think about her future with optimism."

I didn't really understand what she meant when she said that she's thinking about her future with optimism. I said to myself that it could have something to do with her health. A person's heart is like that—the spark that lights its way never goes out, it remains burning, however dimly.

Leila goes on as if to reassure me: "It seemed to me from the way she was speaking, from the tone of her voice, which was responsive and generously accepting of the world, that she had found what she'd been searching for. It seemed as if her days had become bright once again. I haven't seen her, nor have I heard her voice since that conversation. I don't know where she is."

I ask Leila about her illness.

"Illness? What illness? I know nothing about it."

I drink the glass of water slowly, as in need of another moment to think.

Leila says, "She didn't have to give up singing. She always needed work to maintain her balance."

Perhaps she sees that her sadness has transferred to me and, trying to comfort me, she says, "You can still fix what's been broken."

I nod, although, frankly, I don't know what it was that has broken. We part at this point. My conversation with Leila has only made things more ambiguous.

Evening has fallen by the time I return to the house. I ask the neighbors for a bucket of water and wash my face, as some sand is causing a sharp pain in my eye. I finish washing. I drink a bottle of wine in less than half an hour, expecting the gendarmes to knock on the door at any moment. It's not a good idea to have the gendarmes arrest you on the charge of fleeing the battlefield, even though at first I thought that would have been for the best. I stretch out on the bed, trying to put off thinking about the future. I go back to the kitchen and open another bottle of wine. Wine and more wine. I recognize the taste of sand on my tongue, as if I were a drunken snake. It's funny. After walking for several hours in the sand, nothing made me think to stop, and I had no idea what direction I was headed. Was I going north? The sun was burning on the edge of the hills. The sight of the sun didn't interest me, though, because the thought of Mohamed Ali's blood still filled my head.

I didn't know how much time I had spent running toward who knows what when I came to a sudden stop. I didn't see the man and almost tripped over him. He was crouching on the sand, wrapped in a sand-colored aba tinged by the color of the evening falling upon us, so I didn't see him until I almost ran right over him. He was listening to a radio he held up to his ear. I greeted him. He offered me some water from a small canteen. I needed his water. There were a number of amulets around his neck. I sat next to him. I saw a camel lying down not too far off. He said it wasn't his camel. Under his aba he wore his military uniform. I guessed that he was running away like I was, and maybe the same idea occurred to him as well. I wondered if I should I tell him the story of Mohamed Ali. Instead, I asked him about the war. He said, "These Sahrawis want to establish their own state here in the desert so that they'll have their own set of thieves. Rather than have the same families who loot us seize their possessions too, they prefer that a family or two from their own tribe rob them."

I liked his response. It seemed understandable, reasonable, and funny to me. That's how all revolutions, uprisings, and protests end—they end with you giving your throat over to your own kin so that they can slaughter you and suck your blood.

He asked me if I knew General Bouricha.

"Is he that man who fills his swimming pool with mineral water?" I asked.

He didn't answer right away. He was silent for a moment before saying, "General Bouricha's car exploded while he was on the road to Agadir trucking his oil. His car was completely incinerated. They didn't recover anything from the wreckage except for a bit of bone and half a skull."

Then I told him about his farm—that it had thirty rooms, each with its own chimney, that he had brought in a Japanese architect to design it, that he had a modern oil press attached to the farm, and that he would receive his visitors in a white shirt spattered with oil. He always enjoyed receiving them in that shirt with his hands dripping with oil. The most important thing in life to him was using his own two hands to press his oil, which he would export to the Canary Islands in army trucks. Nine months had passed, with him leaving his farm only rarely. He would receive news and issue orders from his oil press. He would win battles in absentia, he would lose others, and from there he sent one of us to die because he didn't want to marry his stupid daughter. We laughed together while he prepared a cup of tea for me.

I regained some peace of mind sitting with this man. I was looking at the sky as it took on brilliant colors. A purple sky and a purple evening. The air was tinted with the same hot colors. A few date palms and a camel grazing not too far off. The soldier next to me told me about the mission he had been charged with before fleeing to save his skin. He said that he was supposed to supply the enemy with weapons to fight us with, and to lay ambushes so that they could find us. "Once, we arrested one of them and the general told us to shoot him immediately."

I asked him about the cannon and he smiled and said that he was the one who sold them the cannon that shot at us, and that he had sold it *that* time for his own private gain. The man laughed, tickled by his story. A breeze blew over his mind, invigorating his memory. He said, laughing, "And when the general discovered this agreement, I fled."

Then, as if he wanted to find a solution to *my* problem, he said that this was the best place to hide. The desert.

That evening a calm washed over me that I hadn't known before. I thought about whether I should phone Zineb from the first place I came across on my way.

20

I SAT IN THE CAFÉ and took off my tarboosh, trying to make it so that no one would recognize me. I had been deceived from the beginning. It was no use. I put my tarboosh back on my head as if the customers were merely waiting for this in order to be transformed into my friends, acquaintances, and relatives and all that went along with that. The time for friendships has passed, though. I won't be deceived a second or a third time, although I won't hide the fact that a certain amount of pride can overwhelm a man when he suddenly becomes the focus of everyone's gaze, as if the sultan himself is preparing to distribute gifts. The customers smiled submissively, but I was not deceived.

A real fear seized me. There were no longer limits to the customers' flattery, nor boundaries to their friendships. Now they did everything more effusively than necessary. One of them plucked a rose from a pot of flowers and offered it to me with words of exaggerated praise. Another turned toward me and chuckled like an idiot. Another ruse. As a rule, I don't generally frequent these sorts of places, but I came to wait for my wife, Aziza, to pass by. Her mother had sprinkled her black magic on the house's doors and walls in order to get rid of me, and her brother was carrying a knife underneath his shirt. And Aziza? The touch of her skin was so soft. Her mother convinced her to submit a formal court order against me because I left her without support, but what would the judge do when he found someone standing before him who was no longer as he once was? God is great and I put my trust in Him.

Everyone in the café turned toward me and laughed. For some it was enough to smile and wave, as if they expected me to get up on stage to make them laugh. Another customer came and sat in front of me and said that he was the King of Jokes of all of Marrakech. He proposed selling me a joke, but got up before I had had a chance to think about his strange proposal. The strangeness of the idea appealed to me. I'll buy jokes. I'll go around to the different cabarets collecting jokes for five dirhams each, like the ancient poet who used to go around the markets and public plazas purchasing words, with which he would then weave his poems. The idea infused me with a new confidence. Maybe the length of time I had spent in the palace had made me boring and unfunny. I hadn't thought about it from this angle. I always made every effort. I performed every possible prank and ridiculed everyone and it seemed to me that His Majesty's face was always brimming with satisfaction. What had happened, then? I would have to buy some new jokes, by the hundreds, and keep them in a safe place. For next time.

It's not too late, not entirely. That person who'll sell me his jokes wholesale will come. If he doesn't come, I'll go to him. The King of Jokes. Ha!

I sat in my house watching the small fish chase one another. I saw now that the time had truly passed, that no one would come to present his jokes before me. Over the aquarium was a mirror, and over the mirror was my face. Do you, Balloute, know what royal anger is? Royal anger knows no rhyme or reason, or rather it's difficult to know its causes. There are only explanations that may or may not come close to explaining it. You'll never be honored with a reason. He'll never direct a single word in your direction, or even a glance as he passes in front of you, and to show how angry he is at you he'll distribute pleasant words and laughs like gifts to the rest of those who come calling, all except you. You need to listen to his abuses one after the other, and you need to swallow every insult. But they're not insults! As long as you haven't been banished from his presence entirely, there's still hope. The important thing is that you—the one with whom he is angry—must know that your presence is necessary, a duty in fact, so that you can see your master's anger, so that you enjoy it, study it carefully, analyze and explain all aspects of it, and so you taste the flavor of humiliation as you try to understand it as best as you can, even if it is all in vain. You must show that you are willing to drink your shame down to the last drop, waiting and expecting to be pardoned after two days, or maybe eight years. You plead with God to sustain the period of your indignity as long as you are allowed to remain close to the king's presence, even if only in this degrading way. Disgrace is a blessing from God, as long as you are not relegated to this position forever, and as long as you haven't been cast aside with no hope of return. But Balloute has not even been given the honor of thoroughly enjoying his humiliation in the presence of His Majesty.

And do you know what the barber said to me when I visited him yesterday? "Why do you continuously tire yourself out in front of the palace door? Maybe His Majesty has a new jester."

I couldn't bear facing my loneliness at home, and my questions wouldn't find a clear answer, so I had headed to his house for a puff of kif to allow me to forget the bitterness lodged in my throat. What exactly was my friend the barber saying? A new jester! I got up and headed to the toilet. I locked the door and sat meditating in the dark, thinking.

There's a distinct possibility that the king has a new jester, but a human being should not treat others this way. My mood darkened completely, as did the mood of my fish, and the headache that had announced itself without fanfare a few days before now pounded violently in my forehead, and also in my foot, or was it the other foot? I don't know which one is the good foot. I only know that this is my limp.

"Why do you tire yourself out? Maybe he has a new jester." This was the final blow. We live by luck and we die by it, and the barber proceeds to kill me by stabbing me in the back like this. But Si Hussein the barber did say "perhaps." All options are still on the table, and there is the possibility that the king does *not* have a new jester. This "perhaps" that the barber said contains this possibility too. Perhaps he has a new jester, perhaps he doesn't. If only I could be sure. "Perhaps" is a word more poisonous than any other, a word that contains within it all manner of anxieties. It contains the future and the past. Perhaps it ended, perhaps it didn't. And what does "a new jester" mean? It could mean a new minister, or perhaps a new diplomat. What does the minister in the palace do if he isn't jesting? Or perhaps nothing of the sort happened. Or perhaps the barber Si Hussein's head was filled with so much kif smoke that he had lost his mind. Perhaps he wasn't thinking about what he was saying at all. Perhaps . . . perhaps . . . perhaps. . . .

I took the barber's razor. I shaved my head and my cheeks down to the last hair—the final measure, the ultimate trick. A minister called Hamad had resorted to this in order to gain His Majesty's pardon. History books are filled with stories of this sort: influential people, ministers, and great statesmen have resorted to it, and it's not even a trick. Rather, it's a necessary stage of one's professional life. That is what historians write: "bald and clean-shaven, barefoot, with a loose outer garment covering the body." That's how you have to appear before His Majesty, and that's how you have to remain, standing before him for as long as is necessary for him to see you and your humiliation and how far you've fallen, even if you have to stand there for your entire life.

This was how I went out, like the day I was born—naked, barefoot, and seeking the help of an extended hand. I was seeking just a gulp of air so that I might live. I'd buy a wig to put on my head later. Buying jokes and a wig. A full program awaited me in the coming days. As for right now, let me stand in front of the door—the Big Door; the Door of Hope; the Door of the World; the Door of Life and Death—with no hair on my head or whiskers on my cheeks.

"I stand before you a dead man and I want to live. I am a corpse in front of Your Majesty and I want to be resurrected. I have a son whom I sent to the front lines to protect your back. He's still wearing his uniform, ready at any moment to throw himself into battle for you, but I won't let him return to the front until I've been dealt with justly. I gave my son to this country and I don't expect anything more than to be treated justly. Someone like me who works in the palace, who moreover bequeaths his son as a sacrifice for the nation, expects at the very least to be treated in a decent manner in return. Is that expecting too much? I only ask for justice. Let them judge me. I'm ready. But judgment has its conditions."

What judgment are you talking about, old man? I'm hallucinating. "What I'm demanding is not a favor from anyone. Never in my life have I expected favors from anyone. You must choose. Either give me justice, in which case my son will return to the front with his head held high—all of us will go to the front with heads held high—or we will remain in our houses and you won't find anyone to defend you. If you can win your battles without our children, especially one like Hassan who can hold a weapon while at the same time hardening the resolve of the soldiers with his comedy and his jokes, then go right ahead. And Hassan won't stop there. He'll buy more jokes to strengthen the soldiers' bold resolve. We'll walk side by side, lifting the soldiers' morale by jesting, and we'll explain to them the advantages of a man dying while laughing. We won't demand anything in return. Laughter is the right of every citizen, whether he works in the palace or not. There is no difference. That's my opinion, but only God knows the truth."

One of the guards approached and dragged me far away. What was with him? Why was he threatening me? Was I yelling? And, in the end, why shouldn't I yell?

A strange feeling came over me while I was in the street. The windows were all closed. The remnants of the recent disturbances could still be seen—buildings torn apart, the charred remains of cars. People walking stopped as I passed by, and this too was an occasion for feeling proud. Our people are great. They love the pageantry I represent. Should I let them kiss my hand? I don't know where they got this custom—four kisses at least—and don't think that I could extricate myself from them by merely saying no. They lined up along the street, preparing to applaud me. Perhaps they were waiting for me to tell them some jokes. They laughed in advance. Three people were doubled over in laughter. Was I that funny without even having to say anything, without the slightest effort? I had no idea I was that funny. It was all traps and snares, but I wouldn't fall into the trap, kind sirs. The shop owners of the bazaar stood in front of their stores, waiting for me to pass by. They laughed in turn. People have no shame. They have no dignity. They don't know that I understand all of their hellish tricks.

A feeling of optimism, not because the unrest has passed and His Majesty would be able to see to his more serious concerns, at which time he'd remember me, but rather because some wild pigeons flew out from the ruins and pooped on my shoulder. That is always a good sign. I returned to the garçonnière. I took down the last expensive wall clock. I approached the peephole of the guard who was standing at the palace door, perhaps the very guard who threw me out last time (I didn't know, and I wasn't concerned with such generalities). I knocked on the door. For a while I didn't expect the peephole door to open, as if it no longer mattered to me who was behind it to hear my complaints. All guards look alike, whether it's a new guard or an old one, because the first lesson they learn is how to be deceitful—an old guard makes himself look like a new guard and vice versa. Nothing mattered to me except that my gifts arrived along with my complaints and grievances.

I told the guard that I was Balloute, the king's private jester, who had made him laugh for twenty years, and that I was bringing a gift for him. I told him that I had been walking around for days without being able to find anyone who could tell me how I could meet with His Majesty simply to ask him, "Do you have a new jester?" That was it. Was it too much to ask for a jester such as myself who has been exposed to every indignity to try to put things right? No sound came from behind the peephole. It remained closed and the large door remained bolted.

"I just want to know if a new jester has joined His Majesty. I won't cause any fuss over something as simple as that, but it's my right to know. And by the way, I will say to you, my friend, dear guard, that I am innocent of everything that has been said about me, I swear to God. I beg you to deliver this message to His Majesty, or to whomever it may concern. As long as you've made your decision, at least . . ."

I felt the blood boiling in my veins, and I stepped back so I wouldn't feel obliged to charge the door. I moved a bit farther away from the door and turned toward some passersby who had gathered on the sidewalk facing the palace door. Their presence there didn't prevent me from protesting. "That's no way to deal with people. The civilized person is the one who summons you and says to your face, 'Mr. So-and-so, we are no longer in need of your services,' and he thanks you without having to give you anything in exchange. God is the One who gives.'"

I stood before a guard who didn't equal the babouche I wore on my feet, and he didn't deign even to respond to me. I wasn't asking anything of anyone, but the least he could do was treat me with respect, not like an old useless rag. "I'm a jester, if you didn't already know, and the king himself is the one who made me a jester. Everything is allowed for the jester, even heading to the palace in the morning without having to ask permission, and the proof is this protest that so threatens you!"

I approached the gate again, and in frank terms demanded a meeting with the king so that each of us could take his fair share of the responsibility. My sit-in at the gate finally yielded results when I heard the guard say that he was new on the job, and that the orders he had received were not to open the door to anyone. Then he added that he didn't know the palace had jesters. Didn't I tell you? They learn the art of the dodge from an early age. All guards are the same. "You didn't hear, dear sir, that there are jesters in the palace?" Ha! A new guard, he said. Don't make me laugh. New, and he doesn't know who Balloute is and it's not his job to open doors. He's a guard. He neither opens nor closes. I saw him peering out of a small hole almost sympathetically. He asked me to move away so as not to cause him to be fired from his job. What about *me*? Who will give me *my* job back?

The man's wonder was doubled when he looked at me. He saw before him a man in full control of his thoughts, even if he didn't necessarily look as if he was, even if his head was shaved, his cheeks were smooth, and he was barefoot and practically naked save for a light garment. Why so surprised? I'm a normal person and looks can be deceiving. Why did he retreat behind his gate and lock the peephole? I know this type of guard. There he was, standing straight and tall in his gleaming and perfect uniform like an overly important person. Let's see what you look like this evening in your patched and beat-up clothing, sitting in your pitiful den sharing what's left of yesterday's dinner with your children.

The peephole didn't open, as if I were addressing the wooden door. Perhaps I had to be more humble, to become smaller. They like misery, as do their masters. I know about them and their secrets. I approached the wooden door until I could hear the guard's uneven breathing from inside his fortress. "I am Balloute, the king's jester." I took from my pocket a piece of white paper covered with scribbling that the guard couldn't make heads or tails of. I told him that it was the king's personal stamp and I waited. The peephole opened again. He continued to stare at the paper and it appeared that he was starting to weaken in the face of the evidence I was presenting. I kept holding the paper up in front of his eyes, waving it and threatening him, saying that if he didn't open the door he'd regret it until his hair turned white. The guard grabbed the piece of paper, tore it into little pieces, threw them away, and relocked his peephole. Lord have mercy! At that very moment a gust of wind carried off the little bits of paper. The gate in front of me was high and silent, sealing off its secrets. I felt tears coming to my eyes, but my eyes were squeezed into a squint. Should I cry in front of him? What was the use of crying if the door wasn't open? I turned toward the passersby who had dispersed. It would be better if my tears could make the gate fall down. The gate was bolted shut, but it could open at any moment, and why not? It could open if God were to will it and I could enter without having to wait for a sign from a stupid guard who didn't understand anything.

The guard will know what I'm worth soon enough, just as he'll know the value of the piece of paper he has just torn up and he'll apologize, but it will be too late. I won't accept his apology. He'll leave his post and his job at once (if standing in front of the palace was ever even considered a job) and it will be his turn to stand begging for a face-to-face meeting.

I turned around to see if another group of passersby had gathered so that I could bear witness before them as well when I saw him coming. He was moving calmly toward me, filling the decorated cap I had given to him that day. That same hunchbacked man who I thought had been killed by syphilis—Zerwal! He advanced steadily toward the door in his fancy clothes, waddling like a peacock without a neck or legs. I took a step backward and hid my head in my shirt so he couldn't gloat at me. Then I saw the door open for him, thrown wide open before him. The guard received him cheerfully and bowed before him. There was no trace of illness on his face. It was him, just as he was, better even, with his hump and his ugly body and his sick face. Had his ugliness made him less fortunate? On the contrary, he seemed to be in his prime. The guard was happy to see him. He didn't recognize my new look. He didn't turn toward me to acknowledge me. What would he have said if he had seen me looking so ridiculous?

What's the use of laughing? I've practiced all manner of laughter, even a fly's laugh. Yes, I can convince you that what you are hearing is the sound of flies laughing. But now, what's the use of laughing like a cat, or a hyena, or a boa constrictor? What's the use of all the laughter that I've learned when there's no one to hear it? The worker heads to his workplace and the builder goes to his workshop. I'm not a worker, nor am I a fisherman riding in my boat off to sea. I'm a jester. I have only one job, and only one workplace. Strange, isn't it? I can only work in one place, and if it's closed in my face, I won't be able to find another. Should I change my profession and start from scratch, in the Djemaa El-Fna, for example?

I'm sixty years old, I have two wives and two children, my second wife's mother deals in black magic, she has a son who hides a large knife under his jacket, and they've decided to sue me in a court of law. Perhaps my first wife has done the same thing. Why not? Who will prevent them from tightening the noose around my neck? Now I realize why I returned to my first house—so as not to give them the chance to drag me to court, so that they wouldn't be able to establish a new file on me. Pretty sneaky, don't you think? I know exactly what their plans are.

They are preventing me from seeing His Majesty. They are opening files in the courts, inserting money into them to bribe the judges with. They are taking their revenge. For two days they have turned the garçonnière upside down, taking off with every piece of furniture of any value. Can I really attribute this to burglars? And what can I say about the restaurant? Even the restaurant where I eat has changed. In place of the usual stylish ceramic dishes, the waiter puts tin plates down in front of me, and he asks me to pay in advance. How am I to link all the co-conspirators in this plot against me? How can I gather together all of these people waiting expectantly for my downfall? How am I to sort out all of the worries that taunt me? I will choose the worry that is closest to my heart.

I sit in my old room. I look at the wall in front of me. I had taken down the pictures hanging on it, pictures of me with His Majesty in all sorts of places—the Champs-Élysées, the Place de la Concorde, the beloved forests of Ifrane . . . and the two of us leaning over the side of the ferry looking at the sea laughing behind us.

21

Day Nine

THIS IS THE DAY OF the father, a day whose end will be a surprise. People usually die at night. Only jesters die at inconvenient times when everyone is busy—in the morning, for example, which is what happened with my father. They die at these extremely inconvenient times to force people to leave what they're doing, or working on, as if they are continuing to jest after their deaths. The most cunning of them don't die. Rather, they cling to life before your eyes, neither dead nor alive, in order to prolong everyone's suffering as a final form of revenge. All old people savor these difficult hours that can last for years. I woke up intent on asking him for some money, asking myself what other reason he would have for returning home. I thought about it for a long while and came to the conclusion that he was obligated to give me some money. All bets are off with this kind of person, but I didn't want to take the path of a thief. Rather, I said to myself, "It's as if he came home for that rather than for Fadila's wedding, as he claims, or for anything else really. If only he knew that it was the fourth time her engagement had been called off. No, he didn't know anything about all that. Apart from giving away his fortune, his coming here makes no sense. How is his coming so late supposed to benefit us?" Fadila won't be any better off for it. Her second fiancé disappeared. Her first engagement wasn't any luckier.

Two days before the writing of the contract her legs failed her and she no longer had the strength to walk. Then she was confined to her bed, not getting up until the engagement was called off. Dada said that the girl was possessed. Despite all of her visits to the faqihs and holy tombs, despite the harsh séances she endured, the jinn did not leave her body. Will his presence here make the jinn that have been possessing her just up and leave? My mother regained some of her youthfulness, it's true, but only externally. Her misery won't be erased by siwak for her teeth, kohl for her eyes, and the strange paint she puts on her cheeks.

I spent the morning wandering around the house of the doctor and his wife again. When I returned to my mother's house, no one paid any attention to me as they had the day before. An unusual worry inhabited their faces and eyes. My mother and Fadila were sitting in the house's courtyard staring at Father, who was pacing in the bedroom, looking at the pictures hung on the wall. Bald and plucked, like a character who had emerged from some drawing. There were numerous magazines and pictures strewn all over the floor. I wasn't expecting a scene like the one I saw before me now, although I didn't pay much attention to it. I came home because I was in serious need of money, ultimately for Zineb, of whose whereabouts I had not a clue.

When I came in he was barefoot and had on a light robe. His head was shaved, his eyebrows had disappeared, and his eyes were swollen as if he had spent the night drinking and hadn't found the time to sleep. In fact, he had spent the night like this, without sleeping, cutting out all the pictures of himself next to the king and hanging them on the walls or scattering them over the tiles. He would stand in front of one of the pictures and utter a word or two of commentary. Then he would repeat some Qur'anic verses before moving to another photo. One could write interesting stories about this scene, but they wouldn't be funny. After all, what can you say about a bald man with plucked eyebrows raving over pictures hung on the wall?

Fadila's eyes glistened with tears as she said, "Shall I prepare you a glass of tea and a piece of bread before you faint from hunger?"

She had noticed my emaciation and deteriorated condition, but I had no desire to eat. I asked for a black coffee. I sat while Fadila and my mother headed to the kitchen to prepare the coffee. I paused again and wondered what had brought me here. It seemed to me that I had made a mistake. He really looked pathetic. He was standing still, looking at his feet. He wasn't looking at me. Fadila came back in carrying a brass tray with two cups of coffee on it. I took a sip. It was cold.

Father came out of the bedroom. He stood before me. Without lifting his eyes from his bare feet he said, "So you've started to write sketches? You make people laugh like I do? Ha! Do you expect the king of this country to pass by to take you to his palace? That time is gone. Something like that happens once in a lifetime, and it has already happened, thank God."

Now he looked at the table and the coffee cups between us, and without lifting his gaze from the table he asked, "Do you really want to make a living with this sort of work?"

I replied, "It was never my intention to write sketches criticizing the government, but now with all this chaos . . ."

He burst out laughing and started walking toward the kitchen, then turned back to where he was standing before. "How about you write me some stories so that just once I can criticize the government?"

He looked bad. I gazed at him, wondering if I would be able to get the money I needed from a man like this. Had he done one useful thing in his life that would indicate to me that he was a good man? Did he know how we spent our childhood after he left? Did he know that we waited for the neighbors' scraps, and did he know what those scraps consisted of? Potato peels swimming in a bit of broth. There was never a day when we found a whole potato; they were always half potatoes, and sometimes lots of little bits, like chickpeas that other fingers had squashed and played with, but they were delicious to young children who hadn't eaten all day. All while *you* were shaking your belly at parties and growing fat at banquets.

What brought me here? I was furious as I observed his movements and shifty looks. After a few moments he said, "You want to follow in my footsteps professionally? This is why you insult the government, to secure your future at my expense? You're lucky because you'll be able to pass easily through the door. At the door you can say to them, 'I am the son of Balloute the jester,' and they'll open the door wide for you. How can you not consider yourself lucky to have a father who, just about, works as a jester in the palace? Now that this uprising has passed peacefully you don't have to do anything more than present yourself at the first door you come to and announce who you are. You'll never understand how much the good fortune God put into your two hands is worth until the day you realize that work isn't just lying there for the taking in the middle of the road. The only things that you lack in order to replace me in my trade, as far as I can tell, are desire and self-confidence. As for luck, I'm the one who gave it to you. Tomorrow you'll start your new life. I will beg His Majesty to accept you as a second jester next to me. Thus, when I retire, you will have learned the profession. And they need a new jester."

I really was wrong in coming here.

I had walked some distance from the house when I heard him yelling behind me. Fear stopped me in my tracks as if the blood had stopped flowing to my legs. He was barefoot and wore the same rough clothing, and had a strange look that was barely human. He stood there yelling that I had dashed all hopes of his returning to work and to his former life. "Do you want to kill me, you infidel? You want to send me to prison? You attack ministers and make fun of the government? You assault the masters who feed you, you dog! God's curse upon you until the Day of Judgment! I'll go around to visit all of the officers,

ministers, and businessmen that I know in order to wash my
hands of you! I love the king and the government! I love my
country and would die for it! I'll explain all of this to them,
one after the other! Do you want to kill me, you unbeliever?
You're the reason! You've ruined me, enemy of God! There
isn't another son on the face of the earth who enjoys throwing
his father into prison cells to be forgotten. I'll explain to them
that I don't have anything to do with what you do, God damn
you! You've been an ungrateful son since you were a child! In
front of all of these witnesses I'll curse you. 'God's curses upon
him until Judgment Day! God's curses upon him until Judgment Day!' I am not your father, and you are not my son!"

His eyes were red and white foam was forming on his dry
lips. Some passersby carried him home after he fell unconscious. We placed him on the bed. His clothing had acquired
the color of the dirt he had been rolling around in. When
he regained consciousness he began to complain of a headache, as if someone were pressing on his temples and tapping
rhythmically on them to torture him. In the early afternoon,
his pain increased and he began to moan. He said that he had
received anonymous threatening letters. Zerwal the hunchback, who had become a private jester, was ordering him to
leave the country for any exile of his choosing. He really had
a lot of enemies and to catch him they had set many traps.
They asked that he stop telling the jokes at their expense that
he told in the presence of the king. He fell unconscious again
for about half an hour. His friend the barber put a damp
rag on his head, and that woke him up. The barber said to
him, "Do you know who I am?" He paid no attention to the
question. He didn't understand it. He had already entered
another stage of delirium. The last stop. He said that if he
had made a mistake, whatever it may have been, they should
have summoned him, asked him about it, interrogated him
about it like they would have done with anyone else. He said
that Balloute was not a criminal, but was prepared to submit

to any interrogation to clear his name of any charge that had been leveled against him. But on one condition: that the king himself conduct the interrogation. Then he smiled, as if a glimmer of hope flashed in his mind at the very thought of this interrogation. No doubt the king would interrogate him to hear what he had to say. One day long ago he had listened to his story when he had killed the three soldiers. Maybe he'd laugh again, especially since this time he hadn't killed anyone.

"All of you, everyone in the bedroom—you, the barber, my daughter Fadila—knows my story from beginning to end, but you must be quiet and pretend that you don't have any knowledge of it. Perhaps you had something to do with it."

He studied our features and said that he knew each and every one of us; that he knew the traps each of us had set for him. He had known everything from the beginning. Then he grabbed the collar of the barber's djellaba because he was the closest to him and began to shake him violently, yelling at him to confess to the conspiracy.

Balloute was yelling like someone suddenly stricken by a fever: "Why don't they come directly to me, after all of these years, and accuse me to my face? They have consumed my money, stripped me down to my bones, dragged me before the prosecutor, and they don't even possess the courage to face me! I am Balloute, the private jester of His Majesty, and anyone who still has doubts should present himself before me and show me what's what!"

Balloute was moaning, and continued to moan for another half hour.

The doctor came. Balloute thought that he had been sent from the palace, so he began to call him "esteemed officer" and to ask him whether he could leave everything he owned to him so that his children wouldn't inherit a single cent. The doctor nodded, grabbing his arm to take his blood pressure. Father warned him of the perils of marriage. "Don't get married. Don't have children." Then he grabbed his hand and imagined returning to the palace, after which everything would return to its proper course, as it was before. My mother began to cry when he said that he felt cold. The misery she had tried to hide from us had returned to the surface. He asked for a cover, but it didn't do anything to alleviate the chills. The doctor told my mother not to lose hope, and to put her trust in God. When a doctor talks like this it means death is not far off. The doctor gave him an injection, after which he fell asleep for a few moments.

He entered the final stages. He stopped talking out loud, communicating only through sign language. The right half of his body was paralyzed, and his lips contorted until they seemed to touch his ear. The old man seemed small, trivial, and shriveled up, as if he had never been young. He stared at us with his two small, squinty eyes, as if he were jeering at us. He appeared overly disfigured and it was as if this was how he had always looked, having become as ugly as can be. Impossible to think that a woman had once loved him and even kissed his shrunken, twisted, toothless, dry mouth. Perhaps he had been born looking like this—old, weak, toothless.

22

WATER FLOWS OVER MY BODY. The fear that had been winding my watch has disappeared. Tick tock tick tock. The anxiety and the dread, the anticipation and fear of God, all of this has disappeared. My former life was nothing more than a hubbub that, in the end, I have no need for. Lying on a damp plank in the kitchen. They didn't deem it necessary to wash me in my old bedroom, or in a respectable room with a door that locks. The dead have no dignity. Tick tock tick tock. The echo of an empty room. Things become distant. Water flows. The water of mercy. I hadn't felt that I had needed it before now. The features of my old associates have disappeared. I cannot make out a single one of them.

I'm living my life upside down. I have all the time in the world to see what I hadn't seen before. I walk from darkness into light. The light is dim here, and the people under it all seem the same. The same mysterious faces, the same frames, and the same clothing, but their languages are different. Each one speaks his own strange dialect. They aren't angels; nor are they devils, even though they're far from being human. I am among them. I walk through them, but I am not one of them. I walk until I get to the other end of the tunnel. I feel myself advancing through my transition from one darkness to a lesser darkness. Because it is a long tunnel, houses are scattered on either side of it. Cities are spread out along it—entire cities— but few trees, and there are swamps all along the road. They walk along it without complaint, without noticing the awful stench coming from it. I'm pleased how I was able to spend my life on this earth without grumbling.

There was a time when I couldn't stand sitting in the same place for long periods of time. Now every part of me is calm. I feel neither hot nor cold, neither happiness nor misery. Someone is pouring water over me. Man or woman? And why wouldn't it be Aziza who came to amuse herself with how horrible I looked? The way she pours the water is violent, filled with hatred. Her fingers get close to my corpse then recoil in disgust. I hear water spilling. I hear its laughter, the laughter of water. Ha ha ha. My hands don't move, nor do my fingers or my eyes. There are no more surprises in store for me. All surprises are now behind me. Water flows over my head. There's no hair on my head or on my brow. There's no hair on my body at all. I hadn't noticed that before. A complete jester.

My body is sound, nothing wrong with it. No defects on it like Zerwal's hump. We are leaving intact, so that much we've won. The water passes over me. It flows without obstacles. Water infused with rose and clove. The water of mercy. I lack for nothing. Even the change of venue seems to be a mere added luxury. How beautiful it is for someone to stay where he is without faces and words messing it up. As stone he came, and as stone he will go—a stone that made people laugh. I was always a funny person.

What are they doing there in the courtyard other than preparing the water for washing? Are they laughing? And in the palace? And in the barber's house? Everyone's laughing. No doubt they're thinking about my jokes, tricks, and stunts. Ha ha ha. How funny Balloute was . . . funny, and kind to boot. He played his improvised role and went on his way.

But was I funny enough? Did I play my role to the fullest? My jesting never passed without leaving in its wake a full army of people who were jealous of me *and* who adored me, as well as people who were angry with me, enemies, imitators, and fawners. This is a beautiful and pleasant memory that will accompany me to my grave, if my corpse doesn't fall en route. That too could happen. Anything is possible when it comes to people.

23

Day Ten

THREE DAYS WENT BY. No trace of Zineb. I thought about doing some exercise to pass the time until she came back, but I found that my heart and my head were not in agreement. My desire was to sit and wait. I went through some old papers I had written on. They were from a period when I was thinking about writing shows using a numerical language. One day during my long adolescence it seemed to me a discovery worth delving into, truly revolutionary. I was enthusiastic about the project. Shows written according to numbers rather than complicated meters. Save for a few unclear paragraphs, I hadn't gotten very far. I tossed the papers aside and left the house, heading for the bus station. The entire way I was thinking about Zineb. I was unable to focus on anything besides her.

I arrived in this city on a rainy morning. I met with a television executive about a show that I had presented for the students in the Faculty of Science. This executive told me that the television station was interested in my work. Then, a week later, he told me that the contract was ready and all I had to do was come to their offices to sign it. This happened before I was drafted into service in the Sahara. I called him back yesterday after burying my father. The ordeal wasn't easy. We arrived at the cemetery in the late afternoon and the guard had already locked the gate. He thought nothing of sending us back home with our dead body, just a simple matter of him spending an additional night with us, filling us with fear. The guard was adamant in his refusal, saying that we had to come back the following day because the last gravedigger had left the cemetery some time ago. We spent half an hour negotiating, raising our hands in supplication to him and his family, but he wouldn't budge an inch. We had reached the limit of our desperation when we saw a fancy car stop in front of the cemetery gate. A hunchbacked man dressed in white and wearing a red tarboosh emerged from it, as if for an impromptu cabaret show. With his hump and his limp, he looked quite funny. He took the guard aside, whispered in his ear, and returned to the car. The guard hurried to open the gate as the hunchback's car drove away. We exchanged glances. None of us knew who the man was, and perhaps we never would.

I roam the streets of an unfamiliar city thinking about Zineb. She's not at her house or at her sister Leila's house. She's nowhere to be found, which means that she's with the doctor and his wife. It is for her sake that I am making the effort of traveling to earn some money. Would I be able to sell one of my shows to the television network? I'm very pessimistic about this. If only she knew that I had come back. Lots of cars fill the sidewalks and pedestrians walk in the middle of the cavernous streets. Buses don't stop at their stops, they just honk their frightening horns and move along, whereas taxis stop when no one signals for them to do so. Everything is upside down in this city. Pools of water in the alleyways, a cart pulled by a tired donkey with infected sores on its neck, a child poking the sores with a large nail causing the donkey to jump with an impossible effort to move forward, although he can't move forward anymore.

I don't head in any particular direction. I don't know where the television offices are. I lose my way a number of times and when I ask passersby they point in opposite directions. There's a person waiting for me someplace in this sprawling city. It's the general manager, who will welcome me himself, but I'm still stuck asking for directions, waiting for a bus that doesn't arrive, and then hearing a taxicab's brakes screech suddenly before me, its driver suggesting I go to a place that isn't the place I want to go to. Truly a strange city.

The general manager's secretary welcomed me in an exaggerated way and brought me a black coffee while I waited for the boss to finish his morning meeting. She asked me about my father, smiling as if she were sharing a secret with me. She told me that she was the one behind the manager's agreement to meet with me because she had told him who I was and who my father was. She's from Marrakech and knows all the families of Marrakech, from A to Z. I thanked her for her initiative. The same enthusiasm appeared on the manager's face as he grabbed my hand and pumped it up and down repeatedly while he turned to his assistants, who immediately entered the office carrying files under their arms. He apologized for not knowing my works, although he said that he valued and respected them. "Our audience likes to laugh a lot, and God willing, it will all be good."

He asked me to present an excerpt of one of my comedy routines for him, which I did. A few minutes before, while standing on a corner, I had seen a policeman bring his truncheon down on someone walking by, and this is what I was prepared to talk about with the television manager—the story of the policeman and his truncheon, but I nixed that idea because I didn't think it wouldn't work on the small screen. Instead, I presented another one of my sketches to him, which made him laugh long and hard. Summarizing his position, he said, "You just have to change the ending, the whole ending. We don't want any problems with the authorities."

The manager left his office for a while. I rethought the story from beginning to end. This took up almost the whole time the manager was out of the room. When he returned he appeared friendlier and had a thick volume in his hands. I told him the new ending but he paid no attention to it. He placed his hand on my shoulder and told me that he had found the perfect job for someone of my talents. He had come across the epic commemorating the twentieth anniversary of His Majesty's ascension to the throne of his ancestors, and he was suggesting I rewrite some of its passages, which had been written by two well-known playwrights. Because the king would attend the performance personally, it would be necessary to change some scenes deemed inappropriate for him. For my part, I wasn't convinced of the nature of this type of work, or whether I should trust the manager's intentions. Surely he was mocking me, laughing at me. I wasn't interested in his suggestions and the manager seemed to me to be an idiot, despicable, like all managers. Despite that, and because my circumstances required money, I promised him that I would give it some serious thought and return with concrete suggestions in the afternoon. Work is a blessing from above that gives me endless joy, but not this degrading type of work. If not for Zineb I would have slammed the door in his face and left.

When I returned in the afternoon with the papers I had prepared, his private secretary, Madame Razi, met me. She wasn't smiling like she had been that morning. She told me that the manager wasn't there. He had traveled abroad. I had just seen him a few hours before, behind his desk, clapping and rubbing my shoulder and laughing. He had extended his hand to me when I finished performing my sketch about the policeman, but without his truncheon. He told me that he had never laughed more than he had laughed this morning. He thought the idea was quite profitable and added that he would see to my case personally. And this was in front of all of the television station employees. Even Madame Razi was there.

Then I came back in the afternoon to find that everything had changed, that the general manager had flown abroad. How could he have flown without my having seen wings on him that morning when he met with me? Madame Razi said that the manager had changed his mind, that what I had presented didn't meet his standards. I asked her again, clearly and firmly, to see the manager, and she repeated that he had traveled abroad, trying to look busy as if she had no time to waste with me. She told me dryly that if I was interested in the manager's suggestion, she was the one responsible for the epic. She began to discuss the epic and how to revise it. She didn't look at the pages I had placed in front of her. She said that she had another idea. She herself would take responsibility for rewriting the dialogues. It was more than I could bear, especially when the manager came out of his office and stood for a moment listening to her nonsense, smiling and nodding in agreement with her awful observations. Then he went back into his office while I went back to wandering the streets in the most awful mood.

When I left the television office, the orderly said to me, "You won't get anything from that whore. She's the manager's lover and she only accepts projects that her family and relatives bring to her." Rather than get angry, I found that what the orderly told me put me in a better mood. I'm not the only one with worries. We're all drowning in them.

24

Day Eleven

I HEADED TO THE FARM where I thought the doctor and his wife would be holed up. On the way I bumped into a childhood friend who had become a teacher. He hadn't changed much, except for the stupid smile he had acquired from inhaling too much chalk dust. He greeted me warmly and asked for my help in promoting his election campaign because the neighbors respected me. "The local elections," he clarified. Only at that moment did I realize that some sort of elections were approaching, and that they represented his chance to become a chief or a secretary, his opportunity to try out the viciousness he was destined for when he joined the local council to steal the money of the citizens who carried him to office. His party, like all the parties, was enlisting teachers and lawyers such as him, this eternal family of hyenas that smells its prey from afar. His eyes smiled and his stupidity broadened, and as if he knew what I was thinking, he bowed his head. I comforted him and rubbed his shoulder in the same warm manner as he had done to me. Then I left, cursing him and his ilk.

The farm was located outside of the city. On the bus I thought about Zineb, at first without hope, then with high hopes of finding her at the doctor's farm. Despite what her sister Leila had said about her recovery, I still pictured her weak and sick. This was how I always saw her, in constant need of rest and relaxation. Then I thought about how the country air would be good for her and that it would return her to health. She's fragile and needs a lot of tenderness. I picture her always needing me. She could never bear my being away from home for more than a day or two. When I would leave town for a performance, I would see her sad face saying goodbye to me from the front door of our house, wishing me happy travels, and begging me not to stay away too long. At those moments, my eyes would fill with tears. I would tell myself how lucky I was and only hoped that my good fortune could be shared with all the earth's creatures. After the abortion we passed through a difficult period. The bond that joined us together simply blew away in the wind. Our relationship teetered. Her health was no longer what it once was. She had left a piece of herself in the hospital.

Her health returned when she thought about returning to singing—this time seriously, she told me. She had always dreamed of becoming a professional singer, and the time had come. Her previous enthusiasm was renewed. The Zineb I had known two years prior was returning little by little, as if we were coming back out into the light. For a period of some months, a new lifeblood graced the house. The composer would come at ten in the morning, oud under his arm, and wouldn't leave until late in the afternoon, sometimes not until late at night. He was someone she knew from the cabaret where she was working. For the first time in his long life he had been given the opportunity to reveal his hidden talents and excessive enthusiasm that surpassed Zineb's by quite a long way. The old composer had regained his youth. Thanks to Zineb he was to become famous and his melodies would shine in the skies of true music. It seemed like the musician had settled in our house, and from my standpoint I didn't see any reason to prevent him from staying since our renewed happiness was linked to the atmosphere that the musician helped spread to every corner.

From ten in the morning until late in the evening they would spend the day wandering around the house—Zineb singing while he plucked at his oud strings. From the room where I was writing my sketches I could hear her sweet voice singing, "They Reminded Me," and I said to myself that it was she who needed this old man to drag the last remnants of the end of his life behind her to completely restore her to health. She needed someone to set the rhythm of her voice anew. More than this, she needed to regain confidence in herself. Yes, Zineb was right as usual. Zineb loved Oum Kulthum, she loved me, and it was as if she was addressing me directly when she sang, "How could they remind me if I haven't forgotten you?" Her voice echoed all day throughout the house. She was light in her long gown like a bird that has discovered the joy of soaring up high, and in her nightgown when she lay down beside me warbling softly.

On the day of the concert Zineb spent the better part of the morning rehearsing with the regional orchestra, twenty instrumentalists in their somber black outfits, twenty employees, playing and exchanging jokes. Some of them were smoking as if they were doing routine work such as shining shoes or selling bread, or as if they were civil servants. Zineb was not reassured. I spent the afternoon encouraging her. She was scared. Her face was yellow, her lips dry, and her smile pallid. This was natural. Zineb wasn't about to spend the evening singing in the cabaret. Rather, she was facing a new room with new lights and a new audience, accompanied by the employees of the regional orchestra who played as if they were kneading morning bread. When she sang it seemed as if something was annoying her. I watched her from behind the curtain and from time to time she turned toward me. I realized after a few minutes that the band members had raised the music's key and that her singing had begun to sound like screeching. After a few moments she couldn't keep up with the musicians, and in the middle of the song she stopped singing and rushed backstage under the whistling and protests of the audience and the chuckling of the musicians, who were quite happy with their performance. She spent the rest of the night in tears. She didn't sleep. Could anyone who had suffered such a setback ever recover?

In the morning she was unable to utter a sound. She had lost her voice. She would open her mouth but no sound would emerge. It was definitely cause for worry and disappointment. She swallowed some honey and took some pills, but her condition didn't improve. Finally she sought help from paper and pen, writing out her thoughts and desires. For the first few days it was a sad scene. The bird had stopped chirping as if its family had left home. The house was empty and cold. The silence that enveloped the house was not silence; it was closer to frost, as if we had moved to a continent made of ice. Things changed when she came around to the idea of the little notebook in which she would write down what she needed. It came to the point where she wouldn't take a step without the small notebook that hung around her neck, her pen in hand.

Things changed, and little by little the anxiety disappeared, giving way to a new form of intimacy, a new mutual understanding through language, as if we had brought new meaning into our lives. Speaking through writing seemed to me an eloquent luxury, something exceptional. My fondness and attachment to her grew. Even though her handwriting wasn't attractive, we didn't need to speak. I would have preferred a thousand times over to be like her—listening to idle chatter without responding to it—but my profession doesn't allow me that luxury. I am an actor whose bread and butter is words and whose reward is laughter, sort of like my father. In the end, it was all quite funny, at least to us. Her slanted red writing recording on paper the amount of tomatoes, potatoes, and lentils I had to bring home made us laugh for weeks on end. "Two red peppers and a half kilo of squash. Don't let the vegetable seller do as he pleases because he'll only give you damaged vegetables. And milk. Don't forget the milk, and pay attention to the best-before date. . . ."

In the end we sought help from the doctor, as if he had been waiting for just this opportunity to intrude on our lives once again, to renew contact with us and to settle in between us, he and his wife, bringing with them their new party and their new views about change that would include all of society, thanks to their leader with the enlightened ideas.

I arrived at the farm. Flags fluttered above the door, national flags next to those of the party, and below them were pictures of the party's candidate. The woman in the picture was smiling for the camera, having put a black piece of fabric around her head to cover her hair and a large part of her forehead. The smile was sad. The garden inside the farm was neglected but pulsed with movement. Other flags flapped above the orange trees. The cooks were preparing a feast for the evening, but the doctor and his wife weren't there because of the election campaign. The cooks didn't know when they were coming back from their tour that kicked off their electoral project, nor did they know anything about Zineb. My description of her wasn't specific enough. "There are a lot of women at this gathering," the cooks said, and my description could have fit most of them, with nothing that would distinguish Zineb. My description wasn't exact at all. How could I explain that I found it difficult to define the features of her face, her skin, her hair, her eyes, as if walking down a road you don't recognize even though you pass by it every day? Had I really been away for so long? Eleven long days is not enough time for someone to forget the features of the road.

While I was intently devoting myself to recalling these details car horns outside the farm blared. They barreled toward the iron gate, which remained open. They got out of the car, many men and women, among them the doctor, his wife, and Zineb, wearing the black piece of cloth. Zineb, my wife! And with the same smile that was on the poster. The doctor came toward me with prayer beads wrapped around his wrist, which he played with between his fingers. I didn't know who was paler, he or I. He pushed toward me, while the two women remained behind him surrounded by a group of men.

"Is it really you? When did you get back? I can't believe my eyes!"

This was the doctor's response to my completely unexpected appearance before him, as if a mythical creature had come from the world of the unknown. I turned toward Zineb, who was engaged in discussion with a group of farmers. I didn't know where they had come from. She wasn't looking at me as she was busy addressing the peasants. All this time the doctor addressed me, pointing at her.

"She has become an important person. Her popularity has exceeded all expectations. She'll win the elections, God willing. The people here believe in her and her ability to change their lives and social status. Yes, she finally discovered her gift. I always knew that there was something precious underneath her routine life. It's a great day for all of us."

I thought he was joking. But he wasn't. Perhaps the doctor thought I was one of the supporters of his party, which is why he had launched into his trite speech, whereas I shifted my glance between Zineb and her picture on the farmhouse wall. Now I recognized her. I hadn't recognized her at first. Had she changed that much? I looked closely at the details of her face again, waiting for the doctor to finish his speech so I could take her by the hand and return home with her. Now she was addressing the group of farmers, who were crowding around her and appeared enraptured by her words. No, I hadn't recognized her before, just as I didn't recognize her then.

The doctor grabbed my arm. "Don't you know why we're here? Didn't you die in the war? News of your death came to us yesterday. Your family received the coffin this morning. Everyone here is saddened. Look at Zineb. She's wearing black. It's a big day for her, but despite that she's wearing black, mourning for you. As for all of us, we were planning on going to your father's house to attend your funeral. I now see that that won't be necessary. This will allow us to complete our campaign to promote our party's platform and to remain on schedule. Would you like to accompany us?"

More cars had come and lined up behind the doctor's car, honking their horns—truly an awe-inspiring procession. I forgot about Zineb for a moment as I was trying to pull away the spider's web that had wrapped itself around me, looking at the black rosary whose beads danced between the doctor's fingers.

I stood in front of Zineb. I didn't throw myself into her arms as I had expected I would. For her part, she made no move that would indicate any eagerness or longing. What she had been discussing with the peasants still dominated her thoughts. Finally, the shadow of a shy smile formed on her lips. The members of the electoral campaign went into the farm, their playfulness and simmering energy following them. We remained alone, Zineb and I, with the doctor and his wife three steps away watching our meeting, looking anxiously at us as they had before. They were smiling and nodding for no reason. The best response to their bad behavior was for us to return home, but it seemed inappropriate to ask her to go back with me right in the middle of this party.

I don't know exactly what I was expecting from her at that precise moment. I don't know what purpose elections serve. Perhaps they're something good if they've helped Zineb finally find her way. She'd spend the day moving about between villages—that day she was the belle of the ball—and in the evening we'd find ourselves back home once again. Maybe the campaign would last a few more days. No problem. She could be the belle of the ball for a few days after, and then everything would return to the way it once was. This time I'd sever all ties with them, once and for all.

It seemed to me that her condition had truly improved. She was no longer depressed, as I had thought she was just a little while ago. This was Zineb as she was, and as she would remain, Zineb no more and no less, enthusiastic as I had known her before. Her lips whispered a word or two that I didn't hear, as if she were searching for the right words with which to initiate our meeting, or as if what she said just wasn't right, so she retreated.

The doctor approached us, followed by his wife. Nodding, he said, "Despite everything, news of your death came to us as a gift from the heavens."

He said it while directing his smile toward Zineb and continued to talk without looking in my direction, as if he were afraid I would explode before he finished speaking, or as if he were frightened that a hurricane would hit and cut him off.

"We got married a short time ago, Zineb and I. Our marriage was in accordance with religious custom, attended by witnesses from the cinema club and some friends, with the expectation that *God accomplish a matter that was already destined.* We got married about . . . about . . ."

I turned toward his wife, who finished his sentence: ". . . before she got pregnant."

Then the doctor picked up the thread of what he was saying. "Yes. The abortion wasn't what anyone wanted. It was a real problem for all of us. It was necessary because at that time she wasn't sure of anything, whether she loved you or not. She didn't know herself, nor did she know what she wanted out of life, but things became clearer to her little by little. Little by little she became sure that she wanted to live with us—with Suad and me. We make a very harmonious trio."

His wife nodded in agreement, as did Zineb. His fingers continued to fiddle with the beads for a few moments. I watched the fiddling, unsure of what I was supposed to do. All I know is that for a long while I didn't move, as if I was waiting for them to offer me their condolences.

The neighbors gathered at the door near the hearse. The two soldiers standing in front of the door would have prevented me from entering were it not for my glowering face. The house's courtyard was full of mourners gathered around a coffin made of wood. Four men dressed in white djellabas surrounded the coffin to prevent the mourners from getting too close or from trying to open it. You wouldn't have known that they were soldiers except for their heavy shoes and khaki uniforms showing from under the djellabas. The boards were firmly nailed shut, and inside it there was me, or Mohamed Ali without a head, or Naafi without a leg, or Brahim, who had perhaps fallen into some other snare. My mother was weeping, for me, or maybe for all four of us—Mohamed Ali, Brahim, Naafi, and me.

The soldiers wearing the djellabas walked out carrying the coffin on their shoulders, placed it in the hearse waiting by the door, and hopped inside. Then all of the mourners lined up behind it yelling, "God is great!" Fadila came out crying. She stood in the doorway with my mother, supporting her so she wouldn't fall. The procession set off and the women went back inside. Little by little the street emptied out. I followed the procession on foot. The procession got farther and farther away until it could no longer be seen. I was walking in no particular direction. My only thought was to get far away from there. I thought about Aissa. What was he doing right now? He was probably preparing the props for a new performance, or setting a trap for a mouse he hadn't yet figured out how to get rid of, even though he'd say that they had become friends. The mouse no longer annoyed him at all. Quite the contrary, he found something useful and real in his presence, something that made him forget his own loneliness. I'm not like them, and I don't possess his naïve optimism. I am a ruined person who has reached bottom on my own. I picked up a cigarette butt to complete my new image. I stood in front of one of the cafés. I reached my hand out toward a nearly empty cup of coffee while glaring angrily at the young man sitting before it. He didn't say anything. He appeared gentle and frightened.

I drank down the last gulp in the glass, violently slammed it down in front of the young man, and cursed the weather. The little money I had in my possession I had scraped together over the last three days.

I've neglected my exercises, forgotten about them. I need to think about them. I'm an artist. I'll discuss this with Aissa. He needs to forget about his mouse for a few days. We'll prepare a new show. The theaters are closed to us, Aissa. Theaters are filthy and havens for lovers, drunks, seamstresses, and railroad workers. Still, they're forbidden to us. His Majesty's governors have forbidden us to go to them. We won't present our show to them. We don't need television either. We don't need governors and officials and their permits, or television and its director. They put their permits on chairs and sit on them! We'll present our show in the cemetery for our dead friends, for Mohamed Ali and Naafi and Brahim, and for me, the newcomer.

The alleys of Marrakech became dark, no light at the end of this tunnel. Then a glow like that of a candle appeared in the distance. The more I walked toward it, the farther away the light became. Sometimes a brilliant, blinding light appeared, so close I could almost touch it and feel it burning the tips of my fingers, and sometimes it receded and slunk back so that it could only be glimpsed. At times I walked and at other times I ran, as if in one of those dreams when you see yourself panting behind the same light, unable to stop or turn back. On the walls were pictures of Zineb with her new look, with her confounded smile. I turned and saw a beautiful white cat walking alongside me, looking at me as if it were calling out to me, as if it were smiling at me.

I thought about Zineb, about that day we went down to the beach and were rolling around on the sand kissing one another when two gendarmes came and stood over us and asked for our marriage papers. I gave them another piece of paper, a ten dirham note. We laughed afterward, Zineb and I. We laughed a lot. It's true, we used to hide in all sorts of isolated places in order to live out our love freely. Another time four young men came out from behind a cactus fence and threatened to rape us. Again I took out the magic piece of paper that quelled their anger. Lots of funny stories happened to us that made us laugh for a long time. But this time she was in the doctor's arms, lying down next to him with his wife on the other side of the bed or in the next room waiting her turn. Her place wasn't there next to him. Her place was next to me. It always was and always will be next to me, not in anyone else's bed. If only she knew what sort of trap the doctor and his wife had laid for her. My sadness transformed into overwhelming hopelessness and grief. I thought about how to pull her away from him. Zineb. Her natural place was in my arms.

Our first kiss. The honey of our first kiss was still in my mouth. I was at home lying on the bed with nothing in particular bothering me—a fever of the senses in the excitement of waiting, a fever of the soul approaching the source of life. I heard the rustling of her pink dress. Zineb approached on tiptoe, worried about me. She looked at me and smiled. Her halo of coal-black hair lit up her smiling face. Her face approached mine and she placed her hand on my forehead as if she were taking my temperature. I could see her breasts under her light top. She passed her fingertips over my hair and my stomach fluttered. Her smiling face got very close to mine and I could see the nipple rising above her breast, so close to my thirst, and that just made me more feverish. Our gazes met. My lips were dry, as if blood no longer flowed to them, maybe having stopped flowing in my whole body at that moment. My wretched soul appeared naked before her. My heart beat so violently in my chest that I imagined it could be heard. Then, slowly, her hair got closer and lowered its darkness over my face as she scraped her delicate nails across my neck. I closed my eyes. Her naked breast lay calmly on my chest and her lips gently touched mine as if in a dream. I was like someone soaring in the clouds. Then our lips came together with all the thirst and violent passion that we had been carrying for months.

While I was walking I remembered the star that had died hundreds of years before but whose light still shone. Like it I have died, and what I was seeing could very well be a nostalgic memory for something that had finished, but whose echo still resonated, waiting to fade away forever. I bought a bottle of wine with what remained of my money and headed to Aissa's house. I'll get drunk and I won't go to sleep. I won't regret a thing, especially when I go to the cemetery tomorrow to attend my funeral.